MW01125618

AN IMPROPER EVER AFTER

BILLIONAIRES' BRIDES OF CONVENIENCE

BOOK FIVE

NADIA LEE

An Improper Ever After
Copyright © 2017 by Hyun J. Kyung

To my reader group members.
Thanks for reading, thanks for cheering me on.

ONE

Annabelle

ELLIOT HASN'T BEEN IN BED ALL NIGHT. I know the moment I open my gritty eyes, and my heart is heavy with regret and pain. I swing my legs to the other side of the bed and check the pool. It's empty.

He didn't come back from wherever he went last night. After our world came crashing down.

Will it ever be right again?

I drag myself slowly and mechanically to the bathroom. It feels weird—wrong—that I have to keep up my morning routine when there's a huge knot inside me, one that's so big and ugly I don't understand how I can still function without crumbling. I brush my teeth, splashing my face with cold water to wake up. Eight hours in bed last night, but I didn't sleep well. Most of those hours were spent tossing and turning. And it shows in the puffiness of my listless green eyes and the pasty complexion of my face. My flat and lifeless hair sticks to my skull like matted blood.

God. What a sight. I snort a humorless laugh. If Elliot were to see me like this, he would run the other way, screaming in horror. I stick my fingers into my hair, trying to get it to look better, but it's no use. After a half-hearted attempt, I give up. He's not home anyway, so what's the point?

I manage to shrug into a robe and go downstairs. Nonny's up—I can hear her moving around in her suite—but Elliot, of course, is nowhere to be seen.

If he *did* come home, he's probably in his office. I reach the door that leads into it and put my hand on the cool handle. Clammy sweat coats my palm; suddenly I'm unsure. The muscles in my belly clench and flutter, and I inhale slowly, girding my loins for what needs to be done. I couldn't tell him everything the way he wanted, but it wasn't because I was trying to hide things from him. My life has been a series of failures since my dad was exposed as a fraud, and nobody likes to talk about failure.

The well-oiled hinges move silently, and I take a step inside. My head feels like it's full of wet cotton balls. I ache all over, like I've been beaten with a bat, but I know it's more psychological than physical. As predicted, Elliot isn't in his office... although there's a tumbler on the desk with lip prints. I pick it up and sniff. *Alcohol.*

I leave the office and grab my phone, wanting to call Elliot. We *have* to talk about what happened. Hopefully he'll be less upset than he was yesterday.

The browser reloads when I unlock my phone. I clicked it shut last night after I saw all those hateful headlines about my stripper days. Not even days: *one day*, since I only lasted that long. But tabloids aren't interested in the truth. It's more fun to speculate, because speculation sells more copies.

The headlines have been refreshed, and the first one catches my eye.

Already Straying? Billionaire Seen with Escort.

Underneath is a shot of Elliot entering a hotel. It's dated yesterday.

I shake my head. His being at a hotel doesn't necessarily mean anything. And the tabloids could be lying about when the picture was taken. But I see another one with a redhead going inside, too. The unnamed source says she's the mystery woman he's been seeing for a while now.

My heart squeezes painfully. I've never felt such an inexplicably profound connection with another person. Nor did I expect the intense joy from such a bond. Knowing that it's been ruined…maybe for good…cuts more deeply than I could have ever imagined. He and I were cocooned together in St. Cecilia. The realization that there was a chance I could've salvaged our relationship by being honest with him from the very beginning… That's the unbearable salt in the wound.

I don't know what I expect now, but I call Elliot anyway. We need to talk, and I'm going to tell him everything he wants to know and more.

The door to the balcony opens, and he walks inside. His deep brown eyes are slightly bloodshot, and his hand is closed around an empty bottle of scotch. The hair that usually has a dark chestnut sheen has lost its shine and is sticking up on his head. The first three buttons on his black dress shirt are undone, the fabric as worn and tired as his handsome face. The sight hurts. I know I'm the one who put the misery there.

Despite the empty bottle, he's walking straight. It's like he's immune to alcohol. "You called?" he asks, his voice gravelly.

"Yes, I wanted to talk." I wipe my clammy palms on the robe and straighten my back, try to put a little more strength into my voice. "Want some coffee?"

He inclines his head once.

My mouth dry, I start a pot and give him a mug full of the fresh brew. My hands start to shake and I hide them behind the robe. *Calm down. You can do this.*

Instead of drinking it, he studies the steam rising from the dark gray cup. The outside of it reads TRUTH HURTS in blood red letters. I wince inwardly. I didn't see the logo when I reached into the cabinet.

He takes a few sips—finally—then says, "What do you want to talk about?" His voice lacks inflection, and that chills me. I can deal with emotion, but this...*void?* It's scary because I don't know if I can fill it the right way so we can fix what's broken.

I clear my throat. "I'm sorry about the way you found things out."

"So you're sorry I found out?"

"No. That's not what I mean."

"Then what do you mean?"

I inhale. I suppose I deserve the cold treatment from him. He probably feels betrayed that I kept things to myself. "Elliot, I never mean to deceive you. I honestly didn't think any of it mattered."

"The fact that Grayson set you in my path, all the while telling you I needed a wife, wasn't worth mentioning? Even when I asked you point-blank to tell me if there was anything that would impact the both of us?"

I have no excuse…except that I was too ashamed to talk about the kind of control I let Mr. Grayson have over me.

Elliot doesn't give me time to respond. He continues: "What about Dennis? He probably wasn't phoning you to reminisce. So what did he want? Or does that also have nothing to do with me?"

"Elliot…"

"Spare me," he scoffs, suddenly animated and slashing the air with a hand. "You would've *never* told me any of this on your own. And now suddenly I'm supposed to stand here and believe that you're going to be one hundred percent honest? How can I know that you're telling me the truth—all of it—without having my PI dig into everything?"

"That's not fair."

"What's not fair is you never trusted me. I trusted you enough to tell you about Annabelle Underhill. Do you think it was an easy story to tell?" He finishes his coffee. "At least what you said about your roommate checked out."

"You checked?"

"Of course I checked. Had to make sure I had all the facts."

He comes closer until I can smell coffee and alcohol overlaying his warm flesh. My heart thuds, and I wet my lower lip, wondering what he'll do next. "You know what I hate the most about all this?"

I shake my head.

The back of his forefinger brushes along my cheek. The gesture is unexpectedly tender, which just makes it hurt more.

"I still want you in spite of it all." His words are so soft, they barely whisper across my skin.

"Elliot…"

"I need to shower and do some work." He drops his hand like a guillotine and stalks away.

Closing my eyes against the pain, I bury my face in my hands. How can I fix our relationship when he hates the fact that he still feels the connection between us?

I can't keep running. I ran before, when things went south in Lincoln City. People blamed me for being my father's daughter, and there was nothing I could do to change that. But things are different here. Elliot doesn't have a problem with who I am…it's just what I've done.

I can work with that. I can find a way to make him see that I won't do it again…and convince him I didn't do anything to betray him.

I am not like the Annabelle from his past.

TWO

Elliot

MY FINGER STILL TINGLES AS I VICIOUSLY yank off my clothes and dump them on the bathroom floor. A button from my shirt hits the tiles, and I curse under my breath. Fuck it. The housekeeper will have to find it, or else the dry-cleaning lady can just replace it. I really don't give a damn.

The shower is heating up, turning the room steamy. I put an overly large dollop of toothpaste on the brush and start scrubbing my teeth with more force than necessary, as though that will somehow stop me from going back downstairs and kissing my wife's lush lips.

I should hate her for what she's done. I *do* hate her. But somehow my hormones become entirely too active when she's around.

I rinse my mouth out and step into the shower. The hot water erases the rest of the fatigue weighing on me. I didn't sleep a wink last night. Impossible, when all sorts of thoughts were spinning and bouncing around in my mind like a BB in a pinball machine.

My wife's betrayal hurts. In fact, it enrages me. Maybe time has dulled my memory, but I don't remember betrayal causing this kind of anger before. Not that I wasn't furious when Annabelle announced her engagement to my father, but the intensity wasn't like this…this…all-consuming fire.

Squeezing my eyes shut, I bow my head under the water.

"Elliot."

Belle's voice shatters what meager calm I've been able to gather. I pull back from the spray and glare at her standing on the other side of the glass stall. She's still beautiful, her green eyes dark and solemn and her soft mouth like a lush flower in that finely carved face. The flimsy silk gown skims the gorgeous body that I spent hours worshipping just a few days ago. Was it just yesterday that we came back from our honeymoon?

Knowing what she is changes nothing of my reaction to her.

I let my mouth curl into a sardonic line. "Didn't you hear what I said about shower and having things to do? Unlike you, I actually need to work."

She hugs herself. The gesture makes her look oddly alone, and I instinctively want to reach out and comfort her. "Don't use that to shut me out," she says.

Damn her. Damn me! I curl my hands into fists instead and keep them hanging by my sides. "Like you didn't shut me out when you kept your secret?"

"You're being unfair."

I bark out a laugh. "There it is again. *Unfair.* That's rich, coming from you."

"When was I supposed to tell you? When you were shoving money into my G-string? When you were telling me to get down on my knees in exchange for three thousand dollars? When you were manhandling me at owm?" She flings an arm out. "Or how about when you told me you wanted to marry me for a year so you could 'fuck me' and put your hand between my legs?"

That's it. I'm not going to stay in the stall and listen to her try to justify what she's done. I cut the water and come out, grabbing a towel. "How about the time I asked you to tell me your secrets? How about the time I told you my ugly past with Annabelle Underhill? I've been many things with you, but never a hypocrite."

"As far as I'm concerned, Mr. Grayson is my problem. I owe him money, and I figured once I pay him off he won't have any leverage over me. Why do you think I wanted to get a job?"

"And you could've told me then, too. When I told you it was pointless to get a job since I would be providing for you. You also could've told me what was going on, and I would've paid Grayson off on your behalf." And seen if I could squeeze any information out of the man, given his connection to Keith Shellington, the Embezzling Asshole.

"I was *embarrassed*, okay? It was stupid to take his money. But…I was desperate." She bites her lower lip. "You know how things were when we first met. We just started to have a decent relationship, and I didn't want to ruin it by asking you to pay off my debt or talking about all the ways I screwed things up after I left Lincoln City."

I toss the damp towel on the floor and glare at her. "So it's my fault that you couldn't come clean."

"You're twisting what I'm telling you." Unshed tears spike her eyelashes, and she looks at me as though I'm the monster.

The same way Annabelle Underhill did when I called her out on her fucking scheme to marry my father. We were in a small closet where various dresses and outfits were stashed for their ceremony and reception. It was one of the few places we could have some privacy.

You're twisting what I'm telling you, she said. *If you hadn't kept your plans secret…*

"If we hadn't such a rocky beginning..." my wife is saying.

I close the distance between us in three big steps and grip her wrist. I can feel her pulse spike against my thumb. "Then what, *wife?* You would've told me everything?"

She tilts her head to look up at me. The motion pushes her tits forward, and I wonder—quite cynically—if it's a calculated move. Annabelle did the same then...and then let her mouth quiver...just like my wife is doing right now. The two women start to blur. And I finally realize why I'm more furious now than before. I assumed Belle would be on my side, that she would never betray my trust because she'd thrown some crumbs about her past my way. But of course that was an error. A very stupid one.

Belle's breathing shallows. With fear or something else...I don't know and I don't give a damn. The edges of my vision dim and redden.

"Elliot..."

"I should've stuck to our agreement," I spit out between clenched teeth. "Trying to change that, as though we could ever have anything meaningful for a year, was my mistake."

Infuriatingly enough, my mind tells me I should stop now, before I hurt her too much, but I can't. I want to devastate her the way she's devastated me. I want to be contemptuous, make her feel as much self-disgust as I do.

And I can't stand myself for wanting her. My cock's so hard I could use it to split timber. I twist my hand into her hair and pull until she's arching into my body. Her pointed nipples stab into my bare chest, and I growl deep in my throat. My dick presses against her belly, and she gasps.

Before she can regain her equilibrium, I crush my lips against hers in a punishing kiss. There's no gentleness or finesse as I plunder her mouth with every violent emotion that whips through me. She needs to know what she's done, and I don't even know why that matters so much. The likeliest scenario is that she doesn't care, because all this had been coldly calculated, and everything between us is just one huge farce. I exert more pressure, my teeth almost cutting the tender flesh of her lips. I brace myself for her reaction—a recoil of shock and distaste, an attempt to slap me away, a struggle…

But none of that comes.

Instead she's kissing me back with wild abandon, like a woman on a mission to prove she wants me. Her tongue tangles with mine with an aggression that stuns me…then stokes my need.

She tunnels her fingers into my hair to keep me close. Blood roars in my head as I push her robe and nightgown away with unsteady hands, revealing smooth, sun-kissed skin. Her warm, delicious scent is a narcotic; as I crush her hair, I can smell faint apple from the silken strands.

Need pulses in my veins, throbs through me. My dick aches so hard it feels like it's about to break.

Desperate to maintain some semblance of control, I cup her breast, kneading it, toying with it. My thumb brushes over her beaded nipple more lightly than a feather, but she shudders violently.

"More," she moans, breaking away from our kiss long enough for that one word. And I give it to her, circling the tip with my thumb, my touch light and teasing. Her fingers in my hair tighten until my scalp feels the sting. I pick her up and prop her on the vanity; her thighs part wide to let me stand between them. She rocks shamelessly, her cunt wet.

She can't fake this. She can't will her body to be this ready for me. She either wants my dick in her pussy or she doesn't. And I'm inexplicably grateful for that bit of honesty from her, then ticked off with myself for feeling anything positive.

She is wanton, her eyes barely slits as she looks at me, her body liquid and undulating with desire. Her nipples are so tight I know they have to hurt every time she draws a breath. She digs her small, even teeth into her swollen lower lip. I'm so attuned to her, I know what she wants, but I don't want to give it to her. Not like this.

"Beg for it," I say. "Tell me exactly what you want; don't leave anything out."

"You." She shudders. "Your mouth on my breasts—one after the other." She licks her mouth, and the muscles in her throat works as she swallows. "You on your knees as you eat me out." Flush tints her cheeks. "Your hands in my hair as you"—the flush spreads to her chest—"fuck my mouth and my hand between my legs so when you come, I come too."

I order myself to be disgusted—the way I felt disgusted by the other Annabelle when she moaned and writhed against me in the closet while the wedding guests milled about on the other side of the door. But instead my wife's words are like flames, burning away my self-control. I want to give her everything that shaky voice of hers is asking for.

Because I know she means every syllable. Her voice might be quavering, but her gaze has been steadily on my face the entire time.

She drops her eyes to my cock, her lips parting softly. I look down and see clear beads of liquid dripping down my thick shaft.

Unable to stop myself, I step forward and take her mouth in a kiss. This time it's lush, the intent to arouse and pleasure.

Belle clings to me desperately, and I reward her by tweaking a nipple between my fingers. She gasps against my lips, and I feel myself growing even harder.

I pull away to take her other breast into my mouth. I suck it deep inside, my tongue running over the hard nub. Her back arches, and her sharp cry echoes around the bathroom walls. I run a hand along her inner thigh, and she spreads her legs wider. Her wet heat beckons me closer, and I dig my fingers into her slick folds.

"So fucking hot," I groan.

"Don't stop," she begs.

I laugh darkly. A horde of barbarians wouldn't be able to tear me from her now. I tease her opening, feel the muscles clench with emptiness. This intimate, I can sense everything—her sweet scent, the tiny quivers of her flesh that say she is dying for what I can give her, and the shuddery breaths she takes to control herself.

Except I don't want her in control. I want her out of her mind. I want her shattered.

I switch to the other breast and plunge two fingers into her.

She cries out, her inner muscles clutching the digits like her life depends on it. I give her time to adjust while I suckle her breast. It isn't long before she's rocking against me, needing me to move.

I leisurely work my fingers in and out, making sure to stimulate the front wall of her vagina, as my thumb circles around, and then over, her swollen clit. Her breath grows more jagged and rougher, the sounds in her throat primal and raw. She tightens her grip in my hair as though that will anchor her. I drive her ruthlessly, relentlessly until her body bows and jerks helplessly in climax.

Remembering what she's begged me to do, I lower myself and thrust my tongue into her dripping cunt before she's come down from the high. She shakes violently as I start in, her arms barely holding her up. Her leg muscles tighten, her toes curling. Her heels dig into my back, and I relish her reaction. I lick at her, suck her in and thrust into her until her muscles spasm in another orgasm. She shoves a fist against her mouth, and I grip her thighs hard.

"Don't you dare muffle your reaction to this," I growl against her quivering flesh. "You're going to come again and scream until your throat is raw."

"Elliot, I ca—"

I don't let her finish. I push her to another climax, then another and another and she screams through them all until her voice breaks.

She collapses, clinging to my shoulders. After a short moment, she pulls me up and kisses my mouth, her tongue gently licking at my lips. If I didn't know better, I'd find the gesture tender and loving.

I'm just about to pull away, but she wraps her hand around my straining erection. My vision turns hazy for a moment as pleasure courses through me. The pressure in my dick is relentless and brutal. I could come after just a couple of strokes from her, but I'd rather die than lose control like that.

Her lips brush over my hammering heart. "Thank you, but you forgot something…"

I should move away, but I can't. I'm a man, and I want what I want.

She drops to her knees before me and takes me deep inside her mouth. My eyes roll up and it's all I can do to keep my legs stiff.

Belle doesn't drive me to an orgasm with single-minded focus the way I did to her. Her mouth is sweet as she pleasures me. It's as though she is making love to me in the most primitive way, and even as my mind rebels, rejects the idea, my body is helplessly drawn to her, craving more of her tenderness.

When she cups my balls and pulls me hard and deep into her mouth, I'm lost. I shatter with a hoarse cry, and she drinks me in, her soft gaze on me.

And in that moment, I realize one thing I've tried to deny since discovering her deception.

No matter what, I crave her with an intensity that borders on madness.

THREE

Annabelle

I stay at Elliot's feet as he gathers his breath. He braces his hands against the edge of the vanity, and stares down at me, his chiseled face stark with the recent orgasm.

Finally he squeezes his eyes shut and tilts his head back. Then he stands straight and says, "The shower's yours. I have a few conference calls."

Slowly I push myself up. My legs are like soggy pasta, the flesh between my thighs hypersensitive. His right hand twitches, then he clenches his jaw and leaves me alone in the bathroom.

I inhale deeply and review what just happened.

If I'd been thinking more clearly, I would've known nothing would change from sex. What just happened was great—it's always been fantastic between us—but it isn't enough to fix what's broken.

Have hope. He isn't indifferent.

I can work with anything but indifference. Maybe one night isn't enough time for him to cool down and regain the proper perspective. With more time he'll be willing to listen—*really* listen.

I've been telling myself what Elliot and I have is only for a year, so it doesn't matter how things pan out between us. But I care about what he thinks, how he feels. I wasn't just saying it when I told him I loved him. I did and still do love him. So even if all we have is a year, I don't want it to be a bad year. I want to leave my mark on him so he'll always think of me with…well, something warm and sweet, even if it's not love.

By the time I step into the shower and wash, I feel better. The warm water is soothing. Back in the closet I pull on a simple sleeveless yellow dress. I'm not going to make a move against Mr. Grayson until Elliot and I have a calm talk. Mr. Grayson knew about Elliot needing a wife, so maybe whatever he was having me do actually had more to do with my husband. Elliot and I should come up with a game plan so neither of us is working against the other inadvertently.

Just as I enter the kitchen, Nonny emerges from her room. She's put on a black dress and matching sandals, and her hair is pulled back in a high and tight ponytail. A thicker than usual layer of concealer betrays the fact that she has dark circles under her eyes. Anger and shame simmer in equal parts in her eyes…which won't meet mine. I don't know what she and Elliot talked about yesterday before he left the penthouse, but whatever it was didn't solve the problems between us.

I go to the kitchen and hand-wash the crystal tumbler I left in the sink earlier. Nonny watches me, then looks away.

Guess she isn't making the first move.

"Cereal?" I keep my voice as neutral as possible. Trying to pretend that nothing's happened is an insult to both of us, but I don't know what else to do.

"No."

Nonny walks to the fridge, making sure not to touch me, and takes out a small tub of strawberry-flavored Greek yogurt. She stands, waiting until I move out of the way, then opens the top drawer for a spoon.

"I'm sorry."

Her motion's jerky as she stirs the thick white stuff. "You did what you had to do." Still, she keeps her gaze on the food in front of her.

"If you know that, why won't you look at me?"

She snaps her head up and stares at me. Her face is set in a positively mutinous line, something I've never seen on her before. "Happy now?"

"Nonny…"

Her brow creasing, she looks back down at the yogurt. "You should've told me."

"I'm sorry."

"Forget it." She polishes off the yogurt in three big spoonfuls. "I'm running late."

I glance at the clock on the wall. She has plenty of time.

"We need to talk."

"Yeah, like weeks ago."

"I'm trying to talk now."

"Like I said, I'm running late. I have some things to do before school." She turns around and goes into her room.

I make myself fresh coffee and drink it silently, blinking away the tears burning in my eyes. What do I do now? I've never felt so alone before. Even though the people in Lincoln City turned their backs on me, Nonny has been always by my side. I didn't realize until now how much that meant to me.

She leaves the condo soon after, backpack slung over one shoulder. She doesn't say goodbye, doesn't even look my way. It's as though I'm dead to her.

My phone beeps. I pick it up listlessly, then notice a text from my best friend Traci. She's from Lincoln City, like me, and her family lost everything because of my dad's Ponzi scheme. It's a miracle that she's gotten over the betrayal and anger, and I'm grateful. I can use a friend.

Are you okay? I saw the articles about you and Elliot. You know I'm here for you if you need a shoulder or sounding board or anything.

Suddenly it seems like a great idea to see her. Traci's smart and discreet. If nothing else, she'll cheer me up and help figure out what to do about Nonny.

I text her back. *I'm okay, but I could use a friendly person to talk to. You have any free time?*

Her response is almost instant. *Of course. Today or tomorrow? I can take an early lunch.*

I look at the closed door to Elliot's office. *Today is good. Time?*

Eleven thirty at Galore? It's a sandwich shop not too far from the office.

I remember that place. Elliot took me there after our courthouse wedding because I was nearly fainting with hunger. Has it been only two months since we got married? *I know the place. See you there.*

I check the time. *Almost ten.* I write a short note for Elliot, then go back to the bedroom to put on some makeup. Traci won't care, but I don't want to run into any acquaintances of Elliot's and cause embarrassment by looking so haggard and tired. Everyone already knows about my stripper past and will have drawn whatever conclusions they're going to draw. I don't want to look pathetic over it. I haven't done anything illegal or unethical.

I carefully apply concealer and foundation to hide the dark circles under my eyes, then put some color onto my cheeks. The lip-gloss adds a nice shimmer to my mouth, and I pull my hair back in a ponytail and put a pair of big sunglasses over my face. I'm not ashamed of what I've done, but at the same time I don't really want to deal with people recognizing me either.

By the time I step inside Galore, it's only eleven twenty. I shrug mentally. Being early never killed anyone.

The sandwich shop is nice and cool inside, A/C running low and ceiling fans doing the rest. The dark wooden tables and chairs are empty now, but soon they'll be crowded. I get an order of a ham and cheese sandwich plus chips and Coke Zero and take a table in the back, thinking it'll give us the most privacy. Traci shows up at eleven thirty five.

She struts in like a model, dark brown curls bouncing around her shoulders. Her carefully mascaraed hazel eyes are bright on her round face. She's dressed in a fashion similar to before— her tight skirt a little too short to be professional but long enough to pass muster. The deep purple sleeveless top has a plunging V-neck, but again, it covers just enough to be okay for an office setting. Her stilettos look like something Torquemada might have designed, but she seems perfectly fine in them.

She spots me easily in the nearly empty shop and joins me with a bowl of chicken and veggie soup, a half sandwich and an iced coffee. I stand up, and we hug tightly before taking our seats.

"That's all you're eating?" I ask.

"Yeah. Don't have time to work out these days, so I gotta cut calories."

"I had no idea you were so busy."

"Hey." She reaches over and squeezes my hand. "I always have time for my best friend."

"Thanks, Traci. It really means a lot to me."

"I'm just worried about you, that's all. But you seem to be taking the…well, you know, the *news* pretty well."

"I don't care what the tabloids say."

She peers at me while sucking her coffee up through a straw. "Is Elliot okay?"

"I…" I hesitate. Elliot is okay with my past as a stripper, just not the other stuff. But something holds me back, and I can't tell her the whole truth. I don't know if it's because of the way she abandoned me when I was at my lowest or if it's something else, but my gut tells me to keep my mouth shut. "I mean, he already knew, so…" I shrug, not wanting to lie outright to her face.

"But it's one thing for him to know, another for it to go public."

"I honestly don't think it matters to him that much." His siblings and parents, on the other hand... I have no clue what they think about all this. Oh no...*Elizabeth*. His saintly sister is probably scandalized.

"Probably not," Traci muses out loud. "It's not like he's a choirboy. I mean, he has that sex tape in his past, so I can't see how he'd be upset with you about this. His family, either. They should be thanking you for marrying a guy with a reputation as wild as Elliot's."

"Right." Except his family knows why we married in the first place, so they probably aren't feeling all that much gratitude. Not that I would ever tell Traci. It's strictly Elliot's family's issue, and I can't make an executive decision to share something that isn't mine to begin with.

"The problem is Nonny," I say, not wanting to talk more about Elliot. "She's really upset."

"Oh no. The poor kid. She didn't know?"

"Well, *no*, of course not. It's not something I wanted to tell her."

"Is she being bullied because of your...previous job?"

I pause for a moment. I've never thought of that. I just assumed she was embarrassed, but maybe other kids in school are teasing her. Even though she seemed to have gotten some cool points for being related to Ryder Reed—distantly, through marriage—kids can turn on one another so fast. *Lord of the Flies* isn't a classic for nothing.

"I don't know," I finally answer.

Traci sighs. "You might want to find out. See if you can do some damage control." She taps the rim of her glass. "But I think that the biggest thing that can fix the situation—if she's being bullied or something—is for you and Elliot to make up and put on a good public show as a loving couple. Maybe, I don't know, go to some kind of Hollywood party together or something? Once people see that you guys aren't bothered by your past, maybe the kids in her school will leave Nonny alone too. It's not any fun to pick at a wound that doesn't exist."

I frown. "You're right." Except…Elliot and I don't have any special event we can attend together while looking like we're in love. Even if there were one, given his reaction in the bathroom this morning, I don't know if he'd go for it.

"I just want you to make up with him and be happy. And take better care of yourself."

I force a smile. "I am taking care of myself."

She gives me a pitying look. "Come on. I've seen zombies with more pep."

"I…"

"Don't worry. Most people wouldn't have noticed, but who am I? Traci, your best friend since kindergarten, that's who. And I can tell."

I swallow and nod.

"Seriously. Multivitamins." She gives me a small smile and squeezes my hand. "Feel better now that we've talked?"

"Yes."

"Like I said, I'm always here for you if you need somebody."

"Thanks."

We finish our lunch while chatting about her job. I'm not interested in what's going on at OWM simply for altruistic "I'm being a good friend" reasons—although I am curious about how she's doing under a boss who seems as demanding as Gavin Lloyd. I want to know what's going on there because of my ex-boyfriend, Dennis, who seems convinced that one, my husband is out to get him, and two, I'm the only one who can stop him. I swear he's gone paranoid. There were signs when we were living in Lincoln City, but he was never this bad. Is this recent worsening somehow the result of what his father did? Jack Smith joined my dad in the Ponzi scheme, and when it fell apart, he gunned down my parents and then blew his own brains out with the last bullet. And Dennis's been very careful to hide his true parentage from everyone.

Of course, steering the conversation the way I want it to go isn't easy. Traci is somewhat stuck on her immediate supervisor Hilary, and Gavin.

"It's like he can't live without her. If I didn't know better, I'd swear they were lovers or something. But they have zero chemistry that way. Besides, they're both too happily married."

I tilt my head. "Maybe she's just good at her job."

"She is. I'm hoping she keeps me because being so close to the boss comes with some great advantages, even if I'm not that high on the totem pole." Traci flushes, then sips her coffee, lowering her eyelashes. "I can learn from watching him and then maybe leverage that into getting a more lucrative position at the firm."

"Right." I grin. "You are totally crushing on him," I tease.

Traci meets my gaze straight on. Her eyes are unusually bright. "What if I am?"

I gape at her. "Wait. You're seriously saying that you are?"

She shrugs, although her mouth is smiling. "He's a very…charismatic man, and I'm not dead. But"—she sighs—"I know he's married. So…"

"Don't they have other unmarried hotties at the firm? It looked like it was full of young, ambitious men the last time I was there."

"Yeah, but they aren't the same. Gavin's the alpha male." She adjusts her top, smoothing it so it lies perfectly against her enhanced cleavage.

So that explains her outfits. I don't know if she's consciously choosing to wear them or not, but I hope she doesn't do anything stupid. Unless I'm mistaken, Gavin is utterly in love with his wife. I open my mouth to say something, then stop. It seems a bit presumptuous of me to lecture Traci when she already knows about his marital status and we've just reconnected after a couple years apart. Unlike me, Traci's been smart enough to make something of herself, so who am I to act like I know better?

"Although... There's this guy in accounting with this totally hot look. But I hear he's gay. Pete's handsome too, but he's taken." She sighs again. "It's always something."

Finally. I perk up. "You mean Pete Monroe? Dennis's boss?"

Traci nods. "He's Gavin's brother-in-law. Really yummy, but engaged to some interior designer."

"What's he like?" I lean forward. "He's handling my account, so I'm curious."

She whips her head my way. "Wait. You're a client?"

I nod. "Didn't I tell you?"

"No. You didn't." Her eyebrows pinch together as she quickly drops her gaze for a moment. She inhales. When she meets my eyes again, the frown is gone, and she's smiling again. "He's pretty amazing from what I heard. Gavin trusts him, and he's very good at what he does. Dennis is lucky to be doing his internship with him. You couldn't ask for a better man to mentor and guide you."

Perfect. "How's he doing? Dennis, I mean."

"Pretty par for the course, from what I can tell. I think he's stressed out because he's really hoping to make an impression and get hired on full-time. OWM doesn't take that many new analysts."

"How come?"

"Turnover's too low." She nibbles on her lower lip. "By the way, I asked around about an opening."

"Oh?" I'd almost forgotten that I asked Traci about a job. "And?"

"There is one. It's not a great position or anything. A junior assistant to one of the VPs. Her current assistant's going on maternity leave in eight weeks, so it's sort of temporary, if you don't mind that. But she'll be gone for at least a year—"

"A year?"

"What can I say? OWM has a great maternity leave policy." Traci pushes her curls over a shoulder. "Anyway, it's a temporary position, but it'd give you a chance to network and get some office work experience for your résumé. A foot in the door."

I consider. I want to say yes right now, but things are fragile at home. It'd be better to discuss the matter with Elliot before committing to anything. I don't think he'll object, but our fight has been about me keeping things from him. I want to show him in every way possible that I won't do that anymore. "Let me think about it and get back to you."

"No problem." Traci checks her watch. "Oh, shoot. I need to get going. Gotta prep for a meeting."

I wish we could linger—I don't want to go home right now—but of course she has to work. We walk out together, chatting animatedly. It's somewhat forced on my part, but it's better to pretend I'm fine.

"We should do this again when you don't have a crisis going," Traci says. "It was fun."

"Definitely." I smile.

Talking things out with her has definitely improved my mood, even if we couldn't come up with a solution to my problem with Elliot. I can't tell her much, not like in the old days, but just knowing that I have someone I can talk to makes me feel better.

We hug each other goodbye outside the door, and I watch her trot off down the street. When

I turn to leave, something cold splashes all over my chest.

"Oh shit," comes a dismayed male voice. "Sorry about that. Are you okay?"

"Uh, yeah…I guess." I tug the wet dress from my chest with a grimace. The iced coffee drink—probably a latte—really did a number on my outfit. It's turned the yellow into a semi-transparent brown, and I can feel it soaking through my padded bra, making my breasts cold and uncomfortable. A couple of large rivulets have also dripped all the way down to the hem; several drops land on my shoes.

"Really, really sorry." He pulls out a pale cream handkerchief from his jacket and hands it to me.

I take it and do what I can to salvage the dress, but it's no good.

"Ah jeez. I've I ruined your clothes."

I finally raise my eyes to look at the man who's being so apologetic. A lot of guys would've been like, "Watch where you're going" or given me a token "sorry." But he's different. He genuinely seems upset.

The guy is probably in his late thirties or early forties, although I'd put my money on the younger half of the range. He's impeccably groomed, with neatly cut sandy brown hair and a cleanly shaven face. A dark navy suit hugs his tall, lanky body, making him look like a banker or a lawyer. The only somewhat disconcerting thing about him are the eyes—light gray, and penetrating as he studies my reaction. I feel like a lab rat under the gaze.

"Don't worry about it," I say. "I should've been more careful."

"I wasn't watching where I was going." He smiles sheepishly and shrugs. "On my phone."

"It happens."

"You can't go around like that. Let me buy you a new dress."

"Not at all necessary."

An eyebrow rises like he can't believe I'm turning down a free outfit. "Are you sure?"

"Quite. I'm on my way home anyway."

"Still. I insist. You're soaked."

"Tell you what. You can pay for the dry cleaning." I don't want to go anywhere with this man. There's nothing really *wrong* with what he's offering, but…

He reaches into his pocket and pulls out a money clip. He hands me a bill and a business card. "This should cover it. But really, no joke, if your cleaner can't get the stain out, let me know and I'll have your clothes replaced."

"Okay."

"I'm serious."

"I'll call if there's a problem. I promise."

He points a finger at the card clutched in my hand, raises his eyebrows significantly, and walks away. I look down. The lunatic has given me a hundred-dollar bill. Where in the world does he get his stuff cleaned that it costs a hundred dollars for a single outfit?

His business card is printed on stock that feels thick and expensive. It has three numbers— mobile, office and fax. There's no business title or anything else, just a name. *Keith Shellington.*

Sighing, I stick the money and card into my wallet and head home.

FOUR

Elliot

I CAN'T FOCUS ON ANYTHING. I WANT TO BLAME my inability to concentrate on a lack of sleep, but I can function on two hours for three or four nights in a row so long as I make up for it later.

After having read the same email five times without understanding what my assistant wants, I close my laptop in disgust. My mind keeps drifting to my wife. I can't stop thinking about the way she felt, the way she came against me and the way she sucked me off. I'm doing my best to convince myself it's just the sex—I'm a healthy guy and I love it. But the truth is, there's something more going on. No one's ever gotten to me like this, making me feel like a piece of me is breaking with desperate want of her.

Stop obsessing about her.

Easier said than done.

"Damn it." I get up and kick my chair. It wheels away across the room.

Needing to give myself something to do, I pull out my phone and call Lucas. The bastard predictably ignores me. He isn't doing it because he's upset with me. He's just become something of a hermit ever since the accident that left him scarred and slightly limping two years ago. Actually, he doesn't really limp usually, only when he's tired. I might've thought he was embarrassed about his scar, but I know my brother. He's not that vain, and he certainly isn't worried about what people think. And I have proof: he's only hermit-like when invited to social events. For professional stuff, he's available—albeit very selectively—and people seek him for speeches and consulting services for his brilliant mind.

Pissed off, I text him a name: *Keith Shellington*, and think *Now let's see how long it takes for you to call.*

A few minutes later, my phone rings. The screen flashes my twin brother's face along with LUCAS in all caps.

"Finally, you bastard," I say.

"Um. Hold on a minute, please," comes the familiar woman's voice, and I pinch the bridge of my nose. It's Lucas's personal assistant, Rachel. I actually like her, so I'm annoyed she got the greeting meant for her boss.

"Lucas," my twin says finally.

"Your finger broken?"

"No. Rachel likes to be useful."

"You're an ass."

"And you texted *Keith Shellington* to tell me this? Watch it. Next time I might not call back at all."

"I know where you live."

"Ah, but do you know my schedule?"

Touché. Lucas has been traveling over the last two years, and I haven't been able to catch him, not even by barging into his home unannounced.

"So. What's the meaning of your text?" he demands.

I prop my butt against the edge of my desk. "Watch your back. I think he's up to something."

"Like?"

"Who knows? He's a rat."

"Yeah, but he won't jeopardize what he has by trying to fuck with us. He got away, stealing from us, and he knows the only reason he's able to continue is because we never pursued the matter. Nobody wants a money guy with even a hint of embezzlement attached to his name."

"Maybe not. Still, he blames me for stealing 'his' millions."

Keith raged at me when I confronted him. Face mottled, he yelled, "You fucking bastard, you have no idea what you're doing. It's not stealing if you plan to pay it back!"

Sort of like it's not shoplifting if you plan to give it back. That logic didn't fly with me, and I didn't like the way he set his assistant up to take the fall that should have been his. By the time the forensic accountants were through, I had all the evidence I needed, but our business mentor and advisor Marlin thought it would be better if we just moved on, and Lucas agreed.

After all, Keith didn't get the millions of dollars he would've received if he'd been honest, and that would have more than made up for the money he stole. He was a small-thinking rat back then too, only helping himself to a few tens of thousands here and there. Then again, if he hadn't had such tiny balls, he would've been caught much faster.

"You're being paranoid," Lucas says. "He knows you have evidence of his embezzlement. He wouldn't want to provoke you into releasing that and killing what he's managed to build since then."

I sigh. What Lucas is saying makes sense, but still… "He's approached my wife." Admittedly, not directly…but then that isn't his MO. He needs a fall guy.

"You sure?"

"Positive."

"For what?"

"He probably wants to use her to get something. I just don't know what."

"Maybe he's going to convince her to divorce you and take you to the cleaners."

I shake my head. "Not possible. Prenup."

"They can be gotten around. You saw what happened to Ryder's uncle, right? That prenup was supposed to be unbreakable."

Shit. That's true enough. I heard some whispers about that from a few people, mostly those whose sole purpose in life is to keep track of juicy gossip. But Belle doesn't seem like the type to do something like that. It's just…low and not like her. If she were, she wouldn't have been cleaning toilets for a living. "I'm having a hard time wrapping my mind around it," I say finally.

"Well, get your mind-wrapper fixed. ASAP. You know how people can be when there's a lot of money involved," Lucas says, his voice quiet. "I'm not the one who discovered the embezzlement. Keith blames you more than me for the fallout. So be careful, Elliot." He hangs up.

I grind my teeth. Suddenly everything about life is pissing me off. I have an old enemy making a move against me…and a wife I crave but can't trust. Whenever I think of the times she told me she loved me, my skin crawls. I can't help but wonder if it was genuine or attempted manipulation, and then I feel hollow inside because I want her love to be real.

I grip my phone hard. It's that or hurl it against the wall, and I'm likely to regret the latter.

I march to the kitchen. It's a quarter after twelve, so Belle should be downstairs, about to have lunch.

I don't want to eat. I don't want her to eat. I want to hash it out, yell at her, have her scream at me—

The kitchen's empty.

The fridge has a note stuck to it.

Elliot,

I'm going out. I won't be home for lunch, and I may be out for too long to get something for you on the way back. So you'll have to fend for yourself. See you later today.

–B

The note deflates me, and I don't know why. I'm *not* not angry. But I assumed she would be around, waiting for me.

To do what?

I sit at the counter and stare at the note, running my forefinger along her neat handwriting. She's smart enough to know I'm still upset and that lunch with me would be unbearable. Who could blame her?

I raise my eyes from the note, gazing around the penthouse. The silence practically screams at me, and I can't help but think that the place looks cavernously empty somehow.

Annabelle

ELLIOT'S IN HIS OFFICE WHEN I COME BACK FROM my lunch with Traci. Without saying anything to let him know I'm back, I change into a T-shirt and denim skirt and go drop my dress off at the dry cleaner, which, unfortunately, can't guarantee anything about the giant coffee stain. But if they can't clean the dress, I'll just throw it out. I'm not calling this Shellington guy to demand that he replace it when I have so many clothes in my closet. I need an awkward conversation with a stranger like a restaurant needs a rat in its kitchen.

When I return, Elliot's in the kitchen getting another coffee. I say, "Hi."

He merely nods.

"There's something I want to talk about."

He raises an eyebrow and waits.

The silent treatment. Fine. I don't let it get to me. If he expects me to cringe or something, he has another think coming. "I met Traci today for lunch, and she said there's a temporary opening at owm. I thought maybe I should take it."

A small muscle in his jaw flexes, and he breathes audibly through his mouth. "I'll take care of the money you owe Grayson."

"It's not really about the money. I don't think this is a well-paying job, given that it's a junior assistant position." When he merely stares at me, I fidget. "Like I said before, I want something to occupy my time." *Especially if you're going to treat me like this.* "Besides, it'll be good for me. Something to put on my résumé, plus it'll get me out of the house…maybe make some new friends."

"Then you should take the job."

The lack of inflection in his voice twists me inside out. He used to be so animated, eyes bright and words full of emotion, even when he was trying rather crudely to proposition me. I'd rather have that than this.

"Elliot…"

"That's what you want, isn't it?" He sounds reasonable. Too reasonable.

"Yes, but you can tell me if you have any misgivings. It's your friend's company."

"Why? Do you have to hand over any secrets to Grayson?"

My face heats. I can feel blotches of red blooming in my cheeks, neck and chest. "That's uncalled for."

He shrugs.

I put my hands on my hips. "You know I could've just applied for the job on the spot when Traci mentioned it, but I wanted to talk to you first."

"Why?"

"Because you made a big deal about talking things over first, and the last time we talked about me getting a job, you seemed standoffish about the idea."

"You can do whatever you want, Belle."

"You want me to beg, don't you?"

"If you want."

My teeth grind together, but I force myself to relax so I can talk with some outward semblance of calm. "I already said I was sorry. And I am sorry. I honestly didn't think it would matter so much to you, or that it would be such a betrayal. I haven't told Mr. Grayson anything, or done anything on his behalf. I don't even know what he really wants." The only thing I am pretty certain of is that he doesn't just want his money back from me, except...I can't imagine what he thinks I can do for him.

"Have you considered the fact that if he knows about my needing to marry, he might know how long I need to marry as well?"

I tilt my head. "No. It never crossed my mind."

"Then now you can see how he could've asked you to divorce me before the year is up."

"Except I wouldn't. You and I signed a deal." His expression doesn't change, and I know I'm not convincing him. So I add something he'll understand. "I want that million dollars."

Elliot's mouth slants upward in an unpleasant smile. "He could top that amount. Easily double it."

Would Mr. Grayson go that far? I shake my head. "Well, I don't care. I still wouldn't do it."

"Why not? You said it yourself back then—you needed money."

"Yes, but a million is more than enough. Besides…" I sigh, suddenly tired. "I love you, Elliot."

His eyes shutter. The only thing that betrays that he feels anything is a light flush streaking his lean cheeks.

He is shutting me out, and I ache. There's something so painful about telling a man you love him and having him reject it. Did it have something to do with me telling him that I didn't think I could love romantically? Back then I believed that because my experiences were less than ideal, and I couldn't let myself be that vulnerable. But then Elliot had to show me another side of him that I couldn't resist. It was more than sex, more than just kindness. It was as though he knew exactly what he needed to do to heal my soul.

My eyes prickle, and I blink quickly. I won't have him accuse me of using tears to get my way, but I'm not going to look away either. I'm not lying and I have nothing to hide.

"I don't care what you think," I begin, "but it's the truth. God knows..." My voice breaks along with my heart. "I didn't want to love you."

With that parting remark, I go upstairs to my room, feeling Elliot's eyes boring into my back. I need to text Traci that I'm interested in the position, and I need some time alone to lick my wounds. In addition, Nonny's going to be home soon, and I need to mentally prepare for the cold shoulder I'm undoubtedly going to get from her. I refuse to lose my temper or break down.

I can get past this.

As I feared, Nonny is aloof. She makes an effort to be more pleasant when Elliot's around, but when it's just me and her, she's frigid.

"Is school okay?" I ask.

"Sure. Why wouldn't it be?"

You know why. "You'll tell me if anything's wrong, won't you?"

"Yeah." She shrugs, then disappears into her room.

The strain between us weighs heavily upon me. I'm not used to this with my sister. No matter how awful things got, even when everyone else turned their back on me, we were always a team.

But now...I'm really alone.

FIVE

Annabelle

THE REST OF THE WEEK PASSES SLOWLY, every day as awkward as the one before.

Clearly, time isn't going to make anything better on its own. Nonny is still standoffish. If Elliot notices, he doesn't let on, and I don't say anything to him, since it's something I need to work out with her. The longest she's ever been upset with anyone is a week. I'm going to give her that much time and hope that she comes to the realization that everything I've done is for us.

But her attitude doesn't improve. And Elliot...

We no longer talk much during the day. It's impossible to hold a conversation when the other party doesn't say more than a syllable or two. I don't sit on the deck and watch him swim, either.

It hurts too much. We're like polite strangers from dawn to dusk.

But once night descends…

He comes to me in the dark, when I'm in that state of half sleeping and half awake. He takes me hard, but he doesn't kiss me or drive me like he is punishing me. It's as though he's on a mission to exorcise a demon from his mind.

The first night, I told him I loved him, and he quickly put a hand over my mouth. Since then he always muffles my declaration with his palm or mouth.

I might resist if he were a selfish lover, but he isn't. He always painstakingly coaxes my body to mind-obliterating orgasms. And now I'm so primed for him that I grow wet every time I sense him slip into bed. Pavlov's wife.

Even as I lie in the dark, my body sated and covered in sweat, I know something has to change soon or I'm going to go mad. Maybe other women can continue like this, but not me.

Saturday morning, a dress box arrives. It has my name outside on the otherwise spotless matte black exterior, and its sleek look reminds me of the place Josephine took me to replace my wardrobe. I take it to the bedroom and open it. Inside is a note:

Thought this would look best for tonight. Let me know if you have any questions.

–J

I stare at the floor-length ice-blue gown. The color will contrast beautifully against my hair. There's only one thin strap to hold the dress up, and the rich silk will flow over me, skimming every curve. It's obvious I won't be able to wear anything underneath, and I can see why Josephine thought it would look good on me because it will. I'm just not sure why I need it toni—

"I see you got Josephine's package."

My head snaps up at Elliot's comment. His voice is devoid of emotion, and the indifference slices me. I push the pain aside; there's not a lot I can do about it at the moment, especially with Nonny right down-stairs. "Do you know what this is for?"

"Elizabeth's charity dinner. It's tonight."

"What charity dinner?"

"The one Amandine mentioned."

Now I remember. When we dined together at her home, Amandine asked if we were going to attend. "I thought we weren't going."

"Why wouldn't we?"

"Things have...happened since then."

"That doesn't mean we get to back out. Elizabeth's expecting us."

Of course. Elliot would hate to disappoint his sister. He loves her, trusts her with everything.

And as petty as it is, I'm envious of Elizabeth for having that special place in his heart. I'm beginning to see how precious and rare his trust is. "Elliot—"

His heavy sigh cuts me off. "If you really don't want to go, we can cancel. I can tell her I'm not feeling well."

I almost want to. Being out in public and pretending that we're fine is going to take a lot out of me, but I recall what Traci said. Maybe it'll be good to be forced into acting like a loving, newly wedded couple. If nothing else, it'll remind Elliot we had something amazing just a week ago. "Of course not."

"Then you need to get ready," he says. "You have a full spa treatment. I emailed you the confirmation, with directions."

"I have all day." I drop the dress back in the box, unable to bear it. "Can we talk? It's been a week—"

"You need to hurry." He's looking right through me, and he might as well be filleting me with a fish knife. "We're flying up to San Francisco. She's hosting the dinner at the Sterlings' Bay Area mansion."

He turns around, and I tell his retreating back, "One day, Elliot, *I'm* the one who might not want to talk."

He doesn't acknowledge me, but I know he heard me from the way he hesitates for a fraction of a moment before shutting the door behind him.

Sighing roughly, I force myself to get up and go to the spa. It's more or less unavoidable if I don't want to embarrass myself at the event. The kind of people who drop tens of thousands of dollars without a thought spend a lot of money and time to be seen and admired.

By the time the spa people have worked on me for a few hours, I look like I'm a model about to strut down the runway. The only thing we disagreed on was the nail color. They wanted something more newlywed-like—dreamy and soft—and I wanted an assertive, bold color...maybe something like blood red. But the style coordinator insisted it would look too garish, especially with the blue dress. So we compromised on a glossy, dark coral. The staff keeps remarking how beautiful I am. But I feel woefully unprepared for what's to come, a public event where I'm supposed to pretend I'm happy and not at all bothered by what the media is saying about me.

A pair of huge sapphire drop earrings and matching necklace and bracelet complete the look. To all appearances I'm the lucky Cinderella who got herself a rich prince. No one would ever guess that I'd trade all the trappings of wealth for a warm word or smile from Elliot.

When the spa people are finally finished, I climb into the waiting Bentley. The black car stops in front of the penthouse, and Elliot joins me. He's in a tuxedo that fits him perfectly. It emphasizes his broad shoulders and trim waist and the power inherent in his body. It's like tuxes were invented just to make him look fabulous.

Suddenly all I can feel is the vibrant energy of him—his dynamic personality and magnetism. My skin prickles as though I'm surrounded by electric current, and I'm left breathless.

And it hurts that I can't just reach over and run my hand along his arm or link my hand with his the way I want to. A week ago I would have. And he would've given me one of his long sideways glances, appreciation glittering in his eyes.

Now he barely looks at me. I clasp my hands together and gaze out the window, blinking away sudden tears. It's that or throw away every shred of pride. I don't think I can do the latter when we have an audience.

Elliot and I fly in the private jet with the butler. Parker is as solicitous as before, but I can't take any pleasure in our trip. My mind keeps churning, and I can't decide what I feel anymore.

"It won't kill you to smile," Elliot says when we're in the limo on our way to the mansion.

"Do you want me to rub myself all over you

and coo about how handsome you are while I'm at it?" It's out before I can stop myself.

"If it'll help, why not?"

I clamp my mouth shut. I don't want to add a pointless argument to our existing issues.

When our car stops, he takes my hand and guides my face toward him, his index finger under my chin. "Relax and fake it for the evening. I timed it so we'd arrive late anyway." He presses a quick kiss on my mouth just as the door opens.

Thankfully there aren't any photographers with flashing cameras surrounding us. The Sterlings—the family that owns the mansion in front of me—don't take kindly to paparazzi of any type—or so I read when I looked them up while getting my hair done. And what the Sterlings want, the Sterlings get. Apparently Elizabeth is good friends with Nate Sterling, younger brother to the new head of the family.

"Why are they having the dinner here?" I whisper as Elliot leads me to the huge main entrance. The three-story mansion is beyond grand, with soaring columns and a giant portico. Every window on the first and second floors is ablaze with light, creating stark silhouettes of socialites, tycoons of industry and celebrities.

"It gives more oomph to the event because it comes with Justin Sterling's stamp of approval.

Without it, she wouldn't have been able to use the venue."

"Does it really matter?"

"Yes, since Barron's more or less retired and not interested in making his presence felt these days." Elliot frowns. "It's a good thing for Elizabeth's foundation. A lot of people want to be on good terms with the Sterlings, and they'll give more than asked for to support her cause."

The security people at the door are in crisp tuxes, like the guests, but their body language is totally different, alert and watchful. Also, the earpieces are unmistakable. They nod as Elliot and I walk inside.

The place is unbelievably crowded, given how big the mansion is. Occasional loud laughter breaks the steady hum of conversation. Somewhere an orchestra is playing a classical tune. My guess is Mozart, because that seems to be everyone's default composer for something like this—cheery and inoffensive, yet genius. When Mom hosted Lincoln City's social gatherings, she always picked Mozart, declaring you could never go wrong with his music, and suddenly I miss her. I remember the way she would coax my dad out of a bad mood and make Nonny smile no matter what, and I can't help but think that she would've known how to fix the problem I have with Elliot…and the cold, untenable situation with Nonny, too.

I stick close to Elliot, my cool hand in his. What seems like hordes of people come over to introduce themselves or say hello, and it's all I can do to smile as faces and names blur and my head starts to spin. Most are courteous, but some stare outright, like I'm some kind of circus freak on display. And it's not just the men. Some of the women give me a cool once-over, running their eyes up and down my body as if wondering what I looked like hanging off a stripper pole.

Elliot pulls me closer, and he says something I can't quite make out over the ringing in my ears. Then he peers at me. "Are you all right?"

"A little overwhelmed."

His gaze skims over my face, and something in his gaze shifts. A hopeful part of me wants to believe it's concern. He starts to raise his hand, and I think he's about to touch me…but then he drops it, and I hurt.

"If you don't feel well, we can cut the dinner," he says.

"Elizabeth—"

"Doesn't care. She already got the money, and I can tell her we had to go."

I shake my head. "No, don't. I know you want to support her, and I just need some fresh air."

"If you're sure. There are benches and places to sit and rest in the back and on the second level." Elliot dips his head. "Upstairs might be better. There are balconies."

I glance upward and see a giant interior balcony connected to the stairs. "Okay."

Reluctantly I let go of his hand and take the winding stairs. A few guests pass by, but they don't give me a second look.

Once I make it to the second floor, I pluck a glass of ginger ale from a server and plunk myself down on an empty bench. There are fewer people up here, and being away from the crush lessens the claustrophobic feeling. I decide maybe I don't need the outside air after all.

From here I can see everyone below. Elliot is chatting with a group of men and women— all couples. The women are a bit older than me, not by much, but they seem so much worldlier in exquisite designer dresses they pull off with aplomb, flutes of champagne in their bejeweled fingers. Their relaxed stances say this is their scene, their domain. They offer chirpy comments that make everyone laugh, including Elliot.

I feel like a piece of cubic zirconia among Cartier diamonds. What I wouldn't give to have the wit and sophistication those women do. I'm certain none of them would let a problem fester as long as I have with Elliot, because they would know exactly how to cajole him out of his anger.

"Your first event?"

I start at the question, but manage a warm smile as Elizabeth sits down next to me. Always beautiful, today she's positively radiant. Her golden hair is pulled into a sleek updo accented with a gorgeous leaf-shaped, diamond-and-sapphire pin. A few curls frame her model-perfect face, softening it. The makeup makes her brown eyes appear larger and brighter, and the lovely pink on her mouth emphasizes the fine lines of her lips. The white silk cape dress she's in makes her look both regal and ethereal at the same time.

"You look amazing," I say, slightly awed.

"And you look *fabulous*. I'm so glad you came! I haven't been able to catch up or anything since you came back because I've been super busy with last-minute stuff for the event." She makes a vague half-circle with her hand. "But I saw pictures from your honeymoon. You guys looked so cute and happy together."

"Yes, it was a great honeymoon," I say, forcing a smile. I don't want to discuss the tabloid articles about my stripping. It's easier to pretend that none of it happened, even though we both know better. Even though she said she's been busy, I doubt she's been completely isolated from news and social media sites.

Elizabeth leans closer. "Are you all right?"

"I'm fine."

She studies me, the angle of her head so similar to Elliot's that it takes my breath away for a moment, then she nods. "Okay. If you're sure." She turns to the crowd below. "Just so you know, Elliot probably brought you here because he wanted you two to make a good show together. A united front, you know?"

"Um…I don't, actually."

"He hates charity events. Finds them boring, although he attends one or two a year for appearance's sake. He says 'money counts more than attendance.'" She leans toward me, lowering her voice conspiratorially. "The couples he's talking to over there…"

I look at the women who made him laugh earlier.

"He finds them dreadfully dull, but he can playact. Sort of. I guess Ryder's rubbed off on him."

Right. Elliot apparently hangs out a lot with his actor brother Ryder Reed. Or at least he used to, before he married me.

"I generally don't mind them. They always support my causes. I…"

I glance her way. She's suddenly pale, and her lips are parted, but I know she's holding her breath. If she hadn't been sitting down, she might've fainted.

"Elizabeth, are you all right?"

I reach over and take her hand. It's like ice. She doesn't acknowledge me, her eyes focused somewhere on the first floor.

I swivel my head, trying to identify what's caused her distress. But there are too many people below, and I can't figure out what she's seen. I then spot someone I recognize in the sea of faces—Annabelle Underhill—and my gut goes cold. What's *she* doing here? She isn't with her husband—at least I don't see Stanton anywhere around. She's talking with a man, but he's angled so I can't see his face at all.

Then I realize that it can't be Annabelle Underhill who upset Elizabeth. Elliot said he didn't tell anybody about what happened between him and his ex. So…who?

"Elizabeth," I say, this time laying my hand on her shoulder and shaking her slightly. "Are you all right?"

Finally, she blinks and turns to me, the movement more of an automatic response than something conscious. I sense a tiny tremor under my palm, and frown.

"Do you need to lie down?" I ask in a low voice.

"No," comes her barely audible croak. She shakes her head. "No." This time it's stronger, but her voice remains hoarse. "Sorry. I think I'm just caught up in the excitement of the moment..." She gives me a smile designed to make me think she's all right when she's anything but. I recognize it because I often used the same smile with Nonny after our parents were gunned down. "I haven't been sleeping well. Hosting an event of this size at the Sterling mansion has been a bit...taxing."

"Maybe you should just sit here and rest for a few minutes."

"Probably a good idea." She lets out a shaky laugh. "Gosh, I'm so embarrassed. I'm the host, after all."

"Can I get you anything?"

"Vodka, please."

Hard liquor seems like an odd choice, but I don't say anything, too unsettled by her reaction to probe. It's like she's a stranger.

SIX

Elliot

I WATCH MY WIFE CLIMB THE STAIRS. A SMALL part of me wants to join her, wrap my arms around her and make sure she's all right, but another part of me wants to stay away so I can stew over our last seven days.

She confounds me. She doesn't run, she doesn't hide and she doesn't try to get sneaky reinforcement from Grayson or Keith or anyone else. She bears Nonny's virtual ostracism with patience, far better than I'd be able to. She responds to me with honest passion. I know how girls play those games, and I can spot a fake ten feet away. And I know my wife isn't that great of an actress when it comes to sex.

She stands tall, with her shoulders pulled back and her chin high, but when she thinks she's alone her body seems to bend a little, like an old tree under the weight of its own branches. And every time, I want to reach over and hold her up so she can remain tall.

But I don't, because I remind myself why I'm upset…why I can't take everything she says and does at face value…then become furious at both of us. We could've had something special and wonderful. In spite of what she might think, I want to be the one to hold her up, share her burdens.

One of the women around me says something inane, and I return my attention to the group and laugh because everyone else is laughing. It's either that or be rude, and I prefer not to create unpleasantness at Elizabeth's events. Her causes are worthy and deserve my support, even if it costs me a few IQ points.

My eyes find my wife again and I see that she's gotten herself a drink and a nice, empty bench. Elizabeth soon joins her, and I turn away, oddly relieved that she's not alone up there.

"Is it true?" one of the women asks breathlessly.

Given that she's looking at me expectantly, I guess she's been talking to me. Too bad I wasn't paying attention. "Is what true?" I say, not bothering to hide that I wasn't listening to her.

She rolls her eyes. "About your wife having been a stripper."

Imbecile. I snort. "I expected better of you. Does she look like a type to strip?"

"Not really," another one says. "She's hot though. If she played for my team, I'd go for her."

"She doesn't. Besides, she's married, and only wants me."

The couples around me smile, and a few of the women titter like sparrows, probably thinking I'm being overly possessive.

But I know it's true. Of all the ways a woman can betray a man, Belle would never commit adultery.

Suddenly the tittering stops, and my skin prickles with awareness. I feel my wife's presence before I see her. I turn and put an arm around her to show everyone they can shove their pointless speculations up their collective asses. I can sense the stiffness in her muscles, and it makes me tense. Still, I put on a big, affectionate grin. "There you are, beautiful. Feeling better?"

She smiles, but it doesn't quite reach her eyes. "Yes, thank you."

"You need a drink," one of the women says.

"You know, you're exactly right. I was looking to get some vodka."

Vodka? I do a double take. Given her history with alcohol, she would never want something that strong. She didn't even drink champagne on our wedding night.

Then I remember she was with Elizabeth, and vodka is my sister's drink of choice when she's stressed.

"Of course, Belle," I say smoothly, leading her away from the avid gaze of the couples. I lower my head. "What happened?"

"Elizabeth wants some, and I couldn't find any on the second floor. They only had wine and champagne." Belle touches my arm lightly, then yanks her hand away as though she's just realized what she's done.

My chest tightens, and I swallow.

She looks away. "Um. I think she saw something that upset her, although she won't say what. If you want, you can go find her."

"Got it. I'll take the vodka to her."

"Great." She hesitates, then gives me a quick glance. Before she looks away, I catch a glimpse of pain in her eyes, and I feel like I'm being flayed.

"I need to use the ladies' room," she says. "See you at dinner?"

I nod. "Don't forget we're in public. Smile and look happy." *Don't let me see you in pain.*

"Right. Happy." She puts on a fake smile, tilting her head to make sure I see it, then walks away.

Damn it. I rub my face, exhaling roughly. She can make me feel like scum so effortlessly.

I order two glasses with four fingers of vodka at the bar and take them up to the second level.

Elizabeth is easy to spot. She looks like a queen in that white dress. She doesn't look upset now, but she's always had great composure. If it cracked, even momentarily, whatever shook her must be bad.

I sit down and hand her a drink.

"Where's Belle?" she asks.

"Bathroom." From up here, it's easy to scan the people on the first floor. I take a sip of the alcohol. Vodka isn't my choice of poison, but I can drink it if it'll get her to talk. "So what happened?"

She starts to gulp it down, then catches herself and takes a couple of dainty swallows instead. "What do you mean?"

"Belle told me you didn't look so good."

"Did she?"

"*Elizabeth.*"

She shrugs delicately. "It's nothing. All of a sudden, I just felt faint. I've been working really hard on the event, and I think it just caught up to me. And the whole thing with Grandpa's paintings and all… I haven't been sleeping well, and…" She smiles brightly. "I'm just tired. Nothing a good night's sleep won't cure."

I squint at her. I believe about half of what's coming out of her mouth. She might be saintly, but she is also excellent at glossing over things, especially when they're distressing.

"Stop looking at me like that. I'm telling you the truth. Besides, if you have the time and energy to worry about me, you should worry about your wife."

"What do you mean?" Did Belle say something?

"She looked lonely…and a little bit miserable up here. Kind of unusual for a woman who just came back from her honeymoon."

The soft words put me on the defensive. "Don't."

"Are you upset about the articles saying she was a stripper?"

Elizabeth's making me feel like I kicked a puppy. I take another drink of the vodka.

"You're such a hypocrite. You released a sex tape, and you're the one who wanted to marry a stripper in the first place."

"It's not like that," I bite out. Elizabeth has no idea what's going on between us, and I'm not telling her.

Elizabeth nurses her vodka. "Sometimes we get blinded by emotion and push too far, say and do things we shouldn't." Her voice is low, but her words are perfectly clear. "By the time you realize you've crossed the line, it's too late. And you're never able to take it back and fix the damage you've done to the relationship. So consider if it's worth destroying what you have with Belle before you step over that line."

The vision of my wife walking away from me flashes through my mind…then her standing alone in the penthouse we share, looking so tired and alone. Suddenly I've had enough. "It's not about the articles. I knew what I was getting into, and I'm not a hypocrite."

"Then what?"

"Her secrets." I clamp my mouth shut.

Elizabeth regards me. "That bad?"

"Yes, and I'm pissed she didn't tell me. I've given her chances."

She finishes her drink. "Maybe she couldn't. People think our family has everything because we have money and connections…but we can't just do whatever we want, and we certainly don't have everything. Imagine how much harder it is for someone with so little. And the stress… If she messes up, she isn't just risking herself but a younger sister who depends on her."

I look away, not wanting to hear her tell me what I already know but don't want to admit.

Elizabeth continues, undeterred, "She might've had good reason to keep things to herself. As shocking as it may sound to a man of your ego, it might not be about you at all. I think she genuinely cares about you."

My wife has told me she loves me. Repeatedly. And she tried to over the last six nights, even though I covered her mouth so I didn't have to hear it and have it lance through me again.

"Did she try to talk to you about...whatever it is?" Elizabeth asks.

"Yeah. *After* I found out." I try to soften my tone for my sister's sake, and fail.

"So you didn't let her explain."

"What's the point?"

"Unless you honestly don't care, you should give her a chance to share her side of the story before it's too late."

"What do you mean, 'too late'?"

"If you wait too long, she may not want to anymore. Who wants a love so shallow that it doesn't come with a bit of trust?" With a long sigh, she stares into the empty glass in her fragile hands. "I have to go downstairs and mingle. Make people feel good about helping those less fortunate than we are."

I nod, relieved that this conversation is going to be over.

She squeezes my shoulder. "Just...don't be too stubborn and turn her tender feelings for you into pain. Because the next stage will be indifference."

My knuckles turn white around the glass. It's a wonder it hasn't shattered.

"Don't give me some bullshit relationship advice you read from *Cosmo*, sis," I say, trying to dismiss the panic her words have brought on. Of all the outcomes I've considered, Belle's indifference isn't one of them.

She tilts her chin. "It's not."

The thinly veiled pain in her words makes me snap my head her way. For a second I think I see something shattered and bleeding in her gaze, but she blinks and it's gone. I look harder, but her face is composed, serene and calm, and the alcohol has given her cheeks a light glow.

"See you downstairs." She kisses me gently on the cheek and walks away.

I watch her make her way through the crowd. People stop her to say hello, and she responds, her face lit up with a sweet, welcoming smile. She's at ease and relaxed as Nate Sterling comes over and puts an arm around her waist. Her hand rests on his shoulder, and when he dips his head, she whispers something in his ear, which makes him grin fondly. It is as though she didn't say any of the things she just told me.

The idea of my saintly sister having any kind of strong emotion for stuff other than saving the world is preposterous. I have to be projecting my own feelings onto her.

My eyes search the crowd for my wife. What's

her breaking point? She's feisty—a fighter underneath the delicate appearance. She wouldn't…

What if she's already reached the point of no return?

What the hell is wrong with me that I'm freaking out like this? It isn't me who screwed up. Belle fucked it up, and there's no reason for her to feel she's been treated unjustly.

Except…

Elizabeth said Belle looked lonely and maybe a little miserable, and I know my sister's right. And I know I'm the chief reason.

But loneliness and misery aren't indifference. So that means I haven't pushed my wife too far.

Yet.

Annabelle

THE BATHROOM IS HUGE AND LUXURIOUS, DARK marble with gleaming gilt faucets. It's obviously designed with guests in mind: two big sinks and several stalls with doors that reach all the way to the bottom of the floor. The toilets are Japanese and high-tech like nothing I've ever seen, with covers that raise and lower themselves automatically, the seats heated.

When I come out of the stall, I bump into the one person I prayed I would never see again—Annabelle Underhill. She's as gorgeous as ever. Her face is expertly made up, expensive rubies around her throat and on her ears. Dark brown curls frame her heart-shaped face, and a red chiffon dress hugs her toned and tanned body. The eyelashes seem even longer than I remembered.

She puts a tube of lipstick into her clutch and gives me a sideways look in the mirror. "Well, well, well. Don't you clean up nice?"

I ignore her and wash my hands.

"Didn't anybody teach you any manners?" She smiles, then gasps. "Ohhh, right. They must have *stripped* them off you at that job you used to have."

It's a stupid thing to say, but the blatant mention of the asterisk-marked portion of my past stuns me. Nobody at the party has breathed a word about it, and I'm certain they've all seen the lurid headlines, if not the actual articles.

"I knew Elliot could be wild, but I thought he would choose somebody with a more stabilizing influence." The smirk she flings at my reflection is extra catty. "After all, opposites do attract."

That pulls me out of my shock. "That can't be right, or you'd be married to the Dalai Lama."

She snaps her clutch shut and faces me. "You think you're so clever?" Hateful condescension twists her face. "Yeah, I guess you do. So you know Elliot doesn't need to stay married to *you* to get what he wants, right? He just needs to be married."

Her triumphant viciousness leaves me dazed. As my brain kicks in again, I gape at her. How does she know this? Elizabeth swore that only her brothers, father and stepmother know the truth behind my fake marriage to Elliot. I haven't known her for long, but I'm certain she isn't the type to lie.

"Surprised?" Annabelle flutters her eyelashes at me. "You shouldn't be. Everyone knows."

My throat constricts for a moment, but I manage to say in an even voice, "Everyone?"

"Everyone who counts." She gives me a smarmy, used-car salesman smile.

I rally myself. I'd rather bite my tongue until it bleeds than let her see how she's upset my equilibrium. "So you *can* count. I was wondering. Well, at least I'll be going home with a hot, young husband tonight."

"You'll never satisfy a man like Elliot."

"Apparently you didn't either. Which is why he passed you off to his father."

Her eyes flash. "Elliot enjoys slumming, but at the end of the day, a man wants a lady by his side."

"A lady who hasn't married his father, surely."

"Always so naïve. If that were true, we wouldn't have been fucking in a closet after the ceremony." She smirks. "What? You didn't know? Oh yes, it's true. He's always wanted me." She strokes her chest, breathing shallowly as though she's turned on by the memory. "He's just too stubborn to admit it to himself. He's always been stubborn."

To hide how shaken and sickened I am by the revelation, I start drying my hands.

"Give it up and leave him," she continues. "I don't want to have to hurt you or your sister, but"—she shrugs—"you've led such an *interesting* life. I would hate to release all those little nuggets, but I will…one by one if you're too dense to understand what I mean."

Fury sears my cheeks, and I itch to slap her. "Don't you threaten me."

"And why wouldn't I? Who you gonna tell?" Annabelle leans closer until our noses are almost touching. "Elliot?" she whispers. "He'll never believe you."

My misery is nearly complete because I know she's right. He won't even listen to my explanation about Mr. Grayson. Why would he believe anything I say about Annabelle Underhill?

After a long moment she pulls back. "That's what I thought. Well, cheer up. It's not like there's no way out of the situation. All you have to do is divorce him. No…big…deal."

She leaves. I brace my hands against the edge of the vanity and try to drag in air through my mouth. My head throbs like Annabelle's just slammed the back of my skull against the wall, and my stomach roils.

If Annabelle Underhill follows through on her threats, I'm screwed. Nonny will never forgive me, and Elliot will grow even colder and more distant.

Why did I ever think I would have a fresh new start? Fresh starts are for the lucky few. I'm not that fortunate.

SEVEN

Elliot

WHERE IS BELLE? SHE'S BEEN GONE FOR too long. She isn't in the dining hall, and I remember how pale and withdrawn she was earlier.

I walk toward the ladies' room and spot Ryder, who's in a black tux that fits him perfectly. Despite the fact that we're half-brothers, we look nothing alike. I often joke that I'm the handsomer guy. In reality, he is one disgustingly good-looking bastard. He takes after his mother—the almost-black hair and arresting blue eyes combined with a face that people gush over in breathless wonder. Underneath the pretty mask is a decent brain as well. He's monetized his appearance quite effectively, much to our father's fury.

A small throng of people has gathered around him—can't be helped, since he's the biggest thing in Hollywood right now. The moment he spots me, he extricates himself and walks over. "Didn't know you were planning to attend," he says.

"Me? What about you? You hate these things."

"I'm trying to make a few appearances with Paige."

I nod. He doesn't have to explain further. He's trying to put on a good show for Paige's sake. There are still those who think she "stole" Ryder from more deserving women. What they don't know is that nobody "steals" Ryder unless he wants to be stolen. His relationship with Paige started out much like mine—a simple contract. But he is crazy about his wife now, and they're expecting a baby together. He would've never impregnated her if he wasn't thinking forever.

"So where is she?" I ask.

Ryder gives a mock long-suffering sigh. "Another potty break."

"Pregnancy, bro. Get used to it. Any morning sickness?"

"Nah, she's fine. Just needs to go to the bathroom a lot."

"Wait'll the baby pops out. You're gonna wish she was still just pregnant."

"How would you know?"

"Some of the managers have newborns. You would not believe the complaining."

"Can't be *that* bad," he mutters.

"Sounds like it is. And it's going to be extra bad for you. Your genes, remember?" One of our father's pet complaints is what a fussy baby Ryder was.

An inscrutable expression crosses my brother's face for a brief moment, and it pulls me up short. *What the hell?* He hesitated when I asked him whether or not he wanted the baby a few weeks back, and now this? Is he still feeling ambivalent? If so, it's too freakin' late now. Paige is having the baby.

I take a step closer to quietly ask what his deal is, but I never get the chance; Paige walks out of the ladies' room.

Even before pregnancy, she was never a small woman, unlike a lot of the Hollywood crowd. Her voluptuous body is full of generous curves. And she's pretty. Her loose golden hair tumbles behind her back, and her brown eyes are warm and friendly. She's in a bright purple dress with an asymmetrical hem and an empire waist. The baby bump is obvious now, and she glows like only a woman in love can.

It reminds me of the way Belle used to glow. Now she doesn't. And the fact sits in my gut like a knotted lump of cold noodles.

Ryder wraps his arm around Paige's waist and pulls her to his side. "Missed you."

"I was only gone for a few minutes," she reminds him.

"My heart doesn't care." He kisses her on the forehead. "It misses you even when the absence is measured in seconds," he says, in a faux-Cary Grant accent.

"Silly," she says fondly, beaming up at him and putting her hand on his. "Elliot, it's good to see you."

"Likewise. You look amazing." I smile easily, as always. "By the way, is Belle in the bathroom?"

"Um, no." She hesitates for a moment, stealing a quick glance at Ryder. "We should catch up soon."

That makes me raise an eyebrow. Paige and I have known each other for four years, but we don't exactly have the kind of relationship that requires catching up. Still, I nod. "Sure. Call anytime."

"I will."

The firm tone of her voice indicates she's not saying it to be polite or friendly. *Huh.*

Ryder frowns at me over the crown of her head, and I give him a small "I have no idea" look. After a brisk nod my way, he escorts her off.

Not in the bathroom. I wonder where the hell Belle is, worry beginning to gnaw. She's been so pale. Did she feel bad and have to lie down somewhere? That wouldn't surprise me a bit.

I pull out my phone, about to call her, but stop when I spot Annabelle Underhill. Her jewelry is expensive enough to scream, "I'm a trophy wife." But then, she doesn't marry men with less than a billion dollars in assets. And her skintight outfit leaves nothing to the imagination. If she thought she could get away with it, she might've shown up nude. Annabelle is a woman who instinctively understands how to use her body for maximum effect and to get what she wants. What wouldn't I give to see her in her forties and see if she'll still strut around like she's some hot shit. But she will be completely out of my life by then.

Her gaze zeroes in on me, and she starts walking in my direction, her pelvis swaying in an exaggerated motion designed to draw my eyes to her narrow waist and hips. She shouldn't bother. I have nothing to say to the bitch. Actually...I take that back. I have plenty to say, except none of it is appropriate for a venue as public and high-class as Elizabeth's charity dinner.

"Elliot! Fancy running into you here!" She starts to put a hand on my arm, but my cold stare freezes her.

"How the hell did you get in?" I ask tersely, not giving a damn who overhears me.

"Stanton donates regularly to Elizabeth's foundation, and we just happened to buy tickets." Annabelle tosses her hair over a shoulder, then shrugs carelessly. "And thank you for the information. I knew you'd come through for me."

"I didn't do it for you," I say. "I did it for your uncle." I owed the man a favor, now paid in full.

"Does it matter?" She hesitates, then inhales as though she's firming her resolve, but I know why she's doing it—to make her tits rise. Resting a hand on my chest, she moves closer until she's almost flush against me. "What's important is that you want to free me from Stanton."

I remove her hand from my torso, my grip painfully tight on her. The only thing stopping me from shoving her away is that we have an audience and I care about my sister. "If I'd known you'd be such a conniving bitch, I wouldn't have given you the referral."

She gasps. "But you saw the bruises."

And I found them horrifying, but I'll be damned if I let her know that. Annabelle Underhill is crazy enough to twist any gesture of kindness from me into a sign of certain romance. "Like I should care about them."

"Elliot!" she says under her breath.

"You didn't think I'd find out you're the one leaking that shit about my wife?"

"Are you seriously telling me you care about that…that crass little girl you married?"

"First of all, she's not crass. Second, yes, I do care." As I speak, I know I'm telling the truth. I care damn too much about her.

Annabelle tilts her head and looks up at me. Her eyes glitter with malice and something that's equally disturbing. She reminds me of a starving snake ready to strike at anything to satisfy its hunger. I can't believe I found her attractive at one point in my life. Proves I'm not as smart as people think.

"Big, strong Elliot, trying to protect his poor little wife," she taunts me. "I didn't say anything that isn't true."

"No, you didn't. But understand me. You have your share of dirty laundry, too. Don't think I won't air it for shits and giggles if you keep hurting my wife."

"You wouldn't *dare*."

"Oh, but I would"—I give her my most beatific smile—"with immense pleasure."

"You think you're immune to dirt?"

"Nope. The difference is, I don't give a shit if people know about my dirt. Sugar daddies, on the other hand, don't like girls with too many skeletons. And if they knew what I know about you… well, you might find it hard to replace Stanton."

She jerks away from me with a glare. "You're despicable."

"Coming from you, that's a compliment."

"I'm going to win you back, Elliot. We're destined to be together. And no small-town tramp is going to stop me."

I shake my head pityingly. "Your problem is, you're too stupid to realize you never had a chance."

Her eyes narrow until they look like venomous incisions on her face, and she storms away. The smug expression on my face slips.

As enemies go, she isn't particularly formidable. What she *is* is persistent, which, unfortunately, is just as difficult to deal with. Both types of enemies require drastic measures. I'm going to have to cut her off at the knees and make sure she never gets back up.

Remembering why I came to the restroom area in the first place, I pull out my phone and text my wife.

Where are you?

If I could convey emotions with text, it would be irritation. It annoys the hell out of me that she wanted to attend this farce in the first place, and now she isn't around and I have to deal with Annabelle Underhill.

Somebody taps my shoulder. I let a low growl vibrate through my throat. I don't have time for more bullshit chitchat.

I spin around, a curt dismissal on my tongue, then stop. *Belle.*

Her pale face is pinched. Not even the expert makeup can hide the strain. Pain has turned her emerald eyes glassy, and I take her hand. It feels like ice. My irritation instantly vanishes, replaced by concern. I wrap an arm around her shoulders and she sags against me for an instant, as though she's absorbing my warmth and strength. But a moment later she straightens and gathers herself. I feel the loss keenly.

"Are you all right?" I ask, keeping my voice low and soothing.

"I'm fine. Just a little tired. Where's the dining hall? I couldn't find it."

She doesn't meet my gaze, and I know she isn't telling me the entire truth. There is no way she couldn't find the dining area, since the most of the guests went that way. And she is not at all fine. From the listless way she's talking, I know she's autocorrecting her real answer with what she wants me to hear.

Hating the awkward tension, I offer her an arm. She hesitates, starts to slip her hand in the crook of my elbow, then slowly lowers both hands to hang by her sides instead. "Let's go."

I don't want to go. I want to talk to her, make sure she's all right, but what choice do I have for now? I escort her slowly, all the while knowing that I have to do something soon. My problem: I don't know what that something is.

EIGHT

Elliot

THE DINNER COMMENCES WITHOUT ANY drama, but then, people behave them-selves at events like this. I'm annoyed that Annabelle Underhill has been seated in my line of sight, which means she's also in Belle's. What I wouldn't give to have the earth open up and swallow her whole…and then spit her out in the middle of the Mongolian desert.

Interestingly, she isn't with her husband. A man in his late twenties or early thirties is with her, and I recognize him the moment he turns his head and looks straight at me. He has hair entirely too long, the black locks brushing the top of his collarbones. He isn't classically handsome the way Ryder is, but he's striking in his own way, and women check him out with appreciation in their gaze. His icy blue eyes assess me clinically and thoroughly, and I return the favor. He's a self-made billionaire himself, most of his money made in real estate and online media, if I remember correctly. What the hell is he doing with Stanton's wife?

And if she has him as her *friend*, why the hell did she try to feed me that line of bullshit earlier about us being fated to be together? Her date is a much better target than I am. He's plenty rich, and—unlike me—probably doesn't know what kind of a viper she is.

But I dismiss the two of them. I have other things to worry about—mainly my wife.

Belle is seated next to me. She is stunning, absolutely gorgeous in that ice-blue dress. It brings out the fire in her hair and deepens the color of her eyes to forest green. More than a few men look at her admiringly, and I give them a warning glance. Most get the hint; for the ones who don't, a second long, cold stare while fondling my steak knife gets the point across.

This isn't like me. I don't usually go all caveman over a woman, but I don't give a fuck. Belle is my wife, and I'll be damned if some loser is going to drool all over her. Even the huge Asscher-cut diamond and wedding band on her finger seem inadequate to show our union, and it doesn't help that she's careful to not touch me…which, perversely, makes me want to touch her. And I do—my elbow brushes hers and I let my fingers caress hers when I hand her the salt. Each time, she gives me a reserved smile. She gives the same smile to the other people around us, but it becomes strained every time she happens to glimpse Annabelle Underhill.

Belle's mood affects mine.

No, that isn't entirely a fair assessment. It is her mood plus Elizabeth's vodka-infused comments earlier.

I study the way my wife lets her mouth smile. Her eyes are watchful and dark. Never once do they brighten with good humor.

Is this how people slowly retreat? Is this what happens when they start to become indifferent?

Even as I wonder, resentment stirs inside me. Why should she be upset when I'm the one who was wronged? I've given her chances. If she'd come clean at any of those times, I would have never held it against her—

"Great fish," a man who's been sitting to my right says, looking at me expectantly. He's at least in his late fifties, his hair more gray than black.

I look down at my plate. Sure enough, it's some kind of white fish with some kind of white sauce, and I've already had a few bites. The problem is I don't remember how it tasted. "Yes…succulent," I manage.

"Your sister always knows how to put these things together."

"That she does."

I signal for more wine, and drink while pretending to enjoy the meal. Gavin and Amandine didn't come—she isn't feeling well—and now I wish I'd canceled, too. Elizabeth wouldn't have minded as long as she got my donation.

"Your brother and his wife seem to be quite the happy couple," the man continues.

"Ryder would've never married a woman he didn't love, and I can say the same about Paige," I answer, taking a quick glance in their direction.

Ryder whispers something in her ear; she flushes and giggles, slapping his shoulder affectionately. Even if I had no clue how they really felt, watching them would dispel any doubts. My brother can pull off the lovesick routine. He's a brilliant actor, after all. But Paige? She couldn't act for shit, even if her life depended on it. Her reaction to him is one hundred percent genuine.

"Surprising, isn't it? Didn't really seem like she'd be his type." The man looks at me expectantly, like he honestly thinks I'll pursue this brain-cell-killing line of conversation. When I ignore him, he says, "Don't you think?"

"Think what? Who says she's not his type?" I ask tersely.

"Um. I'm saying…she's a little on the heavy

side. Not"—he clears his throat—"your usual Hollywood beauty."

Shallow asshole. "Ryder prefers inner beauty. At least it doesn't decline with age or need periodic plastic surgery to maintain."

"Ah. You're probably right." He leans forward and looks at my wife. "Inner beauty. That is indeed important."

Doing my best to rein in my temper, I put down my utensils. I turn to face the annoying bastard fully, my tight fists on the table. "You have a point you'd like to make?" My nerves are frayed, and if the other man weren't so damn old, I would've knocked his teeth out by now, Elizabeth's function or not.

"Nothing, really." He eyes my fists uneasily. "It just seems odd…you and your brother marrying so quickly, back to back."

"Maybe true love found us *back to back*." I give him a hard stare. "What's odd is people being ungracious about others' good fortune."

The man flushes and turns away. He starts chatting with the woman seated on his other side, but I can sense he's talking about what I said about Ryder and Paige. Just what the hell gives him the right to question what Ryder and I do?

My wife excuses herself and leaves the table, her face pale and strained.

I watch her go. That expression probably isn't convincing anybody that we're happily married.

That she's gone for the rest of the dinner and the following dance and social mingling doesn't help either. Other women come over with pointless smiles, and I pretend to be happy dancing with them, but I'm not. I want to leave, and to hell with everyone. This is why I hate coming to events for my sister. I have to behave for her sake. After a fourth dance with a simpering socialite who makes my teeth grind, I've had enough. I go to the bar. "Scotch. Neat. To the brim."

The crisply dressed bartender raises both his eyebrows, but gives me what I want. I hand him a twenty and chug it down rapidly.

"Goodness, is that scotch?"

I sigh at the rotten timing. "Yes, Mommy," I say, turning to face Elizabeth.

She eyes my drink with disapproval, then raises her gaze. "Come on." She takes my hand.

I resist when she tugs. "Can't. Waiting for Belle."

She takes a quick look around, then leans upward and whispers into my ear. "She's not coming. There's been an accident."

NINE

Elliot

I T TAKES AN HOUR TO REACH THE STERLING-
Wilson Medical Research Center. And during
the entire trip, my heart stays in my throat. I
don't know what the hell happened. There aren't
any security cameras inside the mansion, and the
staircase is very well lit.

Why would my wife fall down the stairs?

I don't believe it was the heels, even though
she isn't used to wearing them. Besides, people
who aren't used to them tend to be more careful. The steps have been specially sandblasted to
prevent slipping. In addition, there's a very sturdy
railing.

Nonny's late night comments slither over my
mind. Apparently Belle tried to hurt herself the
same way when she was younger. But surely her

life with me isn't so miserable that she would do this.

You haven't been exactly open and understanding. She never got a chance to really talk to you. For all you know, she might have an ongoing propensity to hurt herself when she's under stress. If my conscience had a hand, it'd be wagging a finger at me.

I grit my teeth. I refuse to believe my wife would harm herself that way, no matter what. She's too strong, too responsible.

It was probably an accident, I tell myself, since that's the least objectionable scenario. It doesn't matter I don't quite believe it, either; the other possibilities are intolerable.

Thanks to Elizabeth's quick thinking and discretion, the people at the dinner have no idea what happened to my wife. It doesn't hurt that the hospital was built with the Sterling fortune or that my sister helped raise millions for the hospital's pediatric hematology-oncology department. By the time I arrive at the nurses' station, there's an admin waiting to whisk me away to the private room where my wife's been stashed.

"Take your time. Nobody knows she's here," the man says before leaving.

A doctor is examining her pupils, flashing a penlight into her eyes, when I arrive. She then checks Belle's reflexes and asks her a raft of questions. Contrasted to the doctor's ebony skin, Belle looks like a ghost. The harsh fluorescent lighting hides nothing. My wife's left cheek has been scraped, the spot red and angry, and the back of her right hand is bloody with a couple of cuts. A hint of a bruise darkens her jaw, and I can tell from the way she's sitting, slightly hunched, that there's more damage underneath her clothes.

Goddamn it. My legs start to shake, and I place a palm against the wall for support. Now that I'm seeing her in person, I feel weak and lightheaded…except that won't do at all. Somebody has to be strong here.

"What happened?" My voice is unsteady, but I can't do a thing about it.

The doctor turns to me. "You are…?"

"Elliot Reed. I'm her husband."

"Finally." Her dark eyes are solemn behind a pair of rimless glasses, and her mouth is flat. The seriousness of her expression sends a frisson of alarm through my system. "I'm Dr. Lisle."

"Is she all right?"

"I'm sitting right here," Belle says hoarsely, barely audible.

I ignore her.

"Yes," the doctor says. "Just some cuts and bruises. Nothing broken, no head injury or concussion. She was *very* lucky."

Lucky. The word keeps circling in my head, and I let out a long breath. "Thank god."

"You should definitely thank something. I heard it was a long flight of stairs."

"I'm *still* here."

Belle's peeved tone, more than anything, else lets me know she's going to be okay. The scrapes will mend and the bruises will fade.

"She needs to take it easy," Dr. Lisle is saying. "I'm assuming you can manage that. And I'm prescribing a muscle relaxant just in case. Absolutely, positively, *no* drinking *or* driving after taking it."

"I don't want—"

"Anything else?" I ask. Neither Dr. Lisle nor I even glance Belle's way.

"Your wife asked to be discharged tonight," the doctor says. "She can go if that's what she wants, so long as you can promise she'll take it easy."

I purse my lips. I understand why Belle wants to leave. I hate hospitals too, but she just took a tumble down what had to be twenty yards of stairs at the Sterlings' mansion. Even if nothing's broken or permanently damaged, I prefer that she stay at the hospital overnight.

Belle is watching my eyes. "Elliot, I can't stay here. This place makes me…" She seems to grow paler and smaller.

I breathe out harshly. *All right.* "I'll take her with me, doctor. And I promise to keep her in bed and resting."

Belle sags in relief, and Dr. Lisle nods. "If you notice anything wrong...even something small, you need to bring her back. Immediately."

"Got it."

"Go do the paperwork or whatever to get me out of here," Belle says. "I'll get my things and meet you at the nurses' station." I hesitate, but she flicks her wrist a couple of times. "Please."

If she'd said anything else, I would've stayed, but the imploring *please* gets to me. Despite myself, I do as she asks.

Once we're in the limo and on the way to the hotel, she leans back with a long sigh, her eyes closed.

"Are you all right?" I ask.

She doesn't open her eyes. "I'm fine. Just a little bruised, no big deal."

I study the lines on her face and the tightly pressed lips. A little bruised, sure. I pull her until she's leaning against me, her back to my chest. She must be hurting worse than she lets on. I arrange her so she can rest her head against my shoulder, but she stiffens. I don't let go, though. I need to hold her and know she's okay...for my own sake.

"What happened?" I ask after a moment.

The muscles in her back and shoulders turn to stone. "Didn't you get the answer you want from the doctor?"

"Don't. I don't want to fight. I just want to know how it happened."

"What's there to know?"

"Elizabeth said one of the wait staff found you at the bottom of the stairs." I didn't hear the rest of what she said over the panic roaring in my head.

"Then you know what happened."

"Belle…"

"I don't want to talk about it. I'm banged up, and I'm tired."

Part of me wants to push until she tells me everything, but she feels so small and fragile in my arms. I notice a new bruise on the back of her neck, stark and ugly on the otherwise smooth skin. I'm afraid if I push too hard, she might shatter.

A hotel staff member opens the door with a warm greeting, and I climb out first and help my wife. Her hand is too cool to the touch. If her injuries shock the attendant, he doesn't show it.

Our overnight bags are whisked away, and we're immediately checked in. A sharp-looking woman in a black dress escorts us to our suite on the top level. She glances at my wife, but doesn't comment. Belle stares at the floor the entire time, unblinking. But I can sense her mind working. I just wish I could figure out what what's going on inside.

"If anything's not to your liking, please don't hesitate to let us know," the woman says in a robotically calm voice as she opens the door to show us in.

The suite is sumptuously appointed with pale, thick carpet, a plushy sectional sofa and an armchair before a huge TV. In the corner is a modern writing desk with a graphite-gray ergonomic chair. I immediately notice several vases of fresh flowers, which perfume the air delicately. Recessed lights set dim keep the large space looking intimate and almost romantic. Through the open, arched doorway, I see the bedroom; there's a huge California king with pristine white covers turned down invitingly. The light from the bedside tables casts a satiny sheen over everything.

"Thank you," I murmur.

"Good night, Mr. and Mrs. Reed. Enjoy your stay." The woman disappears.

My wife lets out a long sigh. Her legs wobble as she steps further into the opulent suite. Tired of watching her trying to be strong, I sweep her up. She lets out a small cry and immediately wraps her arms around my neck. I start carrying her toward the bedroom.

"Elliot..." She blinks up at me, eyebrows pinched together as though she's made up her mind about something. "I think someone pushed me."

Everything stills as I try to grasp what she's trying to say. The notion that somebody might've meant to harm her never crossed my mind. "You mean…at the stairs?"

"You probably don't believe me." The words are barely audible. She bites her lower lip. "Sorry. Doesn't matter." She speaks more loudly this time. "It was an accident."

At first I don't understand. Then it hits me, a shock like I've been backhanded. She didn't want to tell me the truth because she didn't think I'd take her word for it. My whole body tightens in reflex, but I consciously relax, reminding myself of the tumble she took. I don't want to cause her any pain. "It wasn't an accident if somebody pushed you. You should've told me earlier."

"Doesn't matter. Won't find who did it." Her words come out almost garbled, and it's hard to make out what she's saying.

She's right about one thing. We probably won't find the person who did it, unless one of the serving staff or servants happened to see something. But that isn't what stokes my anger. It's the way she turns from me, even though she's clasped in my arms, and the deep shame and disgust I feel for myself at the circumstances I find myself in, the shitty situation in which both of us are mired.

I lay my wife on the bed and strip off her dress, then suck in a sharp breath.

Her injuries are evident—the tender skin starting to bruise around her shoulders, back and hip. Her right knee is going to be at least a medium blue. My body throbs as though I'm the one who rolled down the stairs and had the injuries. If she'd fallen headfirst, she could've died. My hands unsteady, I pull the sheets over her before I lose control and demand that something be done about the fact that she's suffering. She passes out almost immediately. I push her crimson hair away from her face with shaking fingers.

I stand and yank off my tie, my hands rough. I reach into the minibar and help myself to some whiskey, keeping an eye on Belle as she sleeps.

The alcohol dulls the sharp edge of my initial fury. I'm still pissed at the way she behaved, even though I recognize her reaction wasn't entirely without justification. After all, since Paddington's report I've done everything in my power to convince her how little she means to me.

I swirl the liquor around in my glass. I've been trying to convince myself Belle holds no significance in my life. Hearing the truth from her lips hasn't been my primary concern. I've wanted to prove to myself that it didn't mean anything that when Paddington dropped the bombshell, that my anger came from the fact that she lied and misled me, and that her professions of love were most likely a form of manipulation. I didn't think once about my grandfather's painting—the initial reason for our contract marriage.

And that was unacceptable. Unthinkable.

I didn't want to be that vulnerable to someone.

But now...

I watch her broodingly. Her mumbled apology hurt because it was said in such a sad, resigned voice. I have to accept the truth. I was furious because I'd been thinking something more permanent—maybe even a forever—with my wife. There aren't many women I find admirable...and out of those, Belle is the only one who makes my blood boil with desire.

She's worked so hard to build something for herself and her sister. And her pride... I laugh softly. She's so damn proud she basically told me to go fuck myself when I offered her three thousand bucks for a night of sex. You'd think that after two years of poverty, she would have jumped at a chance for such easy money.

And I'm not entirely sure if she would've said yes to my wedding offer—and the million dollars that came with it—if it hadn't been for her sister. Nonny is her biggest weakness, and I exploit it shamelessly. But I don't fight fair. I fight to win.

Except...is this a win?

My wife and I are both miserable. I keep telling myself I'm not, but who the hell am I kidding? My focus is shot, I snap at people and I have to force myself to stay away from her until night falls—acting like a fucking vampire—when I finally allow myself to touch her, telling myself I deserve that much, since my lust for her body is the reason I decided to marry her. Nonny's picked up on the tension, and she's acting out in subtle ways, mostly against Belle. That isn't right, but teenagers aren't often concerned with right or wrong.

I finish the whiskey, start to reach for another bottle…then stop. I have to get my head screwed on right. We can't continue like this. Even the resentment I've felt over the possibility of my wife growing indifferent to me is based on my fear that I might drive her away.

Tomorrow I'll take the first step to fixing what is broken between us. I'll ask Belle to explain the circumstance with Grayson from her point of view…and listen to her—calmly—as she talks.

I have to give us this chance or just let her go before she twists me inside out.

TEN

Annabelle

WHEN I OPEN MY EYES, I SEE AN UNFA-miliar room. I blink, utterly disori-ented for a moment. My body aches like I've been in a wrestling match with an ape, I'm naked except for a super tiny thong and I don't know whose bed I'm in.

Panic rushes over me, and suddenly I'm cold to my core. Memories of the last time I found myself awake, not knowing what happened the night before, pour through my mind; it's suddenly hard to breathe through the tightness in my lungs. As tremors rack me, I squeeze my eyes shut. What happened? What am I doing here?

Then sanity intrudes, piece by piece. The panic recedes as quickly as it came, and I relax my grip on the sheets. I'm not a vulnerable fifteen-year-old who doesn't know better any-more. I'm in San Francisco with Elliot. We attended Elizabeth's charity dinner. I felt awful during the dinner, and the smell of all the rich sauces and fat only worsened the nausea. Fresh air seemed vital, and I went to the balcony on the second level. Then on my way back, I fell down the stairs…

No, not fell. Was *pushed* down. I didn't imag-ine that pair of hands shoving into my back. My only regret is that I didn't see who it was because I was too busy tumbling down the steps.

I hiss out a breath. It was probably Annabelle Underhill. She made it clear she hates me. On the other hand, why would she threaten me in the bathroom if she was going to push me down the stairs anyway? It would've made more sense for her to at least be neutrally pleasant in the bath-room, then go for the sneak attack.

I start to turn to check the time, and groan as my shoulders and upper back burst into blossoms of pain. Holy shit, I feel worse today than yester-day. Not unexpected, though. It was always worse the day after a tough game of hockey.

My eyes shut, I breathe shallowly, willing the pain to go away. I should ask for some ibuprofen. That would proba—

"You're up."

Elliot. My hands twist in the sheet and I pull it up, ignoring the dull throbbing in my arms, as though such a flimsy barrier would stop the sharp awareness of him from prickling over my skin. I feel too naked and too exposed. I recognize my extreme level of vulnerability is coming from the fact that Elliot has never been engaged in our relationship at a deep emotional level. I was the only one silly enough to think there could be more between us.

Elliot comes in and takes an armchair by the window, a hand around his phone. He's impeccably dressed in a white shirt with the two top buttons undone, sleeves rolled up and a pair of light beige slacks that molds to his lean, muscular legs. His dark, glossy hair is almost dry. There is a small nick by his tight mouth, which surprises me; I can't remember him ever giving himself a shaving cut.

An unexpectedly strong urge to run my finger over the wound courses through me, and I stiffen. The period of tenderness is over. I finally see that now, and can accept it intellectually. I just need to get my heart to acquiesce and figure out what Elliot's and my next move in this farce is going to be. His eyes probe as he takes me in, and the unblinking focus is flustering.

"Yeah," I croak, then clear my throat. "Just woke up."

"Want a painkiller?" he asks, unscrewing a small bottle of water.

"The muscle relaxant?"

He nods.

I shake my head. "No. It's going to make me drowsy." I don't want anything that can make me lose control of my faculties. "Do you have anything else?"

He offers me three options from a plastic bag with a pharmacy logo. I accept two ibuprofen pills.

"You've been busy."

"Yeah. Breakfast?" he asks, taking the bottle of water back.

"No thanks. I'm not hungry. But some coffee would be great, if you don't mind."

"Why don't you shower while I call for room service?"

I nod and wait until he turns away to use the in-house phone. Then I hobble as quickly as possible across the bedroom. It's silly—it's not like he's never seen me naked before—but I feel extra vulnerable today.

The bathroom is much bigger than I imagined, with gold-veined marble flooring and polished brass and glass partitions for the shower. A sunken tub with a Jacuzzi jets sits in one corner under frosted windows that let the natural sunlight in. I strip my thong off and step into the shower. The water is instantly hot, and just perfect for relaxing achy joints and pain-knotted muscles.

I let steam build in the stall, then run my soapy hands over myself, rinse off and step out, grabbing a large and very fluffy white towel.

In my experience, the key to feeling better isn't lying in bed all day moping, but going about one's routine. Activity seems to lessen the pain and accelerate the healing process. Still, I've never taken a beating like the one from last night. The stairs at my parents' home in Lincoln City were much shorter...and carpeted.

The reflection in the mirror shows bruises blooming like purple pansies over my shoulders, upper back, hip and right knee. They throb, but aren't too terrible. The scrapes on my cheek are scabbed over, and my jaw is blue along one side. The cuts on the back of my hand are minor, nothing to worry about in the grand scheme of things. I sigh. At least nothing's broken.

I apply concealer with extra care to the injuries on my face. I don't want people looking at them and wondering. Although the hotel staff didn't show any outward reaction last night, it's possible they—or someone else—might think Elliot is abusing me. And that would be unfair.

I place the concealer on the vanity and stare at nothing. I told Elliot that I was shoved down the stairs. Did he believe me? It's hard to tell. I wasn't thinking very clearly last night. He might've assumed I was imagining things. He certainly didn't believe me when I told him I had a good reason for associating with Mr. Grayson, and I don't see how the incident at Elizabeth's event is any different. Of course he'll want to believe that everything at his sister's dinner was perfect. On the other hand, he might take my word for it, since I'm not generally a clumsy person and—

I exhale deeply, suddenly angry and disappointed. This whole line of thinking…it's all moot. I don't want him to believe me on a case-by-case basis. If his trust can't be absolute, I don't want it, just like I don't want his love if it can't be true and unwavering.

By the time I'm done with my makeup and have a robe on, knocks come from outside. "The food's here," Elliot says.

"I'll be out in a minute."

I wrap my still soggy hair in a fresh towel and step into the living room, where a table is set for two. A stiff white cotton cloth covers the round surface, a small centerpiece made with stargazer lilies in the middle. Two chairs are set facing each other; in front of them are two plates with covers and small bowls filled with fresh berries. On the side are a small basket of lightly toasted bread, warmed butter and small jars filled with various French jams, plus elegant pitchers of apple juice and water and a brushed stainless steel insulated carafe that undoubtedly has coffee inside. It's entirely too fancy for a breakfast. It reminds me of our honeymoon, where everything was perfect and romantic, and a shard of pain pierces through me.

He squints at me. "What happened to your bruises and cuts?"

"Makeup." I wave one hand at the food. "I really didn't want anything."

"I ordered extra just in case. You don't have to eat it if you don't want to." His voice is inscrutable. It only adds to my unhappiness. I still can't believe that only a week ago, I thought I could have it all.

In a gallant—and practiced—gesture, he pulls out a chair for me. I sit and let him settle me up against the table, all the while wondering who else he's seated like this. It's a petty and ludicrous thought, but I can't help it when my feelings are all over the place. I didn't care earlier, because at first I didn't want to, and later because I thought we were trying to have a genuine relationship based on affection and caring if not love—it would've been small-minded of me to be jealous of his previous women. It's heartrending to realize I was the only one who thought his being nice to me actually meant something, but it's too late. I'm already emotionally entangled, and won't be able to extricate myself without a lot of effort.

Watching him take the seat across from me, I realize there is a distinct disadvantage to my being in a robe with my wet hair wrapped in a towel while Elliot looks magnificent as usual, his presence born from natural confidence and a self-made success that's bigger than life. I wish I'd taken the time to make myself more presentable. Even if I could never be like him, at least I wouldn't look so…small and pathetic.

Then I shake myself inwardly for even thinking that. Everything that's happened between us in the last seven days told me everything I needed to know about where I stand in Elliot's esteem.

Wordlessly, he serves me coffee. I dump lots of sugar in, hoping that the extra energy along with some caffeine will jolt my brain into gear. He drinks his, watching me over the rim of a white cup, its delicate handle looking almost too fragile for his hand.

The breakfast is a three-egg omelet with two different types of cheese and lightly sautéed mushrooms. Is it Elliot making a gesture? I had the same omelets on our honeymoon in St. Cecilia.

He watches me expectantly, and I take a small bite. It's surprisingly good, and I find myself ravenous all of sudden, despite the tension coiled inside me.

The silence stretches, sitting heavily between us. Only the sound of clinking silverware and china breaks it. Every time I raise my eyes, I see Elliot studying me as though I'm some exotic specimen under a microscope. I'm not certain why he looks at me like that, what he wants to discover. He's already made up his mind about me, hasn't he?

My plate polished clean, I finally place my fork on the table and lean back with a fresh cup of coffee.

Elliot clears his throat. "Tell me about how you met Grayson."

I freeze, then slowly sit up straight, spine stiff and shoulders pulled back. "Why do you care? Didn't whoever you hired to figure everything out tell you?"

"Not everything."

I look away for a moment. Perversely enough, now I'm reluctant to tell him. Maybe it's because I'm resentful of the way he's shut me out. Or maybe I just don't want to bare another piece of myself, only to be found wanting.

"Well...give him some more money. I'm sure he can tell you," I murmur.

"I don't want him to tell me."

"Why not? I'm certain a third party's recounting of the meeting will carry more weight than mine." Elliot's jaw tightens, but the reaction gives me no pleasure. I tap the top of the coffee cup. "It's been a week since you found out." *A week since I wanted to talk, but you didn't.*

He blinks as though he can't believe what he's hearing, then his eyebrows pinch together. "You really don't want to talk about it?"

"I don't see the point."

"The point is not to live in this…tension."

"We have less than a year left to go," I say instead. "We can be polite."

He laughs dryly. "Polite. Jesus." All signs of mirth abruptly vanish from his face. "Do you want sex to be polite? Is it politeness that makes you wet?"

Heat sears my cheeks. Whatever I was planning to say disappears from my mind.

"Does being polite make you scream when I fuck you? Is it politeness that makes your tight little cunt spasm around my dick night after night?"

I concentrate on my coffee cup, my hands unsteady. "Don't be crude. You know I want you— your body." I need to start framing everything into something clinical and unemotional. If I do it often enough, I might be able to convince myself Elliot and I have nothing worth crying over.

Elliot stops, then drags a hand roughly through his hair. "It's not politeness that makes me hard every time I see you. It's not politeness that makes me want to kick myself in the ass for letting you out of my sight last night. It's certainly not politeness that makes me want to kill whoever pushed you down those stairs."

My mouth parts. I didn't know he felt that way about my accident...or anything about me. He's been so...careful not to betray himself around me in the last few days.

"I'm trying to give you a chance to talk. You said you wanted to make me understand. I'm willing to listen now." His voice is surprisingly gentle, like that time back on St. Cecilia. "You and I both know our current situation can't last."

As gentle as his voice is, something unyielding lies underneath. He's not going to give up unless I tell him what he wants to know.

I vacillate. But really, what's the point of not saying anything except to be perverse? He's already given an inch when he admitted he cared more than he let on. I can bend a bit in return.

"Well...all right. Grayson and I met in Las Vegas, a little over a year ago," I begin. "He came to see me at the diner where I worked. It would've been impossible for him to track me down otherwise, since Nonny and I were living in a shelter." I exhale, trying to find enough control to get through the rest of the story. Even now I wonder how I could've had such poor judgment. "He claimed to work for an insurance company, said there was some kind of allowance payout for me, about a thousand dollars a month. Because I hadn't collected anything the previous year, he said I could get a little extra, although not in a lump sum. I signed on the dotted lines he pushed my way to get the money."

"But it was only a thousand dollars a month," Elliot points out, his tone incredulous.

I give him a sad smile. If I ever need proof of how different we are, I only have to listen to him talk about money. "Elliot, it was a *life-altering* amount to me. We couldn't stay at the shelter anymore."

I don't think I've said anything particularly alarming. I've been careful not to. But his eyes suddenly sharpen and his entire body stills, like a predator that just spotted prey and is waiting to pounce.

When I don't continue, he asks, "What was wrong with the shelter?" in a voice so soft that I almost don't hear it over the pounding of my heart. Memories of the place never fail to spike my anxiety.

"The supervisor…" I lick my suddenly dry lips. "He…" I search for the right word, but I can't seem to find it. I blurt out, "He really…*liked* Nonny."

Elliot waits, his eyes unblinking and focused, for me to elaborate…as though I might've meant something unusually abstruse when I used the word *like*. When nothing comes, red slowly mottles his face. He rises to his feet, looking like some kind of ancient colossus. "What the *fuck?*"

The force of the word actually shirrs the water in his glass. Suddenly ashamed and uncertain, I look away.

"Did he pay for what he did?" Elliot asks in a voice so awful my skin crawls.

"No," I whisper. "But Mr. Grayson's money allowed us to leave. And I would've sold my soul to keep my sister safe."

ELEVEN

Elliot

FURY SWIRLS INSIDE ME LIKE A DARK STORM, and I can't stay still. I grip the back of my chair, trying to regain composure, but it's no use. Giving up, I push away and pace. A need for violence throbs in my veins, and I want to punch something. Preferably the disgusting scumbag at the Vegas shelter.

"And yes, you were right that it was stupid and naïve of me to believe Mr. Grayson's story," my wife continues. Her words are weighted with resignation, but she keeps her shoulders straight, her gaze direct. "My gut told me it wasn't the brightest idea to trust him, but...I ignored it."

I stop and stare at Belle. What she's saying is really sinking into me, and I feel like vomiting. Air saws in and out of my lungs, my chest hurts like hell and my throat aches with all the blistering things I want to say but can't. They aren't directed at her. No, they're for me, because I'm such a superior asshole.

Belle's hands are trembling, and she deposits the coffee cup on the table and drops her arms so I can't see them anymore. "I hate remembering that period of my life. Every time I do, I can't help but think of all the ways things could've gone wrong for two poor girls with no education, no friends, nothing. I know from experience how bad it can be for helpless girls…"

My gut tightens like it's been punched. I push a fist against my mouth. I've never felt this searing level of hate and disgust, not even for Julian, not even for Annabelle Underhill. Underneath the rage, my heart is breaking for the girl my wife was a year ago.

"But I never thought that an adult man would try to go after an underage girl. Nonny was just thirteen, and a skinny thirteen at that."

"Why didn't you say something?" I ask when I regain a small measure of control over my emotions.

Her gaze snaps up to my face. "Seriously? When would I have been able to tell you? When you gave me two hundred dollars for the worst stripping ever? When you offered me three thousand for a blowjob? When you took me to that lawyer's office for the marriage contract?"

She's throwing the same events at me again, but unlike before, they hit home this time. My face heats at the reminder of what an ass I've been. Back then I didn't know her. I treated her the way I would any woman who'd sell her body—and more—if it could get her what she wanted.

"But what about after?" I ask hoarsely. "We were supposed to start fresh. That's what the honeymoon was about."

"I didn't want to ruin what we started with an ugly past, Elliot." A bitterly ironic twist of her lips seems to say *like that matters anymore.*

"How can you think it's just an 'ugly past' that needs to stay buried? Is that how you felt about Annabelle Underhill too?" As soon as the words leave my lips, I know I've screwed up.

"She's your ex, she came to your home and she obviously wants you back. I don't know how you can argue she has nothing to do with me."

I bite back an expletive directed at myself. What is it about this woman that twists me, drives me crazy? Women *don't do this* to me. Women are diversions, a bit of fun, not people who keep my emotions running high and erratic, like a train about to derail.

My wife sighs, lifts a hand as though to fix her hair, then drops it when it hits the towel. "You knowing about what happened to me and

Nonny in Vegas wouldn't have changed anything. It had already happened, and it would've only disgust—upset you. And I honestly didn't think Mr. Grayson was going to be a problem. Not one that would concern you, anyway. If I had, I *would have* told you earlier."

Even through the turbulent feelings churning inside me, I catch something in her voice—a clue to what's going on inside her head. "I wouldn't have been disgusted with you, Belle," I say, keeping my voice quiet. I'm trying very hard not to vent the emotions roiling inside me. They push against my ribs, the pressure almost unbearable.

She drops her gaze. "It's not important anymore."

"*The hell it isn't.*"

She's quiet for a moment. "They say it's best not to know how sausages are made because if you know you won't enjoy them anymore. People's pasts are like that too. You don't want to know everything, Elliot."

Then I recognize something that I haven't thought of before. She doesn't want me to know any more than I absolutely have to. She is assuming that I won't stay constant. She's experienced how quickly people, including those who claim to be her friends, can turn on her. "I'm not Traci or anybody else from your home town," I point out.

"I know."

I walk over and cradle her chin in my hand—carefully—then tilt her face until she looks at me directly. "Do you really?"

She doesn't answer. And I realize with sudden clarity this is why I've been furious that she withheld information—because it's proof that she would never trust me, never lean on me or...

"How can you say you love me and not make yourself even the slightest bit vulnerable to me?" The question rasps out before I can stop myself.

She blinks a couple of times, then looks away.

The evasion cuts, but it doesn't just hurt. It infuriates.

I lift her head back to me, but Belle is nothing if not stubborn. She gazes at the tip of my nose, pointedly avoiding my eyes. Her mouth is set tight, her lips almost bloodless. She'll stay like this forever if that's what it takes. I recognize that as the seconds pile up.

Hell if I'll let her.

I slant my head, covering her lips with mine. No matter what, she's always been honest in bed. And this time is no exception.

She kisses me back, her teeth and tongue rough—almost punishing, as though she blames me for all the shit that's gone wrong since we met. I don't give a fuck when she cuts the inside of my lower lip. This is far better than her silent, mutinous retreat moments ago.

I lick her lips and rub my tongue against hers. Her velvet softness stokes my suddenly raging need. Her shallow, choppy breathing tells me she is into it as much as I am. I thank my lucky stars that she's this hot and passionate. *Her past…* God, her past would be enough to kill this part of her if she let it.

Her fingers dig into my hair, nails scraping my scalp and pulling at the strands until it hurts, but I don't care. I let out a triumphant growl, yank at the damp towel wrapped around her head and fling it away. Her hair falls in a loose wet coil, and I wrap my hand in it, anchoring her. She slides down her chair, and I take her in my arms, pulling her until she's sitting in my lap, her sweet ass over my very ready dick.

Still, I pull back with a superhuman effort.

"Don't," she whispers harshly.

"Belle…you're injured."

"I'm sure we can figure out a way to manage." She looks at my mouth.

I hesitate. I didn't start the kiss to seduce her. I don't want to do anything until she's fully recovered from her ordeal.

She undoes the sash around her waist and shrugs out of her robe. The sensational slopes and curves of her body leave me breathless. It doesn't matter how many times I have her or how long I keep her wrapped in my arms. The impact of her femininity is like a nuke going off in the center of my chest.

But the bruises… They dampen what I feel. *God.* I feel like an ass with a capital A for lusting after my wife when she's black and blue.

"Don't worry about it," she says. "I'm fine."

I brush my thumb over a dark purple spot on her hip, meditating on it. "It looks worse than it feels," she says.

Somehow I manage to make my voice firm. "We shouldn't."

"But I want to. Sex is the only time you're close to me." Her words are soft, but they're no less powerful for that.

Feeling as though I've been gutted, I carry her to bed. She shivers as though she can feel the weight of my gaze like a physical caress. The need to give her the closeness she craves is overwhelming—but it's not as simple as inserting Tab A into Slot B. I want her to break me like she did before, when she took me lovingly into her mouth and shattered me inside out. And I want to break her the same way until I have all the pieces of her, every facet of her bared to me—body and soul.

To that end, I rein in the lust raging through

me. I kiss her body—every curve, every inch of her sensitive skin—and breathe in her intoxicating scent. She's so soft, so pliable as desire overwhelms her. Her face is flush with heat, and she begs, "Don't do this…" Her raspy whisper comes to me as I run my mouth over the sweet skin along her inner thigh.

"You want me to stop?" I murmur, letting my hot breath brush the place my lips were just seconds ago.

She shakes her head. "Stop teasing. You know I'm wet."

White-hot lust pounds in my veins. I can smell her most intimate parts like this, feel her quiver underneath me.

Even then, I maintain control. I use my hands and mouth to take her to the brink, only to pull back. Her voice breaks, but that's not all I'm after.

She undulates under me. "Don't you want me?" she whispers, her words barely audible. "Please…"

"How can you doubt it?"

I grind my hard dick against her wet pussy. My jaw clenches with the control I'm exerting over my body. She feels too damn fucking good, and it's all I can do to not drive into her with all I've got. But a part of me tells me I can't let this become just another episode of hot sex. It has to mean more…count for more, even though I'm incapable of figuring out what that "more" is at the moment.

My wife wants closeness. So I'm going to give it to her—sans consummation—even if it kills me.

But before I can pull away, she wraps her legs around me, tilts her pelvis just so and digs her heels into my back. She moves without giving me a second to retreat, and I glide right into her searing, wet core.

A small kernel of logic tries to tell me I shouldn't, but the need overwhelms everything. My blood pulses in my veins, and I just…give up. "Tell me if I'm hurting you."

She looks me dead in the eye. "The only way you can hurt me is by stopping."

No cavalry would be able to drag me away now.

She's so primed that it only takes a couple of powerful thrusts before she starts to climax, her pussy gripping my cock tightly. My eyes roll in my head, but I keep driving into her. Even my lust-addled brain can tell I've lost. But I'm not willing to go down like a man with no self-control. I maintain my pace, sinking all the way in every time.

She orgasms again, her wet hair spread around her thrashing head. Pleasure puts a rosy glow to her beautiful face, and my control slips as two tears leave the corners of her eyes.

When her pussy spasms around me, I lose it. I let go with a deep, guttural groan. I feel like I'm being ripped apart. It's more than a *god fucking amazing* orgasm riding me, it's like being swept out to sea.

Afterward I roll away so I don't crush her, then pull her close so she lies with her side flush against mine. I stare at the ceiling as my breathing returns to normal, two thoughts sliding into my mind like razorblades.

First: It doesn't matter what I've been telling myself. She's got her hooks into me so deep that I don't think I can ever be free of her. And I don't want to be. I've never acknowledged the fact, but I do now.

Second: I know something's happened in the last twenty-four hours. Elizabeth's warning twists in my gut. I teased my wife mercilessly, gave her several orgasms that should have ripped her apart...but she didn't say, "I love you."

TWELVE

Annabelle

MY HEAD IS SPINNING, MY BREATHING shallow. I let myself stay dazed until it deepens, then return to reality.

The almost violent need Elliot has for my body should leave me happy. But instead I'm conflicted. Everything we have is based on primitive, physical lust. If it hadn't been for that, he would've never propositioned me. Anyone would've been okay to fulfill his father's condition.

Admitting that to myself has given me the strength to keep the words inside me. I'm never going to say "I love you" to a man who can't say it back and mean it. I deserve that much in a relationship.

I shift, then stop when I notice the stickiness

between my legs. A sudden chill racks me, and I jerk myself up, a sheet clutched to my chest.

"What's wrong?" Elliot asks, his eyes suddenly alert.

"You forgot the condom," I blurt out.

When he doesn't respond immediately, I look down at him. He is absolutely gorgeous, lying next to me on the bed, and the effect of his magnetism hits me like a freight train, stealing my breath. His thick, silky hair is messed up, but it only adds to the raw, masculine beauty of his masterfully carved face. One hand is tucked under his head, while the other rests on his chest, the arms lean and muscular from regular swimming. I know how strong his body is—I've felt it often: when he carried me like I weighed nothing in St. Cecelia, every time he finally loses control and drives into me…

But there's something else that makes me hesitate. The small hint of insufferable insolence almost always present in his expression is gone, and it makes my internal alarm clang. Something has shifted without my noticing, and I don't know what that is or what it means.

"Didn't you hear what I said?"

"I heard you," he says mildly, as though we're discussing what to have for lunch. He doesn't even move from his rather lazy repose.

"Are you clean?" Even as I ask, I know what the answer is. He's too meticulous to be careless with something as important as his sexual health.

"Of course. You?" he asks in an easy tone that doesn't tell me much.

My face heats. From him, it's a reasonable question, since I'm the one who was stupid enough to get drunk in high school and get... I push the thought out of my head and nod jerkily.

"Well, then."

Why isn't he more freaked out? There's more to the situation than whether or not one of us has an STD. We agreed when we signed the deal: *no kids.* "Maybe the timing's wrong," I say, thinking fast. "Besides, it's only one time."

Even as I say it, my insidious mind reminds me it only took once to get pregnant last time.

Oh my god. *Last time.* I squeeze my eyes shut, bringing a shaky hand to cover my face. I don't want to think about that ugliness at all. This is nothing like before. I wasn't forced, I'm not some naïve clueless girl of fifteen, and the father of this child isn't going to be a mystery *if* I get pregnant.

"If you say so." Elliot's softly spoken words penetrate my churning thoughts. "I'm sure you know better than me."

"Why aren't you more upset?" I drop my hand from my face and study his utterly relaxed body. Just what the hell is going on? I feel like I'm in a middle of a hockey game where the rules have suddenly changed.

"Do you want me to be?"

I don't know how to answer that. So instead I say, "You should've remembered the rubber."

He nods. "True. I apologize."

Oddly enough, his easygoing attitude bugs me more than getting upset would. I straighten and stare straight ahead.

He starts to push himself up, then drops back on the bed and pulls me gently down over him. I settle onto his bare torso, my breasts pressed against his chest. I can feel his strong, throbbing heartbeat, and my heart accelerates to match his tempo. It still astounds me how my body adjusts to his until we fit perfectly. It's either magic or madness. Liquid heat ripples through me despite the strong orgasms I just had, and I don't know if I'll ever get used to this need I have for him.

"This isn't about being responsible or hoping for the best," he says. "I'm not going to worry about anything until…*if* it happens. And I don't want you to worry, either."

I nod, somewhat placated by his explanation. He's being logical, and worrying won't solve anything.

"There's something else. It's about your former roommate—Caroline."

Caroline. The last time we spoke about her, it

was about him checking out my assertion about her betrayal.

"If she ever bothers you again, you have to let me know. I should've told you this earlier, but didn't. Another mistake." He tilts his head while adjusting me, so he can look at my face. "She hasn't bothered you since…the articles, has she?" I shake my head, and he says, "Good."

"What happened between the two of you?" I whisper. "I saw pictures of you at the same hotel."

"Fucking parasites." The muscles in his jaw flex. "Let me guess. They said I was there to bang her, didn't they?"

"Something like that."

"I put the fear of god into her after I extracted some information."

"I see." But I don't. Not really. He didn't have to take her to a hotel for that. And as inane as it is, I don't want Caroline or any woman with Elliot in a location as private and conducive to an affair as a hotel room. Given the events of the last week, I should be relieved that Elliot and I are finally on better footing, but I'm not because I recognize I'm being jealous.

The emotion is entirely pointless. Even though I'm his wife, I know where I rank in his life, especially after our horrible argument on Sunday. The peace between us is temporary, like everything else we have. When Annabelle Underhill goes through with her threat, who knows what will happen? Just imagining how Elliot might react deflates me like a popped balloon.

I close my eyes. My time with him is almost a quarter over. I can do this.

"What are you thinking?"

Why did you choose a hotel to talk to her? "Nothing." I look away, then roll off him. "I should clean up and get dressed. It's late now."

"We don't have to be at the airport for another five hours." His slightly pinched eyebrows say I haven't really fooled him.

"Then let's see a little bit of the area," I say. "I've never been in San Francisco before."

He studies me, his gaze moving over even the smallest lines on my face, then nods. "If you wish."

THIRTEEN

Elliot

BY THE TIME WE CHECK OUT, THERE AREN'T that many hours left before our flight. We end up at a seafood restaurant for a light lunch of shrimp cocktail and grilled wild salmon, then I take her shopping. I figure that should cheer her up—I've never met a woman who doesn't like to buy a handbag or three. Or shoes. Jewelry works too, but I didn't check with the concierge for an acceptable jeweler.

Belle glows like a polished diamond inside the stores. Her unbound red hair frames her face and bounces around her delicate shoulders. The green of her eyes looks even more vivid under the display lights, and the mustard-yellow maxi dress with floral lace trim is casual and feminine, perfect for a lazy shopping excursion. She's paired it with a light, cream-colored cardigan for extra warmth and to hide the bruises.

The weather is chilly compared to Los Angeles, and I'm glad I packed a pair of slacks and a sweater. I shove my hands into my pants pockets, my untucked blue button-down shirt covering my wrists. I watch my wife examine the selection of bags the clerk has brought out.

Although I pretended to be calm earlier to play it down, I'm anything but. *I forgot the condom.* I've never been so careless. I should've known better, protected both of us.

At the same time, it's not like the idea of tying ourselves together with a baby hasn't crossed my mind. That probably makes me an underhanded son of a bitch. How craven I've become with my need for her. It isn't like me to want anyone this desperately. Not even Annabelle Underhill got to me like this.

I study Belle to see if she's in pain, but she seems okay so far…other than moving with extra care to not to bump into anything. I would love nothing more than to find the person who pushed her, but I know the chances of that are nil. If anyone had seen something, Elizabeth would've heard by now and she would've called me. I keep going over potential suspects, but discard them all. Keith is a coward and doesn't have the guts to engineer something like this, not at an event with so many eyes. Annabelle Underhill had a date, although I can't remember if she was in the dining room when my wife left the table. Dad is an asshole, but he's not into physical violence, even by proxy. Sneaking around and backstabbing people is his MO.

Of course, it could be something less sinister. Maybe somebody was moving something—equipment used at the dinner function, perhaps—and bumped into my wife or something…

I shake my head. *Ludicrous.*

Belle runs her hands over various bags, admiring the fine stitching and luxurious leather. Even from here I can tell everything is high quality and ridiculously expensive. Still, she pushes them away.

Undeterred, the clerk brings out more items. My wife smiles wistfully, brushing her fingertips along the supple material, but shakes her head again.

I frown, wondering what's going on. I can't believe she didn't like any of them. A couple items managed to snag *my* attention, and I have about as much interest in women's handbags as a dog does in carrots.

But maybe she doesn't want to buy anything because she doesn't want to splurge on herself. Now that I think about it, she hasn't spent a penny on herself other than when I insisted. I make a face. Belle is entirely too frugal for my taste. I already told her she can charge whatever she wants to her credit card and I'll take care of it.

I push myself off the wall and hand the clerk my plastic. "We're getting this, this and this, and those three over there." I gesture, pointing at the items my wife lingered over in particular.

The salesperson gives me a professionally poised "Very good, sir," but I can see her eyes light up as she takes my card and goes to gather the merchandise. Another clerk immediately comes out with a tray of champagne; I pluck a flute and instruct them to bring out some freshly squeezed grapefruit juice for my wife. A picky order, but I don't care. They can kiss my wife's feet after the amount of money I just dropped.

Belle is staring at me with her mouth slightly agape. "You shouldn't have."

"Yes, I should. Why do you think I carry plastic?"

"You know what I mean."

"Methinks the lady shouldn't protest too much. A husband is entitled to spoil his wife." I scrawl my signature on the five-figure sales slip. Everything is beautifully wrapped and presented in glossy shopping bags.

Belle looks at me, her teeth worrying her lower lip, then finally looks away with a sigh.

"What?" I know she wants to say something.

"Nothing." She shrugs, then shakes her head.

She's entirely too emphatic, and that generally means "nothing" is really "something." I want to force her to say what's on her mind, but I stop as apprehension shivers through me. What if it's something I don't want to hear?

Fuck.

I wish I hadn't talked to Elizabeth at the dinner. Then maybe I wouldn't feel so off balance and unsure. Women are always predictable. They want money first and foremost, and are willing to do almost anything to get it. That's why you see a perfect ten hanging out with a fat guy old enough to be her father. Someone like my sister, who honestly doesn't care about such materialistic things, is rare…an anomaly.

Now I'm with another anomaly—my wife. And there's a sinking feeling that I don't have what it takes to keep a woman like her.

"Want to hit a few other stores?"

"No." Belle checks the time. "We have two hours left until our flight."

Since traffic in the Bay Area can be pretty nasty, I dump all the shopping bags in the trunk of our Audi rental and open the passenger door for my wife. She slides in, one taut and silky calf showing through the side slit in her dress. The second she's seated, she smooths her skirt, and the golden skin is gone from view. Still, it's a hell of a sexy peek. There's an innate sensuality to her that's far hotter than a buck-naked lingerie model.

My body tightens as heat prickles along my spine, and I wipe my mouth with my hand. I'm acting like we didn't spend our morning in bed, fucking each other's brains out.

I climb behind the wheel and start driving. She smells so good next to me—warm and sweet—and her breasts rise and fall gently with each breath, offering a tantalizing view above her modestly cut bodice. I'm so distracted that I almost don't hear her question.

"Last week you said you were going to pay Mr. Grayson off. Do you mind…if I do it?"

"Um…" I blink, trying to reorient myself. "I thought you didn't have the money."

"I don't, but…" She hesitates, then straightens herself. "I want to use your money to pay him off. But I'll pay you back."

"Not necessary," I interject. From the way she tightens her jaw, I doubt she agrees with me.

She continues, "I want to see him face to face…let him know he can't try to control me anymore."

Closure on your own terms. I can understand that. Still… "Isn't he dangerous?"

"I don't think so." She shakes her head. "I mean, yes, I think he is a user and not above-board, but I don't think he's going to get violent if that's what you mean. Also, I plan to meet him someplace public."

I consider. She's probably right. Grayson works for Keith, and Keith may be a snake, but he's also a coward. He won't ever do his dirty work in the light of day, and certainly he doesn't have the guts to get physical. When I discovered he was stealing from me and Lucas, I hit him in the jaw—twice—and he just cowered and covered up. It is as though he's afraid to fight back.

Nevertheless, this is my wife we're talking about, and I don't like the idea of her going out there to confront his agent on her own. I open my mouth, about to gloss my real thoughts and then go ahead and do what I think is best anyway, but stop. If I want to fix what's broken between us, I can't just do whatever the hell I feel like regardless of her wishes. "Hmm… I don't like it."

"I know, but it's important to me."

"How about if I come with you?"

"I don't think that would be wise. Like I said before, he's my problem, and I want to deal with it."

I stare at the red light. Traffic's heavier than I expected, and the bright sunlight reflects off the roofs of the cars around us. I squint through my shades and tap the steering wheel with my thumb. Belle turns toward the window and looks out at the street on her side with various shops and slow-milling pedestrians.

"It is okay for you to lean on me once in a while," I say as the light turns green and I hit the gas.

She doesn't speak or react in any way. We're in the same car, but somehow I feel like we're miles apart.

"Can we start over?" I ask suddenly.

"I thought the honeymoon was the new beginning." She crosses her arms. "Elliot, this isn't some…computer game. We can't just 'start over' every time we don't like the way things are going."

I swallow. She's right, and I can't think of anything to say.

Just…don't be too stubborn and turn her tender feelings for you into pain. Because the next stage will be indifference.

I can't be too late. My wife isn't indifferent.

But I can't help but feel that she's slipping away, grain by grain like sand clenched in my fist.

Annabelle

By the time Elliot and I finally make it to the penthouse in L.A., I'm exhausted. The flight was short, but still felt grueling. My shoulders have been almost touching my pendant earrings ever since we boarded, and the tightness has spread to my skull and mid- and lower back. The pain hurts worse than the injuries from last night. I'd like to think it's the trip making me tense, but I know better.

It's the prospect of facing Nonny.

She's at the dining table, working on her homework. When she spots us, she manages a smile for Elliot, but nothing for me. "Welcome home."

"Don't be cold," Elliot says. "Your sister just took a tum—"

I put a hand on his arm and shake my head. I don't want Nonny to know about the fall and worry her unnecessarily. I also don't want her being nice to me because I had an incident. I want her to be nice to me because that's what she wants.

Her lips flatten and she gathers her things. "I think I'll go back to my room. Let me know when it's time for dinner."

Watching her leave, I let out a rough sigh. I know why she's doing this. She's been avoiding me, treating me like some kind of leper. If she were like any other spoiled teenager I'd have some clue as to what to do, but she isn't. She's always been so perfect, so sweet-tempered. I have no idea how to deal with her attitude or refusal to listen and understand things from my perspective.

A frown creases Elliot's forehead. "This is unacceptable," he says quietly.

I agree, but say nothing.

"How long are you going to let her do this?"

"I don't know, but please don't try to talk to her on my behalf."

That stops him. "You want me to stay out of it?"

"Yes." To soften my curt answer, I add, "She's my sister, my responsibility."

"She's my sister-in-law."

"But she's not mad at you." *And her sister-in-law status is temporary, but she'll be my sister forever.*

Elliot runs a finger softly along my cheek. "One day you'll learn that it's okay to let me help."

I merely smile. It's never wise to depend on people. I've learned my lesson, first in Lincoln City and then with Mr. Grayson. Not even Nonny knows everything, and she's my sister, the one person who's always been by my side.

Thankfully my phone buzzes, pulling my attention away from gloomy thoughts. I check and see a text from Traci.

Are you still interested in that junior assistant job I told you about? And are you free tomorrow at ten a.m.?

I type *Yes and yes* and hit send.

The assistant went into the hospital for some kind of problem, and her doc ordered bed rest. So they're doing interviews tomorrow to fill in the vacancy ASAP. Dress professionally. Bring a résumé.

Oh, wow. So much quicker than I expected. *Okay, no problem. Who am I interviewing with?*

Jana Thompson. Super nice. Don't be nervous. You'll kill it.

I smile and put away my phone.

"What's that about?" Elliot asks.

"It's that job I mentioned. Apparently it's opening up earlier than expected. So I have an interview tomorrow at ten." I steal a quick glance his way to gauge how he feels. But his face stays impassive. Is he still unsure about it because he feels like he should provide for me so long as we're married?

"Good luck," he says. "I think it'll be good for you. Give you something to do."

I nod. "Thanks."

A knot in my gut loosens. I realize I'd been girding my loins for another argument.

As I sag, my hip against the edge of the table, Elliot squeezes my shoulder. "Don't worry. You'll be awesome tomorrow."

Somehow it seems like his voice lacks enthusiasm. Then I shake my head. I have to be projecting my worst-case scenario reaction onto him. He has the upper hand in everything. He doesn't have to fake anything with me.

FOURTEEN

Elliot

I'M NOT THRILLED THAT BELLE WON'T LET ME run interference for her with Nonny. Although the kid's not my sister, at the moment I'm equally responsible for her.

Still, I back off and resign myself to watching the tense byplay between the two of them the next morning over the rim of my coffee mug.

"You have a couple of stains on your shirt," Belle points out to Nonny, her voice kind.

Nonny looks down and makes a face, then spins on her heel and goes inside her room without a word to her sister, not even a thank you.

My eyebrows rise when the door shuts behind her. This behavior is a bit of a shock. My siblings and I may have fucked-up parents, but we've always gotten along among ourselves. No one ever stayed pissed off for long.

At least Belle is recovering from the fall. The bruises are still there, but they aren't livid anymore. I'm grateful.

Belle is in a chic green dress with a V-neck and three-quarter-length sleeves. The skirt is conservatively cut, ending at mid-shin, and the nude pumps she's wearing add to the glamour and confidence of her general appearance. A string of white pearls circles her delicate throat—which I spent a good part of last night nibbling on—and matching pearl studs adorn her ears. She looks classy without appearing ostentatiously expensive, and something about the oh-so-proper office attire fires me up, makes me want to go muss it up and reveal the primal, responsive woman who was writhing underneath me just hours ago.

I sigh inwardly. Looking good for the interview is important to her, and there isn't much time if she doesn't want to be late. I resign myself to waiting and hand her a steaming cup of coffee. The mug reads YOU CAN DO IT! in gold caps.

"Thank you," she says softly, and takes a sip.

Just then Nonny comes back out, changed into a new outfit. Her fitted sleeveless top is long, black and shows off her slim arms, while her jeans have ripped-up thighs in front and are so tight that I don't know how she can move. I squint. I don't remember telling Josephine to buy something so…formfitting. Nonny's just a kid.

"See ya," she says, throwing the words in my general direction and completely ignoring Belle. I grind my teeth. Just how much time does a teenage girl need to get over something?

In the grand scheme of things, Belle's stripper job wasn't even that scandalous. Despite spending her formative years in a small—and apparently uptight—town like Lincoln City, Nonny should've gotten over her prudish attitude after having lived in cities like Vegas and now L.A.

Nonny grabs a granola bar and leaves, mumbling something about being late. Now her manners have gone to hell. Before she used to say a cheery goodbye to us.

Belle finishes her coffee and sighs. "I gotta run, too."

I take her hand, still warm from the mug, and kiss her on the mouth. "Good luck."

"Thanks." She flashes a strained smile and leaves.

The door shuts, and I cross my arms. If the situation doesn't improve soon, I'm going to do something drastic to fix it. My wife won't approve, but I don't give a damn. I don't like this tension, especially not in my home.

And I most certainly don't like to see Belle unhappy every time she faces her sister.

I grab my phone and go upstairs for a swim. Restless or not, tired or not, I always swim. It helps clear my head, and it's good for staying in shape.

I toss my shirt and pants on the closet floor and pull on a pair of trunks. Just as I'm about to hit the water, my phone vibrates. I glance at it and see PAIGE flash on the screen. There is only one Paige in my phone—Ryder's wife.

"Hello, sugar lips," I say—my typical greeting—while gazing at the crystal-clear pool.

"Is that how you answer all your calls?" she says with a laugh.

"Don't you know? You've been with my brother for four years."

"And I think I called you maybe five times during those years."

Ryder likes to arrange our fun times himself. Or did.

"What does your experience tell you?" I ask lightly.

"That you're inappropriate."

"But you love me anyway. So. What's up?"

"I said we should catch up."

Huh. "That you did." I didn't expect her to call so soon.

"Um. It's kind of a serious catching up."

Her tone of voice makes me focus. "How serious? Did Ryder do something stupid again?" He almost lost her over his inability to just…do the right thing where she was concerned.

"Ryder is perfect. It's about your wife."

I sigh and lower myself into one of the poolside loungers. This doesn't sound like it's going to be quick. "What about her?"

"Did she say anything about what happened on Saturday?"

"Should she have?" I ask, my skin suddenly chilling. Does Paige have information about the tumble my wife took?

"Guess not. Okay, well… She had a run-in with Annabelle Underhill. You know, your father's third wife." She clears her throat.

Fuck. "Where?"

"In the bathroom. I was in a stall, and, uh, ended up overhearing them without meaning to. I feel bad about that…but I don't feel too bad because my god, that woman's a menace."

I'm on full alert now. This can't be good. "What did she say?"

"I think she knows about the…deal."

Paige doesn't have to clarify. She's referring to Julian's fucked-up proposition, designed purely to control us. I still don't understand why he thinks making us marry will make any difference, but then, who knows what the fuck our father's thinking half the time? He is the one who keeps marrying younger and younger women, as though it will give him the youth he can never regain. At some point, a man's gotta accept his mortality.

"There is no way she can know," I say. "Julian would've never told her...or anybody. He's a dickhead, but he's not the kind to advertise the fact." Most people think he's an awesome dad because he's spent so much time and energy portraying himself that way.

"You're probably right about your dad," Paige finally says. "I'm sure the only reason he sends me those folders is because of the nondisclosure in my employment contract."

"What folders?"

"Files—actual old-style manila files, like from an office—stuffed with negative reviews of Ryder's new movies every time they come out. Every time. It's amazing just how hard he works to do that."

"Fucker," I mutter.

"Agreed. But anyway, I think Underhill does know somehow. She may not know every detail, but she's got enough. She also threatened to release more embarrassing stuff about your wife to the press unless she divorces you."

"What the fuck?"

"Yeah…" Paige hesitates, then adds, "She, um, told your wife about a wedding closet incident… something about 'fucking in there'…?"

I swear under my breath. It was a terrible, terrible mistake, done in a moment of drunken anger and humiliation. I never suspected she would flaunt it in Belle's face.

"I'm really sorry," Paige says quietly. "Of course I won't tell anyone."

"Thanks." But it's too late. The person I wanted to hide it from the most already knows.

"Talk to your wife. She might be more under-standing than you think. She hasn't heard the story from your point of view."

I say nothing. Paige is sweet to think my spin on the event would sound better than Annabelle Underhill's. The story fucking sucks no matter who it's coming from.

I murmur my thanks, and we hang up.

Tossing my phone on the poolside table, I stare at the water. I wish my wife had told me about this yesterday. Even if she didn't want to talk about my shameful behavior at the wedding, she should've at least told me about the threats against her. Doesn't she know I'll never let any-thing happen to her or her sister?

I've been too lax in my dealings with Annabelle Underhill. That much is clear. Because of the debt I owed to her uncle, I even decided not to punish her for colluding with Caroline to release the info about my wife's past.

But no more. It's time to crush her once and for all.

FIFTEEN

Annabelle

I'VE BEEN TO THE PROMINENT PRIVATE WEALTH management firm OWM first as a janitor, then as a client. Now I'm going as a job candidate, which is kind of surreal. Regardless of the circumstances, entering the cool and impressive marble-and-glass vestibule never fails to awe me. If my life hadn't imploded, this is the kind of place I would've loved to work as an analyst.

Riding up the elevator, I do my best not to fidget in the dress I chose with such care this morning. I know I look professional and good. I just need to ace this interview.

Before coming over, I looked Jana Thompson up on the website. She's thirty-six years old, probably single—her bio didn't mention anything about a significant other or children, unlike some others—and she's worked her entire career at owm, currently managing mostly pension funds. She's an impressive woman too, with a bachelor's degree from Harvard and an mba from Wharton. She chose owm because she's from California and apparently wanted to move back to the West Coast rather than work for one of numerous investment firms in New York City.

The elevator opens and a smartly dressed assistant immediately greets me. "Annabelle? Jana's ready for you."

I paste on a friendly smile, surreptitiously wipe the sweat from my palms and walk inside a corner office with an impressive view of L.A. A large, glass-top desk is absolutely immaculate, not a fingerprint marring the glossy surface. Seven computer screens sit on it, along with two wall-mounted monitors that feed her news from around the world. Jana isn't behind the desk, however. She is in the seating area, papers spread on a low table in front of her white couch. She stands gracefully at the sight of me, and we shake hands. She pumps twice, decisively, her palm bone-dry.

"Nice to meet you, Annabelle. Take a seat." She gestures at another white couch across from her.

I sit down and wait for her to start. She's different from what I imagined. I assumed she would look a bit older, given the high-stress nature of her

NADIA LEE

job. But she's quite youthful. If I hadn't checked her out, I would've thought she was no more than thirty. Her gray pantsuit looks good on her slim figure, and she isn't wearing any jewelry except a pair of diamond studs and a thin golden chain with a small, round locket. Her short, artfully messy hair is so pale it's almost white, and her cornflower-blue eyes penetrate every time she glances up from my résumé.

"Sorry for the abrupt question, but why do you want to work?" she asks.

"Excuse me?"

"I noticed you have an account here, and you're married to Elliot Reed, who's a long-term client of ours. That generally means you don't need to work, and even if you feel like dabbling, you certainly don't need to start out in a position as lowly as my junior assistant. So I'm curious."

Clearly, this is a woman who doesn't like to waste time. Her gaze is direct as she waits for my answer, and I decide I like that. I'm sick of games and bullshit in my life, and it's refreshing to realize maybe I don't need to deal with that with my potential boss.

"I don't want to be idly rich, and at this point, I'm not qualified to be in charge of anything. I don't mind starting from the bottom. It gives me a chance to learn how an organization as amazing as OWM really operates." I lean forward. "Can I be frank?"

She leans back with an unreadable smile. "By all means."

"I've always wanted to work in finance. Always. But when my father's fraud was discovered…"

Her eyes flare, but not with curiosity. She's surprised I'm bringing it up first.

"…well, that dream was put on hold, since I had to survive and provide for my younger sister. Now I don't have to do that, and just to be clear, I'm not going to work as your junior assistant forever. I plan to go back to college and finish my education. And I want to be able to join a place like OWM at some point in the future in a higher capacity."

"Your father's history may weigh against you."

"Which would be a shame, since my father's mistakes have nothing to do with me. Just because somebody has a criminal for a father doesn't mean they'll end up breaking the law themselves."

"Interesting." Jana shifts in her seat. "You do realize if you work here, I'll treat you like any other employee. You won't get any special preference because of your status as a client."

"I wouldn't want it any other way."

A corner of her mouth twitches. "Tell me about how you 'survived and provided' for your sister."

I give her the story as succinctly as possible. She nods and makes a few notes.

"I also read some articles about your rather colorful past," she says.

My face heats.

"Are there going to be more of those in the future? I don't care if you stripped on the side or not, but I do care about personal issues affecting your performance at work."

"I can handle minor gossip like that without falling apart," I say with more confidence than I feel. "After what happened with my parents... Well. Half-baked tabloid junk is nothing."

"I see." Jana studies me, her gaze unblinking.

I meet her eyes, unwilling to cower. This is a job—yes, a job I really want, but I'm not going to let her think she can intimidate me. I answered everything honestly, and if she doesn't want to hire me because of my past, there's nothing I can do about it.

"Thank you for your time, Annabelle," Jana says finally. "Do you have any questions for me?"

"No."

"Well then. Thank you for your interest."

I thank her for her time and walk out. Although it feels like I was in her office for a while, I'm shocked to realize it was only fifteen minutes. Jana didn't ask me a single question about my qualifications. Maybe she's decided she isn't going to hire me, but felt obligated to

AN IMPROPER EVER AFTER

interview me anyway because of Elliot's long-term relationship with Gavin and OWM.

The thought puts a damper on my mood. Maybe Elliot was right to tell me to finish my degree first. I'm certain Jana has applicants with résumés much more impressive than mine.

As the doors to the elevator start to shut, a hand slides between, forcing them to reopen. Dennis walks inside and hits the "close" button.

My breath catches for a moment—not in a good way—at the sight of my ex-boyfriend. His sandy hair is slightly messy, like he's been running his hands through it, and his pale gray eyes are shooting so much anger that if we weren't in public place, I'd fear for my safety. He's been insisting that I need to make my husband back off or some such nonsense. For some reason, he's convinced his trouble at the firm is due to me and Elliot. I drag in air through my mouth and consciously unclench my hands. The elevator has a security camera. Dennis won't do anything rash.

Even as I reassure myself, I feel a growing unease in the pit of my stomach.

"What the fuck is it going to take for you to do what I asked?" he spits out.

"Elliot hasn't done anything to jeopardize your internship here," I say, staring straight ahead to the reflection in the brushed steel doors. He is standing with about a foot of space between us. To anyone looking, we're just polite strangers or acquaintances sharing a car going down. "I want to help you, but I can't make my husband undo something he didn't do. You need to talk with your HR people if you think they're unfairly singling you out for another background check."

Dennis doesn't want anyone to dig into his past because he lied. He even changed his last name to Dunn to avoid the taint of his father. Mr. Smith was Dad's partner in the Ponzi scheme.

"This isn't over, Annabelle." Covetous fury blazing, his eyes rake over my clothes and the huge diamond on my finger. "This is *far* from over."

He gets out on the first floor, and I let the elevator take me further down to the underground parking. The hair on the back of my neck is standing up as I navigate the gray, concrete area full of cars. Every sound makes me jump.

I'm being crazy. Dennis isn't going to run down the stairs to the garage to harass me. Stuff like that happens in movies, not real life. What's more, there are cameras here too.

But I still take out my keys and, in a self-protection move I saw on a video once, clench them in my fist so that three of them stick out between my fingers like claws. And when I finally climb inside my Mercedes and lock the doors, I sag in my seat.

Wrapping my hands around the steering wheel like it's a lifeline, I take a few deep breaths. After a moment, my pulse returns to normal. A car door shuts with a loud thud a few spaces from me, and I jump.

I put a hand over my thundering heart and see a young, slim woman getting out of a Ferrari. She has a huge hat and a pair of sunglasses that covers most of her face. Her long, wavy brown hair hangs loose over her shoulders, and she moves with the entitled arrogance of a woman used to having money. The height, body type and attitude all remind me of Annabelle Underhill—and her threat.

She's declared war, and I can't just sit and wait for her to drop a bomb on me.

I press my knuckles against my teeth, my gaze unconsciously following the woman disappearing into the waiting elevator. I don't have the kind of resources or power to fight somebody like Annabelle Underhill, which means I need an ally or two. And, of course, Elliot is the logical choice.

Oh how I want to ask him for help. But I'm not entirely sure if he'll believe me without any evidence, and the possibility makes my chest ache until I tear up. It took a week before Elliot was ready to listen to me about Mr. Grayson. I don't know if I can afford to wait that long or survive another week of my husband's brooding skepticism. Even now Annabelle Underhill is planning to screw me somehow, and I don't want another thing for Nonny to be angry with me about.

If not Elliot, who? Traci is out of the question. It'd be like throwing two eggs at a rock, and I don't want her getting in that bitch's crosshairs when Traci's just getting her life together.

Elizabeth.

I actually gasp. Elliot's half-sister is so sweet and nice that it's impossible to imagine her saying no. On the other hand, she and I aren't really close enough that I can impose on her like this. But I have nothing to lose by asking, do I? At the very least, she can listen and maybe offer some advice.

My mind made up, I dial her before I lose courage.

Elizabeth answers on the third ring. "Hello, Annabelle." Her voice is so, so soft. "How are you feeling?"

"Much better, thanks."

"I was worried."

"I'm sorry. I should've called."

"Just focus on getting better," she says, her voice full of gentle concern.

I clear my throat. "I hope I'm not interrupting anything."

"Of course not."

"There's something I'd like your advice on."

"Go ahead."

I swallow, my mouth suddenly dry. I wish there was a bottle of water in the car. "It's about something that happened at the dinner."

"Oh?" There's an alertness to her tone now. "What about it?"

I tell her about Annabelle Underhill's threat. Elizabeth listens without interruption or comment, but I know she's paying attention to every word out of my mouth. She is so quiet when I'm done that I almost wonder if the line's been cut.

"Did you tell Elliot?" she asks finally.

"Um… No. Not yet."

"You should."

"I'm not sure…" I bite my lower lip, feeling like a disloyal idiot. "I don't know if he's going to believe me without proof."

"Annabelle, your word should be more than enough."

"Should be, but… It's complicated. I'm sorry, but it's hard to explain." I slowly sink deeper into my seat, my body folding on itself. Now I wish I hadn't called. "Can you help?"

"Of course. But for now, I want you to wait while I look into what she's really up to. Don't do anything rash. My guess is, she wants to rattle you to see if you'll undermine your own position. If she really had anything, she wouldn't have gone after you that way."

"You think so?"

"I know so."

I nod, then remember she can't see me. "Got it. And thank you."

"You're welcome. But you know…" She sighs. "You have to learn to open up to Elliot. He can't help you if you don't tell him."

"I'm worried that he won't help even if I do tell him."

"Oh, I wouldn't. He's surprisingly protective of the people he cares about."

"You know our marriage isn't like that."

"Isn't it? I see how he looks at you. He cares about you more than you think. Don't let his colorful reputation put you off."

"Thanks for the advice," I say, almost in reflex, but I'm not really sure if she understands what I'm going through. No matter how hard I exercise my imagination, I can't picture the man who wouldn't believe every word out of her mouth and wouldn't throw down his life for Elizabeth. She just naturally arouses a protective instinct in people.

"I'll call when I come up with something. And I'm sorry you had such an unpleasant experience at my event."

"Elizabeth, please don't misunderstand. I'm not accusing you of anything."

"I know. But I should've been more… selective."

We end the call. Staring at the concrete wall on the other side of the windshield, I wonder if I'm paying the price for being less than cautious and deliberate with my decisions since my parents' deaths. Right now it feels like everything that's happening is for a reason—my past.

SIXTEEN

Elliot

IT DOESN'T TAKE ME MORE THAN FOUR QUICK laps to come up with a way to disgrace and humiliate Annabelle Underhill and get her to stay the fuck away from me and mine. It is so simple that it's almost laughable. I just need a little time and a few items to pull things together.

After a quick shower, I go to my office and call the front desk to speak to the supervisor of security at my building. The man is quite accommodating when I explain the situation.

Why, of course you can have the footage. Of course we'll be more than happy to email it to you. Terribly sorry that you're dealing with a stalker. Would you like us to blacklist her, should she try to harass you and your wife again?

I'm nothing if not gracious in the face of such cooperation. I thank the man, telling him I would love it if they would ensure Annabelle Underhill never enters the building again. It's been distressing to my gentle wife, who isn't used to such viciousness from people, you see.

Once that's done, I reach out to Elizabeth for another piece I need to put my plan in motion.

"Elliot! Just the person I was about to call," she says.

My eyebrows rise. "What's up, sis? Need more funds for the poor?" She does hit me up often, and I give generously in support. She's my sister, and I admire what she does to help those who are less fortunate.

"Actually, no…although I won't refuse if you want to write another check. It's about your wife."

I'm instantly focused. "Information about her fall?"

"No, it's something else. She called me half an hour ago to tell me about Annabelle Underhill. She wanted my help."

For a stunned moment, I can't process what she's saying. Then the gears in my brain finally start rolling. "Damn it."

I run a palm down my face. The fact that Belle turned to my sister—but not me—cuts deep. I tell myself we haven't had a chance to talk, but I know that's a lame-ass excuse. She's had plenty of chances to lay it out and ask for *my* help.

A beat. Then Elizabeth says, "You know about what happened between them at the dinner?"

"Yeah. Paige told me." Suddenly unable to sit still, I get to my feet and start pacing, the phone glued to my ear.

"*Paige?* How did she know?"

"She overheard."

"Well, at least it was her and not somebody else. What are you going to do?"

"I'm going to ask you to give me all the photos from Saturday."

"For what?"

"To create a narrative to destroy the bitch, what else?"

"Okay. I'll send you all the digital copies, but that's not the main problem."

I say nothing. I know what she's thinking.

"Elliot, maybe…you should show your wife you're the one she should lean on. Not that I object to helping her, but you *are* her husband. You should be her first choice."

"She won't do it. She doesn't think of me that way."

"You two were so happy when you left for your honeymoon. What happened?"

I hesitate, then give her a short summary

166

about how I lost it when I found out about Belle's connection to Grayson…who's working for Keith.

"Good god. I had no idea… Why didn't you give her a chance to explain?"

"I gave her plenty of chances to come clean before I knew about all this. She could've told me then, and I would've believed her because it would have been *her* telling me. But when truth comes from a private investigator, it's not the same."

"Maybe she had a good reason for not saying anything. Sometimes we do stupid things out of fear…or love."

Love. Belle used to tell me she loved me, and it only added to my sense of betrayal when I found out. The love she professed seemed so manipulative—something she tossed out in case she needed cover to protect herself when I learned everything. But I realize it wasn't any of those things, and I want that love back…even though I'm certain I'm not worthy of it anymore.

"When I finally gave her a chance to make me understand it from her perspective, she told me, but…" I dig my free hand into my hair. "The damage had been done."

Elizabeth is quiet for a moment. "Maybe things went wrong from the beginning. Did Annabelle Underhill give you guys trouble before or after your decision to take her to honeymoon?"

"Before."

"How strongly did you nip it in the bud?"

I clench my teeth. I didn't, because I owed her uncle.

My silence is answer enough. "So from your wife's point of view, you didn't eviscerate Dad's Wife Number Three the first time, and she's coming back to cause trouble again. What's she supposed to think?"

"I didn't encourage her, but I couldn't turn her away, either," I say. "She asked me for help, claiming that her husband was physically abusing her."

"*What?* Stanton beats her?"

"She showed me the bruises on her arms." Elizabeth's gasp fills my ear, and I go on. "Trust me, if it hadn't been for that I wouldn't have been so patient with her."

"I never suspected… I mean, Stanton's always so…gentlemanly. Did you confront him about it?"

"No. She just wanted the name of an attorney who could handle her divorce, since she claimed she couldn't get anybody to help her. So I referred her to the Sterlings' lawyers."

"Good god. I never heard about any of that."

"Well…" I pause, my eyebrows tightening. How can Elizabeth be ignorant of something like this? She's too well connected, too well liked. People talk to her, include her in gossip even when she isn't interested just because they want to share with her. They're lucky she isn't an under-cover NSA agent.

"I'll send you what you need," Elizabeth says. "But I also want you think about what I said. I know it's only for a year, but it could be a very good year if you let it."

"I know."

And it could've been more than a year. I realize that I've been subconsciously dreaming of more, and that's why I have such extreme depths of feeling concerning Belle, why I flew off the handle at the possibility she would betray me the way Annabelle Underhill did.

But my past is mine to bear. If I'm not careful, it'll tear us apart.

First... I need to take care of the problem of Annabelle Underhill. I text Paddington: *Tail Annabelle Underhill. I want to know what she's up to.*

He responds: *Anything in particular you're looking for?*

Anything that relates to me or my wife. If she so much as sneezes in either of our directions, I want to know about it.

That done, I stare out the window, thinking about Belle. Her actions prove she meant it when she rejected my offer of a fresh start. But then, why wouldn't she? Words are cheap. And from her perspective, I haven't done anything to *show* her I can make her happy, that I'll be there for her no matter what.

I'm going to need something better than "Let's start anew" to put my relationship with my wife on the right track—a grand gesture that will put me at a risk as much as her should our marriage fail. My palms slicken at the thought. Betrayals early in life have made me cautious, and now I'm always careful to insulate myself. But that path will mean Belle and I are already finished.

I can't accept that. I won't.

SEVENTEEN

Annabelle

WHEN I ARRIVE HOME AROUND FIVE, Nonny's in the dining room, working on her homework at the table. Her biology textbook and notes are spread out, and I hesitate for a moment. The only sign that she notices me is a slight pause of her pencil, then she resumes jotting answers on a worksheet.

"I'm home," I say lamely.

She says nothing.

O-kay. I inhale slowly. "I should change… unless we're going out for dinner?"

"We're not."

"What are we getting?"

Her expression goes scrunchy, like she just bit into a lemon. "Thai." Since she loves Thai food, the facial histrionics are for my benefit.

I press my index and middle fingers against the throbbing points on my temple and jaw line. She really ought to be over it by now.

Sighing, I drag myself up the stairs. Once in the walk-in closet, I immediately dump my purse on the shelf built specifically for purses and toe off my shoes, which feels like heaven. I'm just not used to wearing pumps for hours on end. My toes look red and squished, and god, the balls and arches throb like mad. I strip and get into a loose sleeveless black cotton dress that ends right below my anklebones. It has a side slit on the right that goes up to my knees.

As I start to leave, I catch my reflection in the mirror inside the closet. I look overly tired and maybe even a little bit defeated, my eyes uncertain, my cheeks colorless. Dismayed, I pat my face a few times. Who the hell is going to give me a job? *I* wouldn't want to hire a girl who looks as fatigued as I do.

"One day at a time" has been my mantra ever since my parents were gunned down. Every day that passes is one day closer to the end of The Crappy Phase Of My Life. Surely the rest of my existence can't continue like this.

Shaking my head, I go to the bathroom to splash some water on my face. Maybe the cold will jolt me, help me get my head right. I need to gird my loins if I want to get through dinner without losing it. As it is, I'm strung tighter than piano wire.

When I hear the bell, I make my way down. Elliot heads out of his office to the door, yanking the Bluetooth piece from his ear and shoving it into a pocket. He's in a blue shirt and black shorts, his feet bare. From the closed-off expression on his face, he's had a less-than-great conference call. It still shocks me that he's in such demand that he dictates his own terms and decides who he's going to work with. When you're brilliant and rich, you don't have to hustle like the rest of us mortals.

He hands the guy a few crisp bills and brings the food in. When he notices me, he changes course and places a kiss on my mouth. It's such an everyday gesture, the kind any husband would give his wife along with "Welcome home." The sweet normalcy of it startles me, but I'd be lying if I said I didn't like it. Any semblance of normalcy is good, because my life is anything but.

Meanwhile, Nonny helps to spread the food out on the table—pad Thai, crispy pork with kale, tom yam goon, and a few other dishes I don't recognize but look yummy nonetheless. She also grabs plates, since the delivery place didn't send any disposable ones.

My sister doesn't look at me or say a word. She waits until I take a seat to Elliot's right, then takes the one to his left. He doesn't comment, although his jaw flexes and his eyes go remote in disapproval. We eat in silence for a while.

"My band director made it official. We're going to Vancouver our second semester," Nonny announces suddenly.

"That sounds lovely," I say with a small smile.

She stares at her noodles. Her mouth tightens for a moment, then she says, "I want to go."

"Tough," Elliot says at the same time I say, "Of course you should go."

Nonny looks back and forth between me and Elliot. "What?"

"You don't get to go." He finishes the last of the noodles on his plate and sets his chopsticks with a carelessness that belies the tension pouring off him. "It's ridiculous."

My face flushes. "What do you mean, 'ridiculous'? I told her she could go."

His eyes turn into slits. "So?" he says, then turns to Nonny. "You don't get to go because you don't deserve it."

"Elliot…" She's pale now. "What are you talking about?"

I open my mouth, about to defend Nonny, but Elliot raises a hand, cutting me off. His pitiless eyes are focused on her. "You don't get to condemn the way your sister's been providing for you, then turn around and ask her for money when it suits you. If you don't approve of how she's been taking care of you, do it yourself, but don't you dare expect her to keep supporting you."

Now she's as red as an overripe berry. She stares at him, and although her mouth parts, no sound comes out. Unshed tears glisten in her eyes, and I turn to Elliot.

"You don't get to talk to her that way," I say, suddenly furious at his unreasonable harshness. I'm not thrilled that she's still upset with me, but strong-arming her isn't the way to fix what's wrong between us. Besides, if I weren't going to pay for her trips and so on, I wouldn't have agreed to his marriage contract in the first place. Actually, none of this would've come about, since I would've never taken money from Mr. Grayson and I would've never moved to L.A. and… God. I desperately rein in my rising emotions. Losing control won't help.

"Actually, I do." Elliot is implacable as he glares at me. "When we got married I became her guardian, too, in case you've forgotten."

"But she's just a kid. I promised she could go before you and I met."

"Really?" He cocks an eyebrow. "Was she okay with where the money was coming from?"

"Elliot!"

"*That's enough.*" His tone is hard enough to crack a rock. "I'm not going to sit back and watch her judge you anymore. I'm tired of discord in my home, and if you pay for the trip behind my back, I'm going to cut you off." He stands abruptly, tossing his napkin by his empty plate. "Excuse me. I have a call to make."

He stalks away into his office without a backward glance. The door slams behind him, making me flinch.

Nonny stares into her lap, her eyes teary. I go over to her and hold her limp hand. "Don't worry. I'll help you go."

She finally looks at me. "Why would you want to?"

"Because you're my sister." When she keeps staring, I add wryly, "Do I need another reason?"

Her face crumbles, and tears flow freely down her flushed cheeks. I pull her closer and wrap an arm around her skinny shoulders. She may be fifteen, but she feels so much younger as she clutches me.

"Hey, it's okay," I say. "I'm going to make it okay."

"You shouldn't be saying that." She sounds like a teeny foghorn as she tries to talk and cry at the same time against my shoulder. "I'm a mess."

"What you are is a teenager, and teenagers tend to be…emotional." And don't I know it. My teen years were disastrous. Nonny's a saint by comparison.

She pulls back and wipes her face with a napkin. "I keep telling myself I can be cool, you know? But I can't." Her fingers link together, and she stares at them. "I can't figure out what I hate more—that I didn't know…or that, if it weren't for me, you would've never done it."

Her voice breaks at the end, and my heart aches for my sister. "Nonny, it's not your fault." I hold her sweat-damp hands in mine. "Everybody has goals they want to achieve, and sometimes we have to do things that we might not otherwise. But that doesn't mean the goals are bad. I wish I hadn't had to take that stripper job, but I'm not going to be upset that I have you. You matter to me. You're important—the only family I have left."

She shakes her head. "You have Elliot, too, now."

"He's my husband, and sometimes marriages fall apart," I say, since I can't tell her our marriage came with an expiration date. "But you and me… we're family. Forever. Nothing can change that."

Tears running down her face in rivulets, she launches herself at me. I catch her and squeeze my eyes shut in gratitude. This is the longest we've ever been at odds, and I'm grateful things are going to be okay again.

I wipe her cheeks with a napkin. "Hey, before you get too comfortable, there's something I need to say."

"What is it?" She sniffs.

"There might be more, well, hateful stuff about me coming out. Kind of like the stripper thing."

"What do you mean? Like what?"

"I don't know, to be honest, but some people have a way of looking at everything through an ugly filter."

"Why would they do that?"

I hesitate. I hate to lie to her, but I don't want her to worry about Annabelle Underhill either. "Elliot is sort of famous, being Ryder Reed's half-brother and all. And that makes me a person of interest when reporters are looking for something to write about. So…" I clear my throat. "I don't want you to blindsided. But I swear to you, I've never done anything I'm ashamed of. Even the stripping. If I could go back, I would do it all again."

She looks into my eyes. "I trust you." It's a soft whisper, but it's steady, and I know she means it.

"Thank you."

"I should apologize to Elliot," she says, sniffing again.

"For what?"

"For being bitchy to you. I know he's been sort of stuck between us, and it's my fault. He told me to get over it before, but I didn't."

"You just needed time to put things in perspective."

She nods and gives me a tight hug before heading toward Elliot's home office.

I watch her, hoping with all my heart that she

can patch things up with him. Part of me wants to hover, but I pull back. She needs to do this herself.

I put away the leftovers and rinse the dirty plates. Staring at the hot water spraying the sauces and small bits of food off the smooth white dishes, I wish my past could be made clean just as easily.

But that's not going to happen, so I load the dishwasher and shower. The warm water feels nice beating against my tense muscles. Reluctantly, I step out of the stall, dry myself and put on a nightgown. It's pale lavender with a silken texture that strokes my skin as softly as a baby's breath.

When I enter the bedroom, I almost come to a stop at sight of Elliot lounging on the bed, phone in hand. He's in nothing but a loose pair of black shorts, the waistline resting an inch above his hip bones. He looks delicious—illegally so— with his lean, muscular torso bared, his shoulders impossibly broad from swimming. His legs stretch out, long and strong. I've seen them kick, propelling his big body forward with awe-inspiring power, and I realize I miss seeing him in the water. I can't believe it's been over a week since I watched him swim…

Don't want to go down that path. "Did you talk with Nonny?"

"Yes. She finally admitted what's been bugging her." He shakes his head. "What a stubborn girl. Willful as a mule."

"All teens are willful."

"And some adults." He puts down his phone on the small bedside table and hands me a glass of water and two pills. "Ibuprofen."

"Thank you," I murmur, surprised at his thoughtfulness.

He waits until I take the painkillers. "How did the interview go?"

"It went fine." I check myself. That's a ridiculous lie, and I don't know why I should bother. He's going to find out how badly it went when I get the rejection. "It went okay," I amend. "Well… so so." I wave my hand. "Meh."

He raises both eyebrows. "Keep going. You'll hit 'shitastic' soon enough."

I snort, then laugh. "My potential boss wanted to know if there were any more potential scandals that might come to light, and how they might affect my job performance. I think she was actually more interested in that than any of my qualifications."

"Damn."

"Eh. I should've expected it."

I look around, unsure where I should sit. Before all the mess I would've thought nothing of plopping myself next to him, but now… Despite our talk in San Francisco, I still feel awkward and unsure. Something feels unsettled between us.

But Elliot senses my uncertainty and pats my side of the bed with his palm. I take a breath and settle down next to him, then arrange my nightgown around my legs. He bends a knee, rests his elbow on it and turns his body toward me. His gaze is exceptionally shrewd as he waits for me to go on about my day.

I oblige. "I wouldn't want to hire someone with baggage like mine if I knew her dirty laundry might come out any day. It's bound to be distracting."

Elliot is looking at me expectantly. I gaze back, unsure why he's staring at me with what seems to be a certainty that I'm about to tell him something earth-shatteringly important. The interview was pretty run of the mill. Unless... *Did he put in a good word for me?*

I dismiss the thought. He may be Gavin's friend, but he probably doesn't know Jana. Besides, I didn't get the impression that she's the type you can manipulate easily.

"At least I'll know why I'm getting rejected," I say finally with a lame smile and a shrug. "She seemed like a straight shooter, no bullshit. I would've liked to work for her."

Elliot reclines, propping his elbow against a couple pillows, and cradles his jaw in his hand. Despite the indolent pose, his eyes are sharp. "Is that so?"

I nod. "Anyway, all I have left to do is wait, but I doubt it's going to be what I want to hear, so…"

"Anything else you want to tell me?"

That makes me turn to him, suddenly nervous. I pull on the sheet, needing a cover. "Like what?" He can't possibly know about my uncomfortable encounter with Dennis. I don't want to tell him and cause any hard feelings. Even though Dennis thinks Elliot and I are trying to ruin him, we aren't. I'm certain that as long as we keep clear of him, he'll realize he was being paranoid for no reason.

"You've been gone for a while."

"Oh. I ran some errands and saw Traci."

I didn't, but hopefully he doesn't know that. I took the afternoon off to go to the library to browse the self-help section and skim through some titles before buying an e-copy of a couple that looked most interesting. I feel self-conscious and presumptuous about reading books on finance and career management for new college graduates, because I'm not one. It may very well be that I'll end up unemployable after my time with Elliot is finished because of the baggage I carry becoming public. Regardless, I don't blame him for the unexpected complications. None of us could have known, and I just have to be extra careful with the money I get at the end of our contract.

Elliot frowns for a moment, as though he's disappointed and vaguely unhappy about something. I get the feeling that the "something" is me, although I can't imagine what I might've done to upset him now.

Suddenly he leans over, his tongue licking my lips. I hesitate for a second, then open my mouth for a deep, lush kiss. The heat between us I understand, and I'd rather focus on that than whatever caused him to frown.

He shifts, coming over. His weight settles on top of me like a blanket, and I pull him closer, my fingers tunneling into his warm, silky hair. He continues to stroke me with his tongue. The kiss is gentle but still completely erotic. I clutch him tighter as my blood heats, my skin prickling with rising lust.

I cup his face, holding his flushed cheeks in my palms. The rough stubble scrapes my skin, and I want to feel it against the sensitive spots along my breasts and below.

As abruptly as he started the kiss, he pulls back. His uneven breaths fan my lips, and need pulses through me, pooling between my legs. I stare up into his eyes, so darkly dilated. "I'll never let anything happen to you, Belle."

The words are whispered so softly that I almost don't hear them. I inhale sharply and close my eyes against what I see in his gaze. I don't understand what it is, and I don't want to understand it.

He tilts my head, his fingertips tender on my face. "Look at me."

The command is gentle, but still has steel behind it. I open my eyes and stare up at him. Our breaths mingling, we peer into each other's eyes as though searching for the secret to the universe. My heartbeat grows more erratic the longer we stay like this.

"Annabelle Underhill talked to me on Saturday," I blurt out in a whisper, then cringe inwardly. I wasn't planning to tell him until I could figure out what I needed to say to convince him I'm telling the truth.

"She threatened you."

I gape at him.

"She can't hurt you. I won't allow it."

When my brain kicks in again, I manage, "How...?"

His eyes flicker with something that feels suspiciously like exasperated resignation. "Paige overheard. She was in one of the bathroom stalls."

"I see." I break eye contact and look away. "Well, that was easy."

"What do you mean?"

"If I'd known there was a witness to back me up, I wouldn't have agonized over telling you so much."

His head dips lower, the tip of his nose grazing mine. "I would've believed you without Paige."

"You didn't believe me about Mr. Grayson."

"No. I was furious you didn't tell me." A beat. "There's a difference."

My eyebrows pull together.

"It's one thing if you tell me the truth yourself. It's quite another if I find out some other way." He pauses, and I can see him deliberating, as though choosing the right words for what he needs to say is the most important thing he's going to do this year. "Belle…it isn't easy for me to trust people. In general. It's doubly difficult when I know they're keeping things from me."

I trace the sharp lines of his sculpted cheekbones. "It isn't easy for me to share things with people."

"I know. But this…this is doomed if we stay mired in our old habits."

"What 'this'? We don't even have a year left. Can't we just get along until the contract's over?"

His entire body goes rigid, and I know I've made a mistake…although I'm not sure exactly how. My unease intensifies when a small muscle in his jaw flexes, and an impenetrable shutter comes over his gaze.

Abruptly he rolls over and sits up, his spine stiff. I pull myself up as well, a hand on my throat. I feel cold without his body heat enveloping me. The air between us crackles with tension, and I realize with shock that I'm shivering.

"I've come to a decision." Instead of making me feel better, his terse announcement twists my gut until I feel nauseated.

I wait for him to continue, but when he merely taps his fingers on his legs, I prompt, "Okay…"

"I want us to tear up the marriage contract."

A gasp rips from my throat. Dread floods through me like icy water, swiftly followed by anger.

He circles my wrist with his hand. "Before you jump to conclusions, Belle, I'm not asking for an immediate divorce."

My pulse is still erratic, but I watch him, sitting tight for an explanation.

"We did this all wrong from the very beginning. I see that now." His voice is quiet and firm. "I want to start fresh."

Elliot… "We tried that already. Even talked about it last weekend."

"No. There could never be a new start with the contract hanging over us."

A realization strikes me. "If this is about that one-time indiscretion…"

A dark brow quirks in a silent question.

"I doubt I'll get pregnant."

The incredulity crossing his face is absolute as he shakes his head. "That has nothing to do with what I'm proposing."

"Then why?" If an unintended pregnancy isn't a factor in his decision, I don't know what is.

"It's…" His throat works. "Belle, I want more than a year with you."

Thoughts and contradicting emotions ram into me. He reaches over and takes my limp hand in his. Uncertain hope flickers in his gaze.

I look down at our linked hands. His long, strong fingers stroke the stunning six-carat diamond he gave me. If he'd asked me two weeks ago, I would've jumped at the chance. But now…

"I don't know if that's a good idea," I murmur finally. "We both have *really* complicated baggage. I don't want to live my life wondering if something else from my past is going to set you off, and I'm sure you don't want more of my ugly history to become public and embarrass you and your family."

"I don't give a shit what other people think. You should know better than that. I released a sex tape, for god's sake."

"But you did it on your own terms. Dirt on me won't be like that." Annabelle Underhill vowed she'd dig until she found all there was to know.

I have no doubt she'll follow through and make my life hell. To be honest, I have no idea how Elliot will react…but based on how he was about Mr. Grayson, it won't be pretty. And I can't bring myself to tell him every little thing I might've done wrong in my life in a bid for potential damage control.

His fingers tighten around mine. "Belle, don't. What the media says won't make a particle of difference. I mean it."

Looking into his earnest face, I know he isn't lying. He truly believes he doesn't care.

"If it's about the million dollars, don't worry," he continues. "It'll be yours with or without the contract…although without the contract, I can keep providing for you and your sister."

The only thing I need for the courage to rip up the contract is his love. He's too smart not to know that, but instead he's offering money. It's as though he can't bring himself to offer me his heart, and that makes mine ache.

He brings my hand to his lips and kisses my knuckles. "I think we can be happy together. I wouldn't be asking if I didn't."

I study him. I don't know how he thinks he can be happy tied to a woman he doesn't love…

…and I can't be happy tied to a man who doesn't love me.

EIGHTEEN

Annabelle

E LLIOT'S EYES NARROW AS HE STUDIES ME. Grim determination radiates from him like a palpable energy field, and I hold my breath.

He places his hands on both sides of my head, effectively caging me. The muscles in his shoulders shift and coil as he lowers his head until his nose almost touches mine. My mouth goes dry, and I flick my tongue over my lower lip.

His eyes flare.

I wait, shaky and unsure. Something's shifted between us, and his proposal to rip up our contract is a huge step. But I can't think when he's this close, and his darkly masculine scent short-circuits my thought process. Tension stretches between us, and I—

He dips his head, slants his mouth over mine. The tension snaps, and I kiss him back, suddenly relieved. Lust—this I understand. He's taught me what to do when it hits both of us…and overwhelms me.

This time he doesn't limit himself to using just his tongue. His teeth scrape against the delicate tissue just inside my lips, gently, without breaking the skin. I return the aggression, pull his tongue inside and suck on it, while digging my fingers into his shoulders and back. The air around us feels thick with desire, and I breathe in his scent and sink deeper into the addictive kiss.

His hand slips underneath the nightgown and skims along my calves and thighs. The calluses on his palms feel hard and rough. He pulls the gown off me, baring me to his gaze. I don't have anything on underneath, not even panties. He hisses out a breath. "God, you're perfect."

I know I'm not. But when he speaks so reverently, with such hot admiration glimmering in his lust-darkened gaze, I *feel* perfect.

His lips travel over my body, kissing all the bruises. The gesture is so tender and sweet, I feel like my heart is about to break.

"You have too many clothes on," I murmur.

A corner of his mouth quirks up, and he deftly shucks his shorts and throws them over a shoulder. He is stunning, naked or otherwise, but nude, the strength in his body is more evident. The lean, strong torso gleams under the soft light, his narrow waist…lean hips…the long, powerfully built legs. His heavy erection juts out and up, the head almost touching his tight, ridged stomach.

I lick my lips, and his cock jerks as though I'm tonguing it. The sight is so hot that I push myself up to my knees, ready to take him into my mouth for a taste.

"No," he murmurs, holding me away. When I look at him questioningly, he shakes his head. "Oh, I want your lips around my dick, but this isn't about that."

"Then what is it about?" I ask, my voice husky.

"You."

Before I can demand clarification, his mouth is back on mine. This time it's different. He ravages me, consumes me as though he wants to make me a permanent part of him. I kiss him back, my palm pressed against his cheek, helpless with wanting him. I've wanted him from the first time we met in that strip club, though I refused to admit it then. When we're joined like this, it's as though we're puzzle pieces slotting together.

His hand is on my breast, his thumb tracing the pale blue veins. He kisses my jaw, my chin, then nuzzles the sensitive skin on my neck, his breath scorching. Liquid heat throbs in my blood, making me pant for him. My hands twist the sheet, and he places wet, open-mouth kisses along the curve of my breast. I arch my back, unable to wait, and shiver with a need too painful to bear.

He closes his mouth around my nipple, pulling it in hard, and suckles, his cheeks hollowing, his tongue flattening the tight tip. White-hot pleasure spreads through me from the contact, and I shift my legs restlessly against him, needing more. But he isn't willing to give more. As though to soothe me, he runs his thumb over my other breast, and my hands fist in his hair. He finally lets go, and the cool air makes the wet nipple bead until I feel the tingling sensation all the way to my clit. He lavishes the same erotic attention to my other breast until I can barely breathe.

"Please…" I whisper. "Don't tease me."

"Oh, I intend to deliver," he murmurs against my skin.

His finger strokes my clit then glides down the slick folds. I whimper at the incredible bliss of being touched by him, spreading my legs wider. Sweat mists over my heated skin. I'm beyond shame, beyond inhibition. If he doesn't take me soon, I'm going to die.

He kisses downward over my belly and to the wet junction between my thighs. His breath fans hotly over me, and I moan.

"I love the way you smell," he whispers. "The way you sound…the way you taste."

My eyes prickle with emotion. Until him, I've never felt this—that I am enough, that *I* am what he desires, nothing else. And it makes me want to be more for him…

Rip up the contract.

The thought ripples through my mind, and I almost freeze. I don't think that I can. The contract sets the parameters of our relationship. Once it's gone, I won't know what to expect anymore.

His eyes meet mine. For a fraction of a second, his eyebrows pinch, forming a tight V. I know he can see thoughts jumbling, piling up in my head even if he can't read them.

"No," he says. "No more brooding."

He dips his head. At the first touch of his lips on my clit, my back arches, electric pleasure chasing away all my thoughts. His tongue licks me all over, the touch light, deft and expert. A series of little fireworks seems to go off inside, but it's just a prelude to where he's about to push me. He's too deliberate, too driven.

Cupping my ass, he tilts my pelvis and drives into me with his tongue. My nerves are strung so tight it only takes a couple of shallow thrusts before I'm climaxing all over his face. I cry out, my head thrown back. He doesn't let up. He increases the intensity, overloading my senses. I twist and turn, but I'm helpless in his grasp.

"Stop, I can't…" I sob.

He gives another deliberate lick. "Your taste… God, I can do this all night."

"You're going to kill me."

He chuckles darkly, the sound unbearably seductive. "We can kill each other."

That's the last thing I comprehend before another orgasm barrels through me, hits me like a locomotive dropped from space. It buries me, and I feel like I'm going to faint.

When I can finally drag air into my lungs again, Elliot is positioned between my legs, his face over mine. He's sheathed in a condom, and I can feel his cock throbbing against me.

"Now," I whisper.

He sinks into me, slow inch by slow inch. I start to close my eyes at the amazing fullness.

"Don't," he orders. "Look at me."

I blink, then stare up at him. His face is flushed and stark. Lust and something I've never seen before dilate his eyes. His arms and shoulders shake with tight control, and I place my feet flat on the mattress and tilt my hips, pulling the rest of him into me.

Breathing hard and our hearts beating like hummingbirds' wings, we gaze into each other's eyes. "Elliot," I whisper.

"Annabelle."

Shock stiffens my body. He said he would never call me that because of his ex…

His forehead touches mine, followed by his lips. "Annabelle Reed. My wife."

A huge knot forms in my throat, and it's all I can do to swallow it. "Elliot… I thought—"

He places a finger over my mouth. I can taste myself on it. "I know. But I was wrong." He kisses me with aching tenderness. "It doesn't matter what your name is. You're the one. You'll always be the one. It just took me too damn long to figure that out."

Tears flow freely. He kisses them away as he moves within me. Each stroke is deeper and hotter than the one before, and it doesn't take long before I'm consumed with need and love for this complicated man in my arms. Every time I think this is the end, he does something to utterly shatter me.

He raises himself up and looks at my face. His breathing is shallow and rough, emotion inflaming his beautiful face. A scorching erotic tension coils inside my gut so tightly that it's almost painful.

"Come, Annabelle," he coaxes. "Come for me."

And I do, unable to resist. I arch my body, pressing against him. He drives into me once…

then again and again and again before letting go with a guttural cry.

Making sure not to crush me, he levers himself off and lies to the side. I clutch him to me. I'm unable to bear an inch of separation from him even as desire dissipates and my head starts working again.

I lay my hand over his heart. It's knocking against his chest hard and fast. He has to feel something for me. Maybe it isn't love—not yet—but it's something deeply emotional and strong, because he has no reason to want to rip up our perfectly fine marriage contract or call me Annabelle.

"What are you thinking?"

I hesitate, then murmur, "Nothing."

He puts a finger under my chin and tilts my head up. "When a woman says nothing, it's always something."

I flush. "Sometimes us women say exactly what we mean."

"Sometimes…but you hesitated."

Touché. "Okay. I was wondering… I'm curious why you really want to rip up the contract." When he tries to talk, I put a finger over his mouth. "You made your proposal because you want your grandfather's painting, plus you want my body. You have me now. And I don't think you're going to want the body after a year, not without a deep emotional foundation."

He nips my finger, then licks the sting. "You're right about my initial…plan. But that doesn't mean what I want can't change." He stops. A look of fierce concentration comes over him, and he continues, "You remember the work I did with Lucas, right?"

"Yes. Your algorithm." I give him a rueful smile. "I'm not exactly certain what it's supposed to do, though."

"Basically, it predicts people's future actions based on their interests and previous behavior. So naturally the impression is that someone who can put something like that together is good at emotion and"—he waves a hand—"all that stuff…but I'm not. We were looking at aggregate data and how people who fit certain profiles behaved. But on an individual level, well…it's pretty useless."

I nod, not entirely sure why he wants to tell me this.

"You…defied my expectations. At an aggregate level, the women around me—except Elizabeth—want a fun time in bed, access to my money…and maybe some exposure and a chance to meet Ryder and his agent. And I'm comfortable with that because I know how to handle it. But you…" He shakes his head. "You didn't want to want sex, you've never been terribly impressed with my money and you couldn't care less about Ryder or what knowing him could do for you. And when you told me you loved me…" His eyes take on a faraway look. I feel like he's somewhere in distant space, even though he's right next to me, his warm, bare skin flush against mine. "I wanted that love. It gutted me when I thought you said that to manipulate me. Annabelle Underhill often told me she loved me when she thought I was onto something. If she hadn't, I might've found out what she was up to sooner."

I caress his cheek with my fingertips, hurting for him and hating that bitch with a passion. And she hasn't paid for what she's done. Being dumped by Julian after he used her is nowhere near enough.

"But you stopped saying it, and I can't tell you the kind of panic it created. Then Elizabeth made a point of mentioning that sometimes love can turn into indifference."

"Why would she say that?"

He shrugs, but a certain stiffness of movement betrays his discomfiture. "We were talking and it came up. But she's right. Love can turn into something else in the face of cruelty." He takes my hand and kisses my fingers one by one. "I'm not the type to stay panicked. I went back and thought things through, then realized we never had the right beginning. The contract… It limits what we have, reducing it to a monetary transaction. I don't want that anymore." His hand tightens around mine. "Even though that's what you want."

"Elliot…"

"Everyone learns from watching others and mimicking them. I've never learned how to love. The kind of love you want isn't something I ever saw growing up."

My heart breaks. The skin around my eyes turns hot, and I blink away tears. I thought he hadn't offered his love because he didn't think I was worthy of it. Now I see I was wrong. He promised money because that's the only thing he believed he had to give.

He continues, "I know what I'm asking for is unfair—"

I kiss him to shut him up. I can't listen to this gorgeous, brilliant man feeling like he's less because of his past. "I love you."

Vulnerability and tenderness flare in his eyes. "Annabelle…"

"And you don't have to call me Annabelle." I give him a soft smile, stroking his brow with gentle fingers. "I actually like it when you call me Belle. You gave me that nickname." I breathe in deeply. I am so, so scared—terrified, really—but if I don't take this step, then we have no future. And I want one… Oh how I want a future with Elliot!

"Okay. No rules, no limit to what we can have."

The smile he gives me is blinding.

NINETEEN

Annabelle

THE NEXT MORNING, I GET UP LATER THAN I intended. Elliot is already up. I shake my head. In addition to good looks and a super brain, he also seems to be blessed with inhuman stamina. My brain is still foggy with sleep. He kept me up a good portion of the night. It was for a pleasurable cause, but that doesn't mean I'm not worn out.

"Good morning, beautiful," he says, his voice extra cheery. He's in a pale green shirt that clings to his perfectly sculpted body. It makes me warm just from looking. His denim shorts are artfully faded and frayed, and he has a bright pink mug in his hand.

"You're too cheerful." I start to bury my head back under the sheets, then smell coffee. "Wait. For me?"

"Who else?" He flicks my nose.

I sit up. A man who brings me a fresh brew in the morning is a prince, even if he did keep me up the night before. And, appropriately enough, the mug reads *The Person Drinking Out of Me Is a Princess*. Inhaling the rich aroma, I take a long sip and sigh. "This is so good."

He kisses me on the mouth. "So are you."

"Mmm." I blink away the sleep. The caffeine helps. He turns around, the expertly cut denim shorts showcasing his tight butt. Something clicks into place in my brain. "You don't have your ass tattoo anymore."

He looks at me over a shoulder. "What?"

"FU."

"Oh, that? I got rid of it last year, not that I told anybody."

"Why?"

He shrugs. "I got it while drunk. It was my 'fuck you' to Dad, but then I decided I was through with it. By the way, erasing a tattoo hurts like a bitch."

I giggle. "Good. Then you should let Nonny know."

"She wants a tattoo?"

"Uh-huh." I take another sip of coffee. "One that professes her undying love for your brother."

Elliot makes a face. "Ryder's not worth getting a tattoo over."

"My feelings exactly." I finish my cup. "Is Nonny still here?"

"Leaving in five."

"Okay." I shrug into a robe and we go downstairs to the kitchen, hands linked.

Nonny is just rinsing her cereal bowl and putting it into the dishwasher. She looks fresh and adorable in a sunflower-yellow maxi dress. An elegantly thin silver chain with a piccolo pendant hangs around her neck.

"Morning. Nice necklace," I say.

"Hi." She fingers the piccolo. "It's new."

I raise an eyebrow.

"You know. A gift."

"From a boy?"

Pulling her lips in, she shrugs. From the sudden tinge of red on her face, it's got to be from a boy.

I sense Elliot tense through our linked hands. "Who?" he asks.

"Just some guy."

"The boy from history class?" He scowls. "Algebra too, if I recall."

"Don't you ever forget anything?"

"Nope. I also remember you not telling me how many classes you have with this kid."

Nonny rolls her eyes. "Because it's none of your business. It's not like we're serious." She grabs her backpack from the counter. "Gotta go. Love you." She gives me a tight but super-quick hug and dashes toward the main entrance.

"That necklace looks pretty serious to me!" Elliot calls out as she shuts the door behind her.

I elbow him in the ribs. "You're horrible. Stop embarrassing her."

"I just want to know who it is."

I rinse out my now empty coffee mug and reach for a box of cereal and some milk. "I worry about her too, but I have to believe that she'll be careful or I'll never let her out of my sight." I pour myself a bowl and put everything away. A spoon in my mouth, I settle on a stool at the counter, feet curling over the bottom rung.

"That's why I need to be the bad cop. You won't do what's necessary."

I smile. "I'll play good cop later and talk with her." I want to believe that the kids in her current school are great, but my high school wasn't exactly awash with problem teens, and my parents thought I was safe there…

"Oh, before I forget…" He reaches into the letter holder on the corner of the counter and pulls out an envelope. He checks inside, grunts and hands it to me.

"What's this?" I say after swallowing a mouthful of cereal.

"A cashier's check for twenty-five thousand

dollars. That should be enough to cover whatever you owe Grayson."

I stare at the envelope. "It's probably too much."

He shrugs. "He can keep the change so long as he leaves you alone." Elliot reaches over and places his hand on mine. The contact feels so solid and warm, I lean forward, tilting my chin to look at him.

"You want to deal with him, so I'm not going to stop you. But promise me I'll be the first to know if you need help. I don't want you to feel that you have to take care of him on your own. I'm happy to stand by your side."

The offer touches me deeply. I can't remember the last time somebody vowed to be on my side and really meant it. Certainly none of my friends from Lincoln City did, even after talking about being best friends forever and whatnot. The firm tone of his voice and unwavering gaze tell me Elliot will back me up no matter what.

I can't help myself. I turn my hand over and squeeze his, leaning closer. He is voiding all the rules I've established for myself in the last two years so I could survive on my own. Normally it would freak me out, but right now I'm grateful I have him on my team.

"Thank you, Elliot," I murmur.

"My pleasure."

I finish breakfast, our hands linked the entire time. When Elliot finally has to leave to attend to business, I sit at the counter, staring at the envelope that contains the check. Seeing Mr. Grayson is going to be an unpleasant task. But for our sake…for our new start, I need to do this.

Girding my loins, I call him…and ask for an appointment.

Why, as luck would have it, he has an hour free today around eleven. Would I like to see him then, at the café where we always meet? It would please him immensely to see how I'm doing.

His empty words make my skin crawl. Still, I speak as though I'm calm, totally self-possessed. Of course I would. I'm thrilled he's looking forward to our meeting.

My hand starts to clench around the check, but I stop myself in time. One more meeting…

Then I will be free of Mr. Grayson.

TWENTY

Annabelle

THE LAST TIME I WAS AT THIS CAFÉ, MR.
Grayson wanted me to be a stripper to
snag Elliot's interest. He also bought me
coffee, since I didn't have any money back then.

This time I pay for my own coffee—a latte—
and scan the patrons for the familiar ordinary
face.

There.

Mr. Grayson is in a corner with a cup of coffee himself. He's wearing a charcoal-gray suit with
a neatly knotted blue tie. His dress shirt is white
cotton, only a few shades lighter than his office-
worker skin. His brown hair is professionally
cropped—a cut you could get from any competent
barber—and his brown eyes hold neither friend-
liness nor hostility. His features are even, but

nothing stands out as particularly well formed. The overall effect is one of…singular ordinariness. Assessing him from across the café, I can see him as an insurance company clerk doing his job…or a car salesman doing his job…or any other everyday guy doing any other commonplace job. I always thought it was sort of sad that he was so unremarkable, but I now see it's an advantage. He's a chameleon. He can pretend to be anybody he wants, and no one will look twice.

I take the empty seat at the two-person table and place my purse in my lap. He looks me over with a thoroughness that's almost rude—from my opalescent sheath dress to the platinum chain around my neck and the diamond studs in my ears. I'm glad I took care with my appearance this morning, although I didn't do it just for him. I have another meeting later.

His lips quirk mockingly as he takes in my carefully made-up face. The reaction raises my hackles. I know I look good—better than good. I'm no longer the poor girl who depended on him to put food on the table and keep her younger sister away from predators. I remind myself he has every reason to undermine me before we start. How else is he going to get me to do what he wants?

Without preamble, I pull out the envelope from my purse and slide it toward him across the faux-wood table. "Here. The money I owe you." I take a quick sip of coffee.

"I thought I made it clear I need more than money in return."

"And I'm making it clear that this is all you're getting. Sue me if you don't like it."

"You're entirely too confident."

"I'm not afraid of you, if that's what you mean. What you asked for is illegal anyway."

"Are you sure?"

"I'm certain," I bluff. I'm only about ninety percent sure. I'd like to think that Mr. Grayson is wrong, but sometimes the law surprises me with what is and isn't allowed.

Not even an eyelash twitches as he checks the amount. "Math. Still not your forte. This is too much."

"Keep the change," I say, throwing Elliot's words at him. "A tip for services rendered. Now listen to me. We aren't going to see each other again after this."

Mr. Grayson taps the envelope once with his index finger, the motion surprisingly decisive. "If you do this, you're going to sever everything with me. You won't be able to turn to me for help the next time you get into trouble."

"I want to sever everything with you. I don't want your kind of help anymore."

"Why? Do you believe your husband is going to be with you forever?" He sips his coffee thoughtfully. "You're a pretty girl, Annabelle, but not that pretty."

"Think whatever you want," I say. "You're not important anymore."

He tilts his head and regards me for a moment. "You honestly believe what you have with him is going to work?"

"I do."

"You love him."

"Yes."

"He doesn't love the women who love him."

"You don't know anything about him."

"Oh?" He laughs coldly. "Tell me something. Does he trust you? If I were to hug you and he were to walk in and see us, would he think nothing of it or would he become furious and accuse you of"—he rolls a hand carelessly—"betraying him?"

Mr. Grayson's barb hits home, and I put my hands on the edge of the table to steady them. "He trusts me," I say, but even to my own ear, my voice lacks conviction. But Elliot *must* trust me. Otherwise he had no reason to want to continue our marriage without the contract. I'm not letting Mr. Grayson sow doubts in my mind.

"Sure. I've looked into him, and I know things he doesn't suspect are public."

My breath stops for a moment. Elliot asked if I'd told Mr. Grayson about the marriage deal, but

I never did. He's been aware of it from the very beginning. And Annabelle Underhill knows, too. "Do you work for Underhill?" I ask.

Genuine confusion clouds his gaze. "Who?"

"Annabelle Underhill."

He smiles. "The only Annabelle I know is you."

"Julian Reed, then?" Elliot's father is the next most logical choice.

"I've never even met the man."

Squinting, I take in his measure. Mr. Grayson is no open book, but I don't think he's lying. "How did you know Elliot needed to marry?"

"How much is my answer worth to you?"

I gesture at the check. "The extra not enough for you?"

"You know I can't tell you anything without commensurate remuneration."

I snort. *Commensurate remuneration.* "I'm not owing you anything after I just got out from under."

"At least you aren't a complete idiot." Amusement glitters in his eyes. "You used to be pretty...impulsive."

"What I *was* was desperate, and you took advantage of that."

"You would've done the same if you were me." He picks up the check between thumb and forefinger. "Last chance. You really want to do this?"

"*Yes.*"

He pockets it. "Then we're finished. Don't ever contact me again, Annabelle."

I blink as every muscle in my body abruptly goes lax. "That's it?"

He turns mildly snide. "What did you expect? A drill to the kneecaps?"

I recoil. He's closer to the truth than I'd like. Kneecaps weren't on my list, but I've been bracing myself for something unpleasant.

He laughs. "I'm not in that sort of business. I am, after all, a gentleman." He stands and starts to walk past, then leans over and whispers, "Don't come crying to me when things don't work out with Elliot."

I watch him leave, trying to process what just happened. I'm grateful he didn't get violent or nasty, but he seems awfully confident about me and Elliot breaking up. I shake my head. Of course he is. He wants me destitute again so he can offer up some money and turn me into a puppet. I'm not going to let his poisonous remarks get to me. Elliot and I just made a commitment to each other, and I'm not giving Mr. Grayson that much power.

I toss the coffee, which has gone lukewarm, and leave. Paige and I have a lunch appointment in half an hour.

Although we don't know each other well, she suggested lunch when I called and asked to see her. She chose a venue and texted the info to me along with a note that we have a reservation for twelve thirty. Being Ryder Reed's wife undoubtedly comes with some perks—mainly getting a table at any restaurant in the city.

The Italian bistro is pretty, with black wrought-iron gates and a faux-ivy fence around the outdoor seating area. The intricate workmanship evokes an old European feel, and the interior is bright and sharp, with terra cotta walls and tables covered with pristine linen cloths. The chairs are large and padded, and a crisply dressed hostess takes me to a corner table immediately. I glance through the window. It's pretty outside, the usual fabulous L.A. weather, and there are plenty of empty seats. Then I remember Paige probably doesn't want to be photographed. As Ryder Reed's wife, she's a person of great interest in Hollywood, and often hounded by unscrupulous "media."

"Your party isn't here yet," the hostess says as she pulls out my chair.

"I'm early." She places a leather-bound menu in front of me. Another staff member comes over and pours water. "I'll just wait until…" I gesture at the empty chair opposite me.

"No problem."

I flash her a quick smile and sip the cold water. The operatic duet coming from the sound system is lovely, male and female voices soaring effortlessly, complementing each other. I browse the menu, flipping through the thick, expensive paper. The script is elegant and moneyed. Everything about the bistro says *wealth*.

I'm perusing the long list of salads when Paige arrives. She's nothing like your usual celebrity type. Her face is pretty in an everyday woman kind of way, and she's curvy and soft, with a silhouette that reminds me of a voluptuous beauty from the past. She fits in perfectly at the bistro.

Right now she is obviously pregnant. A teal-blue pleated dress drapes over her rounded belly and stops two inches above her knees. A pair of blue topaz chandelier earrings and a matching necklace sparkle on her.

"Hi, Annabelle. Have you been waiting long?"

I put aside the menu. "No. I just got here."

"Oh good. I hate it when I make people wait."

"Not your fault that I'm early."

She grins. "Still."

When the server arrives, we order. I was planning on being healthy, but then I spot the angel hair pasta with clams in a truffle cream sauce. Paige gets pizza with fresh mozzarella and prosciutto.

"I'm surprised you called," she says after we

get our drinks—a pitcher of peach-infused iced tea. "I didn't think you would."

"Really? Why not?"

She flushes. "Don't take this the wrong way, but you seem pretty reserved, nothing like what I imagined."

"You mean, I don't fit the stereotype of a brash stripper who also does cake work?"

Paige's flush deepens.

"It's fine," I say. "Please."

"I feel bad because I judged…albeit unconsciously."

I wave it away. There's a bit of a silence, and then I can't wait any longer. "Paige…why did you tell Elliot what you overheard in the bathroom?"

She's spared from having to answer when our food arrives. The kitchen must be working extra fast. I take a bite of my pasta. It's divine, the clams cooked to perfection so the meat is tender and succulent without any grit.

Paige nibbles on a slice of pizza, then puts it down. "I told him because I didn't want it to ambush either of you later. From Elliot's reaction, it didn't sound like you'd mentioned it at all."

"I didn't have a chance. At least," I say, hedging a bit, "not a good one."

Her eyes soften. "A good chance never just presents itself. You have to make one happen."

I say nothing.

"Annabelle...can I give you a little advice? Marriage to men as extraordinary as ours can be as demanding as a full-time job. In addition to the usual spouse stuff you deal with privately, there's scrutiny and judgment—people wondering whether or not we 'deserve' men like Ryder and Elliot." She takes a bite of pizza and chews deliberately before swallowing. "I know what it's like and how overwhelming it is. And I do not appreciate Annabelle Underhill threatening you that way. She has no right. Nobody does." Paige's eyes narrow.

"I'm sure you figured out she's Elliot's ex," I murmur.

"I don't care if she's Elliot's soul mate. She doesn't get to talk to you that way, and you shouldn't keep something like that to yourself. Elliot should know who's trying to hurt you. He can help. Surely you realize that."

I nod.

"Lean on him. He'll take care of you."

"I didn't want to be a user," I murmur, since I can't tell her about the whole mess that was festering between us then.

"Tell me something." Paige is contemplative as she finishes the first slice and reaches for another. "If Elliot wanted you to be there for him, would you?"

I answer without hesitation. "Of course."

"Have you ever thought maybe he feels the same way?"

I shake my head. "You know the circumstances of our marriage."

"Yes, but Elliot wouldn't have married you if there wasn't some part of him that really wanted to. Do you know how long he went around, prowling the strip clubs? If the only thing he cared about was his wife being a stripper, he would've found one on the first try."

A memory from last night flashes through me. He wanted a new start—a genuine reboot, with no contract hanging over us. He didn't say he loved me, but he was doing all the things a man would do for a woman he cares for deeply.

"When Ryder and I got engaged, people said horrible things about me, and there were some who wanted us to fail," Paige continues. "Instead of turning to Ryder, I told myself I could handle it, but really...I couldn't. Me trying to do everything on my own almost drove us apart. There's no point in having a relationship with someone if you're going to be on your own anyway when it matters the most."

"You are wise, Mistress Yoda."

She gives me the voice. "Want you to learn the hard way, I did not."

I laugh. "Thank you."

Last night, when I agreed to do away with the contract, I was apprehensive that I was setting myself up for a bigger heartbreak and pain. But now I'm hopeful...

Hopeful that Elliot and I can make this work so long as we both want it badly enough.

Elliot

ELIZABETH'S PHOTOGRAPHERS COME THROUGH. I get an email with access information to all the pictures taken at the charity dinner.

Seated in my office, I go through them meticulously. All I need is a couple that can help me spin a good story, but I don't dare assign my assistant to this. He's good, but he doesn't know everything about my ugly background. And I'd rather not hash it out with him.

The photographers captured several shots with Belle and me together. She's smiling in every one of them, but her eyes...they are either empty or in pain. I remember her telling me she didn't feel well. Regret unfurls as I study her expression. It's all my fault. Next time we go out in public, I plan to have her glowing. She deserves that.

Finally, I spot the perfect photo. Annabelle Underhill and I are together, her hand over my chest. Her eyelashes lowered and her mouth parted, she looks coyly sexual. My lip curls with distaste. Some would find the expression seductive; to me, it's approximately as enticing as a turd—which is about where she ranks in my world.

With this picture, I have the final piece I need. My ex's biggest error is assuming that I actually give a fuck about her feelings. My next move will ensure she never makes the same mistake again.

I put the picture with the others I've gathered and type up some notes. They're concise, sticking to verifiable facts. Facts alone are sufficient to provide drama.

I hear the door open outside. The clock on my computer reads three thirty-six. Belle must be home.

Hurriedly, I finish the document, attach it and the photos to an email and hit send. This should be enough to get the vultures excited.

Just when I close my laptop, Belle knocks on the door and sticks her head in. "Hope I'm not interrupting anything."

"Nothing's more important than you." I gesture for her to come in, unable to do anything but smile at the lovely flush on her cheeks. She's beautiful in a shimmery sheath dress that hugs her gorgeous, curvy body just right, accentuating every mouth-watering line. Her loose hair frames her face like silk spun from rubies, and her green eyes are sparkling brighter than the diamond earrings she's wearing. Maybe her meeting with Grayson went better than expected. I hope he tripped and broke both legs. "What's up?"

"I got a call from Jana!"

I stop for a moment, trying to place the name.

"I got the job!" She twirls around with her arms spread like Julie Andrews in *The Sound of Music*.

Oh…that. I grin, relieved and happy. "Congratulations, beautiful." I get up and walk around the desk to pull her into my arms, soaking in her warm vitality.

"I thought it was a prank when I got the call."

I lean against the edge of my desk and spread my thighs, positioning her between them. My hands span her waist, and I pull her close. "You shouldn't. You're more awesome than you think."

"Thanks. I'm kinda feeling that way."

I can hear her breathless enthusiasm. Then I realize this is the first time she's gotten a job that might lead to a career. Not that being Jana's junior assistant is going to be glamorous—positions like that involve a lot of grunt work. But this is the kind of job where she can make valuable professional connections.

"We should celebrate," I say.

"Totally." She stops, then clears her throat. "Can we invite Traci, too? She called after Jana and I spoke. She heard that I got the position, and wanted to go out."

I blink, surprised that Traci has already managed to put herself on the guest list. "Sure. It's your party."

Although I was initially thinking about a more private celebration, doing something with Traci might not be so bad. Although the dossier from Paddington is very thorough, I don't know anything about what she's like in person. It would probably upset my wife if she knew, but I don't trust Traci that much. As I told Belle before, I don't like "friends" who disappear when the shit hits the fan and pop up again when things are going well. Belle defended her friend, claiming Traci had no choice. Regardless, I don't plan to warm up to her until given a reason to change my mind.

"I'll make the arrangements," I say.

"You mean you're going to pass it off to your assistant."

"Hey. He loves planning stuff like this."

My wife laughs, then impulsively kisses me on the mouth. "That sounds great. Thank you. You're the best."

"You're the one who got the job." I kiss her back, my lips clinging, lingering.

Her response is immediate. She parts her mouth and licks my tongue with hers. She tastes sweeter and richer than freshly whipped cream, but there's an undertone of fiery heat. She's drawing me to her…coaxingly, inexorably. Maybe that unrelenting pull has been there from the very first moment we met. There's no other explanation for what I feel for her, the way my emotions grow stronger with every breath I take.

Desire thickens my blood, and my cock is hard. God. You would think we hadn't screwed last night—or earlier today, before dawn.

On the other hand, it's been hours since I last made her come. Surely that's too long a period of deprivation. I *did* promise to provide for her…

Belle groans softly, angling her head for a deeper connection, and I grin like an idiot against her mouth. I feel like we're finally on the right footing. Was the contract that much of an impediment? Or is this feeling of exhilaration from something else?

My wife said, "I love you," last night. I didn't know how much I needed to hear it again until then. It's a sign that I haven't terminally screwed everything up.

My phone rings. I curse inwardly and ignore it. Whoever's on the line will get the hint.

It keeps ringing, and after a while, it stops. I turn all my attention to running my lips over my wife's delicate jaw line. It's smoothly curved and infinitely precious, just like everything abou—

The phone goes off again. Belle pulls back, breathing choppy and cheeks rosy. "I think you should answer that."

"They'll survive. But I won't…" I dip my head.

Laughing unsteadily, she turns away when the damned phone keeps ringing. "Come on. People are depending on you." She smiles. "Later."

"Promises, promises."

She licks her kiss-swollen lips.

"Keep doing that and I'll throw the damn phone off the balcony."

"And regret it the second it leaves your hand." She walks out, laughing and swinging her hips with an extra bit of provocation.

Annoyed, I hit the talk button. The world had better be burning down. "Elliot Reed," I bark into the phone.

"Got your email."

"You didn't have to call," I say bitingly as unfulfilled lust thrums through my tightly wound body.

"I want to confirm you're really okay with running this."

"Of course I am. Why else would I have sent all that junk to you?"

"It's just such a shitty thing to make public."

"So? You think she's going to sue you for defamation?" I laugh. "She knows everything in there is true."

A short pause and a loud sigh. "You lead an interesting life, Elliot."

"Never a dull moment." I bare my teeth in a smile. "And next time you want to chat, text me." I hang up and roll my neck.

I'm probably going to make enemies with what I'm about to do, but I don't care all that much. The primary focus is keeping my wife safe and happy. And to do that, I would cross the gods themselves.

TWENTY-ONE

Annabelle

THE RESTAURANT WE END UP GOING TO IS contemporary French. The exterior is rustic—pale brick and sun-bleached sandstone. The interior is just as charming, with a huge glass ceiling that opens up to the evening sky and walls that are designed to look like rows of European homes, with stone-and-mortar façades and inset windows. The air is replete with the scent of freshly baked bread and warm butter and herbs. On one side is a huge rack with hundreds of bottles of wine. The sound system gives us a woman singing a soft *chanson*.

It's packed inside, but somehow we have a table reserved. I'm sure Elliot's assistant pulled some strings.

Elliot looks awesome in a white button-down shirt with the collar undone. The sleeves are rolled up, and his dark slacks hang nicely over his trim pelvis and beautifully muscled legs. The overall effect is a casual, masculine elegance that takes my breath away.

I'm in a pair of brand-new jeans and a green sleeveless scoop-neck top. A couple of boxes of jeans came for me earlier in the afternoon, and I couldn't help myself. The arrival of the clothes surprised me, but it was also a sign that our contract is no more—our original terms forbade my wearing pants, ostensibly to give Elliot easier access. I felt almost giddy pulling them on.

Our hands are linked, and I lean closer to him, inhaling the clean soap on his skin and sighing over the heat radiating from his body. Nonny grins at me knowingly, and after a moment I wink at her. It's a little startling to realize she's not a child anymore.

Since Nonny came home late, she didn't change into anything new. But she still manages to look fresh and adorable. She spots Elizabeth at a table big enough for six and dashes toward her.

Elizabeth gets up and hugs Nonny. I didn't think to invite Elliot's sister, but she called him about something, and somehow ended up joining the party. Not that I mind. She is one of the nicest people ever, and I'm delighted that she wants to celebrate my new job. I really want to be good friends with her. I have so few.

Unlike the last time I saw her, Elizabeth is glowing. A royal blue wrap dress is cinched around her already tiny waist, making her look even slimmer. Her hair's curled and pulled into a simple ponytail on top of her head. She's one of those rare women who can make any hairstyle look chic, any dress fashionable. It doesn't hurt that her facial bones are more exquisitely sculpted than most models'.

We exchange quick greetings and sit down. Elizabeth gestures at the glass of white in front of her. "Sorry, started early."

"Not a problem," I say with a big grin.

"I'm so thrilled for you. I didn't know you were looking for a job."

"I was, sort of." I don't want to talk about the real motive that got me started looking in the first place. "Then it happened. I'm very lucky."

"Not lucky. Well deserved," Elliot corrects me. "OWM doesn't hire people who aren't qualified."

"Hear, hear." Nonny grins. "I'm so happy for you, Anna."

Elliot puts an arm around my shoulders for a quick squeeze. His hand stays where it is when the hostess shows up, Traci trailing behind her.

Traci is sporting new side bangs that make her face appear less round. She's in a scoop-neck knit top in magenta so dark it's almost purple. It's cut a bit too low, but not so low that she can't wear it to work. Her tight skirt is the same—just long enough to be acceptable in the office. A silver orchid pendant rests in her cleavage, enhanced by a pushup bra.

She's obviously come straight from OWM and the object of her crush—Gavin Lloyd, the founder and head of the private wealth management firm.

Nonny gets up and hugs Traci. "Traci! I haven't seen you in ages."

Surprise flickers in Traci's hazel eyes. "Hey, Nonny! Wow—all grown up. Great to see you too."

I smile. I never told Nonny about the details of my fallout with Traci. My sister thinks Traci and I couldn't hang out anymore because of our parents. At first I kept it quiet because I didn't want to disillusion Nonny, then later I didn't see the point of rehashing the painful past. Looking at the big grin on Nonny's face, I know I made the right decision. My sister was too young then. She didn't need to know everything and have the past color her perception of the world around her.

Next Traci comes over, and we embrace. "Welcome to the team, girl," she says with a big laugh.

"Thank you. I'm so excited."

"I knew you could do it. Jana loves straight shooters, and you don't bull—uh, beat around the bush." She looks curiously at Elliot and Elizabeth.

I make a hasty introduction.

Elizabeth smiles warmly, as gracious as ever. "It's always a pleasure to meet Annabelle's friends."

Traci flushes. "The pleasure's mine."

Elliot musters a smile, but there is a slight edge to it that makes the hair on the back of my neck prickle. "I've heard a lot about you, Traci."

"Hopefully all good stuff?" she says with a wink and a trilling laugh.

"Of course. My wife adores her friends."

I glance at him sharply. Was there a little bite to "friends"?

Traci doesn't seem to have noticed anything. Maybe I'm being overly sensitive. I know Elliot doesn't think highly of Traci for dumping me two years ago. As far as he's concerned, she's a crappy friend, but he's only thinking about what he would've done. It isn't fair for a man who's never had to struggle financially to make that kind of judgment.

Traci says something, and Elliot laughs. His hand is back on my shoulder, and he strokes my skin with his long fingers as he talks. I shake my head inwardly. I'm overthinking this. Everyone's having a great time, and Elliot isn't judging Traci.

As a matter of fact, he's making an effort to get to know her, and I should be grateful. Unless Traci relocates, I'm sure we'll be tight again. What happened two years ago was a dip in the road, not a cliff.

We order. Since it's to celebrate my job, Elizabeth suggests a champagne toast to start, with Nonny having ginger ale. The server nods approvingly, and I fidget. I know it's a special occasion, and everyone's here for me, but I'm not going to drink. Still, how to gracefully turn it down…

Elliot squeezes my hand and whispers, "Don't worry."

He crooks his finger at the server, who scurries over, and whispers something in his ear. The server frowns in concentration and nods before leaving.

"Dom or Veuve Clicquot?" Elizabeth asks.

Elliot grins. "It's a surprise."

Gratitude unfurls inside me. I've never had anybody who shared my burden before, and it feels surprisingly liberating…and gratifying to know that I have someone who's got my back. And not just any someone. *Elliot.* He's the reason I feel the way I do. I grin at him, letting all my gratitude and love show on my face. "I think he asked for the most expensive vintage."

He brings my hand to his lips and kisses my

knuckles. His eyes are on mine as he murmurs, "Nothing's too good for my wife."

Elizabeth rolls her eyes. "Get a room."

Her gaze lowered, Traci sips her water, hiding a big portion of her face behind the glass dripping with condensation. "I think it's romantic. They're newlyweds. They *should* be all over each other."

"Yes, but I'd rather not think about it. Elliot *is* my brother."

Nonny nods in sympathy. "Totally gross."

"I'm going to need more than one champagne to get over the trauma."

Elliot snorts. "Don't drink too much. You have to drive."

The waiter serves our bubblies. I pick mine up and inhale. It doesn't have the bite of alcohol, just the spicy sweetness of ginger ale.

Elliot raises his glass. "To new beginnings."

We toast and drink. I give him a smile. I didn't realize my life would change like this when he thrust the contract at me. Now I'm grateful for having met him.

The food comes soon after our toast. My dinner is seared beef medallions with a dark wine-based sauce and potatoes on the side. The meat is so tender and juicy, it practically seems to melt.

Elizabeth licks her lips after a bite of fish. "This is really good."

"Is this authentic?" Nonny asks, her eyes wide with curiosity.

"No. It's adjusted to suit the American palate," Elliot says. "And bigger portions. The French take two bites and they're done."

Traci giggles.

"So when does the job start?" Nonny asks me.

"Tomorrow."

Elizabeth quirks an eyebrow. "That's fast."

"It's just training until Friday." I wipe my hands on napkin. "I hope I can learn everything I need to in three days."

"You will," Traci says. "Jana wouldn't have hired you if she didn't think you could. Besides, if you need help, you can always ask me." She grins at me, and I flash her a grateful smile in return.

"Fake it 'til you make it," Elliot says. "Not that I think you're going to need to fake anything for long."

"You're going to finish college too, though, right?" Traci asks, leaning slightly forward.

"I want to. I'm looking to see if I can have all the credits transferred."

"You should be able to," Elliot says.

"Where are you thinking?" Traci asks again.

"Someplace local, but if that's not possible"—I shrug—"out of state, but preferably someplace West Coast." I make a face. "I can't imagine living the rowdy dorm life again, but…"

A strange look crosses Elliot's face. "You aren't doing a dorm."

"Even if I get an apartment, I'll probably need a roommate—"

"No, you won't, because I'll be going with you."

I blink at him.

"What? You think I'm going to do a long-distance marriage when I don't have to?"

"But...out of state?"

Elliot shrugs a shoulder in that careless way of his I can't help but envy. It's the gesture of a man used to getting what he wants. "What about it?"

"But Nonny..."

"I can transfer," my sister puts in cheerily.

"You've already changed schools three times in the last two years."

Traci takes a big sip of wine. "Eh, she's resilient. She'll be fine."

I frown a little. I know she means well and is trying to be supportive, but I hate the fact that I haven't been able to give Nonny the stability I had growing up. I lived in the same town, experienced K-12 with all my childhood friends and never transferred. My sister doesn't have any of her old friends to keep in touch with—especially not after our father ripped off everyone in town—and she's just starting to make some friends in the new school. Uprooting her again seems...cruel.

"Well, pointless to talk about it now," Elizabeth declares. "We don't even know where you'll end up going." And with that, she expertly steers the conversation to safer topics. I stare at her in awe. I guess that's the difference between our upbringings. Nothing seems to faze her. Except that one occasion when we were together on the balcony at the Sterlings' mansion.

After a platter of excellent cheese, I excuse myself to go to the bathroom. Elizabeth stands too, wanting to come with me. I glance at Traci and Nonny, but my sister's too busy munching on the last of the Brie, and Traci tilts her chin, indicating I can go without worrying about her.

This time I make sure the bathroom is empty. The last time I was fortunate enough to be overheard by someone friendly, but I'm not making the same mistake again.

"I'm glad you're adjusting so well." Elizabeth smooths her hair, then clears her throat. "I was worried when you called."

I dig into my purse for my lipstick. "You told him."

"I did." Her reflection makes eye contact with mine. "Are you upset?"

"I was, a little, at the time. But...he *is* your brother, so your loyalty to him would come first," I answer.

She straightens. "It's not about who's first in my loyalty. That was never a consideration."

"I don't understand."

"I wouldn't have said a word if the problem didn't affect him. If you were just unhappy with him and needed someone to talk to, I'd be more than happy to listen and give you whatever advice I could. But you were facing an enemy who threatened the both of you. I thought he should be warned."

"She threatened me."

"Any threat against you is a threat against Elliot. Annabelle Underhill isn't an idiot. She knows that and is expecting him to strike back."

Good god. So it was a deliberate provocation? "Is he going to?" My stomach knots. I wish I hadn't eaten all that food.

"Yes. I'm pretty sure he's set everything in motion by now."

"I don't want a fight."

Elizabeth gives me a curious smile. "You really have no idea, do you?"

I stare at her blankly.

"You're the prize, as far as Elliot is concerned. That's why he's going to hit back."

"But he can be hurt," I whisper. "I met Stanton Underhill."

"You did?"

"On our honeymoon. He and his wife were at the same resort."

"What a coincidence," she murmurs. "What happened?"

"Nothing really, but he didn't strike me as the type to sit back and let somebody take a swing at him without retaliating."

"He isn't, but…" Elizabeth turns to face me. "You have to trust Elliot. He knows what he's doing."

"I do. Still…I don't want him making enemies because of me."

"He isn't. He was never close to Stanton. And from what I understand, Annabelle Underhill has plenty of dirt. She really shouldn't have threatened you that way."

Elizabeth's words don't really reassure me. I don't think Stanton will lose his temper and gun Elliot down or anything. But then, I always thought Mr. Smith was pretty even-tempered, too…

We leave the bathroom together. I do my best to push aside the apprehension nipping at my mind, but it's nearly impossible. The conflict brewing between us and the Underhills seems so daunting. Certainly the stakes are high—because despite what Elizabeth believes, Elliot is the real prize.

Annabelle Underhill is fighting because she wants him. And I'm fighting because I want to keep him.

Returning to our table fails to improve my mood. Nonny is texting someone, teeth digging into her lower lip. Elliot is frowning at her—probably disapproving of the boy she's texting—and Traci...

She's watching him *very* intently.

It's a good thing that I know her so well. Otherwise I might think she's interested in Elliot. But there's no sexual speculation in her brooding gaze. I've seen that look before—when we were about to start a hockey match. She would study the players on the other team, assessing their strengths and weaknesses. I suspect she's heard some less-than-flattering things about Elliot from Dennis and wants to judge for herself. Maybe I should talk to her privately when there's a chance.

Elliot turns his head as though he feels her stare, his eyes as sharp as a brand-new razor, and she immediately looks away and reaches for her wine. He then spots me and Elizabeth, and his gaze warms. "The dessert menu came," he says.

"Ugh. No thanks," Elizabeth says. "I'm stuffed."

"Same here." I look at Traci and Nonny. "Unless you guys want some?"

Say no. The thought pops into my head. It's an uncharitable wish, but I can't help myself. For some reason I don't want Elliot and Traci in the same room anymore.

"I'm full, too," Traci says.

Nonny shakes her head. "I'm good."

Elliot takes care of the bill and Traci and I hug goodbye. Traci says, "There's gonna be a happy hour on Friday after work to welcome you properly to the company." She shoots a quick glance in Elliot's direction. "Hope you don't mind."

"Of course not," he says with a lazy grin, although everything else about him remains as alert as a predator eyeing prey.

I cant my head, but Traci merely flashes me a smile that tells me nothing.

After Nonny slips into her room and Elliot and I are in the privacy of ours, I say, "What was that about?"

"What?"

He unbuttons his shirt with deft movements of his fingers. The more inches of his beautifully sculpted torso are bared, the more I find I can't tear my gaze away from his body. My nipples tighten as though recalling how the hair on his chest feels against them.

"Belle?" he prompts, pulling off his shirt. A small smirk tells me he knows.

I shake myself. "You and Traci," I say, remembering what's been bugging me. "What happened while Elizabeth and I went to the bathroom?"

"Nothing." He tosses the garment into a laundry basket for the housekeeper to do later.

"You guys didn't have a 'nothing happened' vibe when I came back."

He toes off his shoes and yanks his socks off. "She asked me how I knew Gavin, and I told her. That's it." He straightens and faces me. "Ask Nonny, if you like."

I shake my head. "I trust you. It's just…" Eyes closed, I pinch the bridge of my nose. "It's probably nothing." I'm overthinking this. Elliot has no reason to not like Traci anymore. Well, he thought she was a shitty friend back then, but he knows things are different now. If she were still a shitty friend, she wouldn't have helped me. And Traci…

She was probably just making conversation, although I worry about her infatuation with Gavin. She's a smart girl, but she sometimes has a bad habit of mooning over guys who are taken. I don't think she'd cross the line, but I don't want her hurt because her coworkers find out or anything like that. She deserves to be happy with her life.

Elliot wraps his arms around me, pressing his bare chest against mine. "Now that it's just two of us, we should get to the real celebration."

"What are you in the mood for?"

"Oh, I don't know…five or six servings of you?" He nuzzles my neck, his breath hot and humid against my skin.

Heat pools between my legs, and I dig my fingers into his hair. "That sounds like a fabulous idea."

As I let him carry me to bed, I can't help but feel that I'm missing something. But when he bends down and slants his mouth over mine, I can no longer imagine why it should matter.

TWENTY-TWO

Annabelle

I CAN'T BELIEVE IT—I'M ACTUALLY *LOOKING forward* to going to work! And doubly so because I have fashionable clothes to wear—although I make sure not to put on anything ostentatious—and then when I'm done, I'll have a hot husband to come home to.

Life is good.

The first day is going to be spent mostly on orientation and filling out paperwork. I run into Gavin on my way in, who nods at me with a warm smile and walks into an elevator trailed by an impeccably dressed tall and curvy redhead.

When I reach my cubicle, I see a huge bouquet of brilliant red roses. The sight of them and the heady scent bring a smile to my lips. I don't have to read the card to know who they came from.

Enjoy your first day.

–E

I bring the scripted card to my face to hide my widening grin.

"Who's that from?" the assistant in the next cubicle, Jean Bennet, asks with a smile.

"My husband."

"Ooh. Lucky you."

I flush. And that night I show him how much I appreciate the flowers, which made me the envy of every woman on the floor.

"I'm going to send you a bouquet every day if this is what I get," Elliot says when he can breathe again.

I giggle. "You're so bad."

"I simply want to remind you of your despondent husband, waiting with forlorn yet loyal patience for you to come home…"

Eliot's melodramatic delivery—contrasted with the lascivious look on his face—makes me laugh. I kiss him on the mouth. "I think the word you're looking for is 'lecherous,' not 'despondent.'"

"I can't help it that you're hot…and you make me hot." He pulls me down for a deeper kiss before seducing me silly, as though he hasn't just come hard enough to break a window pane.

The second day, Elliot sends me a bouquet of huge pink orchids. I flush with pleasure, but don't get much time to admire the stunning blossoms. Jana is waiting for me in her office.

She's a fair boss. She doesn't look at me like I'm anything special and speaks to me in a cool, no-nonsense tone that conveys both confidence and discretion. I love her for it because I need normalcy, and I don't want my new coworkers to treat me differently just because I have an account with the firm.

Despite her brisk manners, she's also patient. She shows me exactly how she wants her filing done and how I should write messages on her behalf when required. I learn that it's a waste of time to include greetings and other niceties in business communication.

"The main point only. Nobody has time to read 'how are you' or 'hope you're having a good day.' That's what company socials are for."

The previous admin has been gone for over a week now, so I spend my day organizing Jana's schedule and making sure she has coffee—black, no sugar—every two hours on the dot. Apparently a regular dose of caffeine is vital.

"I heard about the happy hour," Jana says at a quarter till four on Friday. "You can go now, but

I'm afraid I can't join you. I have a prior engagement. But we'll do lunch on Monday. Keep the
calendar clear."

"Yes, ma'am."

"Just call me Jana," she says with a slight
smile. "I'm not *that* old."

I take my purse and go to a bar two blocks
from the office. It's a swanky place with gleaming
wood and lots of expensive-looking liquor dis-
played on the shelves. The place smells faintly of
leather and oak and the remnants of hundreds of
opened bottles of wine.

Traci is already seated at the counter. As
usual, she's in an almost-too-racy-for-the-office
outfit. I start to wonder how many V-neck tops
and pushup bras she owns.

"You're early," I say.

"You're right on time. I'm so glad Jana let you
go. She has a reputation. Total workaholic."

"She is kind of intense. But I like her. Seems
very nice."

Traci grins. "Only you would say that." She
raises a forefinger to flag one of the bartenders.
"What are you in the mood for?"

I hesitate. She's expecting me to drink because
I never told her about what happened at the party
and did my best to pretend everything was fine. I
was too ashamed to tell *anyone*, even Traci. When
we were at parties, I'd nurse a Coke or oj while

pretending that it was spiked with rum or vodka, because you couldn't not drink at those events in Lincoln City and still be considered cool. Now I can't decide if I should come clean and tell her I never touch alcohol or get a glass of wine and pretend to nurse it until it's time to go home.

Before she can catch a bartender's attention, she drops her hand and digs through her purse. She takes out her phone and scowls at the screen.

"What is it?"

"A text from Hilary. Apparently she can't come because of an unexpected market movement. Something about the Chinese dumping US treasuries or something… Anyway, she told me I don't need to go back, but to have fun." Her shoulders slump. "Damn it."

"Maybe the others can join us…?"

She shakes her head. "If Hilary can't come, it's because Gavin isn't leaving. And that means nobody's leaving now."

"Oh. That's…too bad."

"Yeah." She sighs. "The Chinese just had to pick today!"

I laugh. "You make it sound like they did it on purpose."

"Feels that way."

"Listen, why don't we…"

I trail off as I look through the window and spot a nondescript gray sedan parked on the other side of the road. A man's inside, his big hands fooling with a camera with a big lens. An uneasy knot forms in my chest, but I shake myself. Probably somebody famous is around here… There's no reason for the paparazzi to follow me, since my stripper past isn't the hottest news item for the bored and nosy anymore.

"Let's go to my apartment and have ice cream and cocktails," Traci says. "I have some good stuff."

"Um…" I'm about to say no, but she's looking at me with a huge grin. Elliot isn't expecting me until at least eight anyway, so why not spend a little time with Traci before heading home? "Sure. Ice cream sounds great."

"Awesome!" She loops her arm around mine. "Let's get going."

Annabelle

Traci's "apartment" is about half an hour from the office. As I climb out of my Mercedes, I can't help but gape. "How did you snag this place? The location's perfect, and just *look* at that!" I gesture at the soaring, glitzy building.

"I know, right?" She grins. "I totally lucked out. My roommate is rich, and paying for most of it. She said she wanted somebody to share the space because she hates it when it's too quiet at home."

How awesome. I'm genuinely happy my friend got such a sweet setup.

The place is fairly new. Two sides of the building gleam, and I realize they are actually floor-to-ceiling windows. The lobby is immaculate marble, chrome and glass with a fully staffed concierge desk. Soothing classical music plays inside a golden elevator.

Traci's place is on the top floor. It's actually a penthouse unit, albeit smaller than the one Elliot and I share. But the open layout makes the place look much bigger and airier than it really is, and there is a fantastic view of downtown L.A. The hardwood floor has been freshly waxed, and a plush rug is custom-cut to lie around a beige sectional couch. The walls are off-white and covered with contemporary paintings.

Traci gestures at a room at the end of the hall. "That's my roommate's, so don't go in. She's a little weird about it."

"Is she going to be okay with me coming here like this?" My old roommate Caroline hated it when Nonny brought someone over.

"Don't worry. She's out of town this week."

I relax and take a seat on the couch, placing

my purse on the floor. Traci brings out two minia-
ture cartons of caramel-and-fudge ice cream. "Ta
da," she says. "Anything to drink?"

"Maybe just iced tea or juice? I need to drive
home, and I'm a lightweight."

"You can't be that bad. You went to a party
school."

I cringe. "I got a big, fat F in Party 101."

"Very funny. I can't imagine you getting an F
in anything. You were one of the smartest kids in
high school." Still, she hands me a glass of sweet-
ened iced tea and pours herself some white wine.
She plops down on the sectional and kicks off her
shoes.

I take a few sips of the tea, which is a little too
sweet. The ice cream is extra rich, and it's difficult
for me to eat much of it. Traci, on the other hand,
doesn't seem bothered. She digs into hers with
gusto.

We chat. She tells me all about her plans,
places she wants to go and things she wants to
do. "I'm not going to be an assistant forever, you
know."

"You won't. You're too smart to not be in
charge one day."

"Exactly. And if that doesn't work, I can
always get myself a sugar daddy."

My jaw drops. "Seriously?"

"Yeah. Why do you think I work at OWM? It's got tons of guys who are making amazing money. And a lot of them aren't that old."

"But…" I blink as my mind struggles to reconcile what she just told me and what I know about her crush on Gavin, who happens to be very happily married. "Uh… Any special candidate?"

"Nah. Just enjoying myself for now, but I'll have to decide on someone pretty soon. No rich man wants an old wife." She laughs and drains her glass. "You're lucky you managed to snag a guy like Elliot. Hey, does he have any bachelor brothers?"

"Yes." His oldest half-brother and twin are single, unless I'm misremembering.

My head is starting to feel a bit fuzzy. Maybe I'm more tired than I thought from working… although my tasks were easier than what I used to do as a server and a cleaning lady.

"You should introduce me, then. We can double-date." She giggles, then pours another glass of wine.

I take a few more sips of tea to wash away the sticky richness from the ice cream cloying in my mouth. Multiple throbbing knots start to form behind my eyes.

Traci peers at me. "Are you okay?"

"Just a little headache," I say. "Nothing serious."

"You want to lie down?"

Traci's voice is soothing. It sounds like a great idea. "Sure." I bring my feet up and lie on my side. The pain seems to lessen. "Ahhhh."

"You have to take care of yourself, Annabelle. Jana hates it when people miss work."

I give her a wan smile. "Okay, Mommy."

"You want me to text Elliot? Let him know you might not be able to come home? It's cool if you want to crash here tonight."

Hmm. That does sound pretty smart. Traci's roommate isn't home anyway. And driving when I feel this awful is probably a bad idea. "Okay."

"Let me text him, then." She reaches into my purse and gets my phone out. "What's your passcode?"

I tell her.

"Your *birthday?* Good god. You can do better than that." She enters the numbers and quickly types something. My phone buzzes about ten seconds later, but she puts it back in my purse. "How did you and Elliot meet?"

My head is swimming, and I don't know why Traci is asking me. I could've sworn I told her. Or did I…?

All I know is I can't tell her everything. I trust her and she's my good friend, but it isn't just about me. "Uh. Work." There. That's close enough.

"I didn't know you worked for Elliot."

"No. Something else."

"Why is he having Gavin look into Dennis again?"

"What?" My brain feels like somebody's dunked it into a vat of syrup.

"If they look too closely, they're going to find out about your past too."

"They already know." I push my thumbs against the ends of my eyebrows. "Dennis lied…"

Traci gasps. "About what?"

I close my eyes. I don't want to talk. I want to… I just want to rest for a while.

"What did Dennis lie about, Annabelle?"

"Something. Complicated."

"Annabelle? Are you all right?" Traci's cool hand rests on my forehead. "Can you open your eyes and talk to me?"

"Mmmm…" I mutter something, although I have no idea what I'm saying. Traci's frantic calling of my name is the last thing I hear before everything turns black.

Elliot

Not feeling too good. I'm spending the night at Traci's.

I stare at the text. I already replied, *I'll pick*

you up. Send me the address, but my wife hasn't answered.

If it were any woman but Belle, I would assume she was in a snit or a manipulative mood. I've had women pull stunts like this before, trying to get me to come after them or give them what they want in exchange for their "coming back." Of course, they learn very quickly that I don't play that kind of game.

But not Belle. If she's mad at me, she tells me so. Jesus, she wouldn't back down even when I was a total asshole after finding out about Grayson. I don't see her changing her MO now.

"You okay?" Nonny asks, tearing me away from my dark thoughts.

"I'm fine. Waiting for a text from Belle."

"I thought she was going out with her coworkers."

"I thought so too…but something's changed."

She nibbles on the end of her pencil. "Huh." She jots down an answer to a history question on her homework sheet then continues reading the textbook.

I give Belle ten minutes. When she doesn't respond, I pull up the dossier from Paddington. It has Traci's mobile, but not her address. Damn it. I call her. If she doesn't pick up, I'm going to have Paddington locate my wife's phone.

"Hello?" Traci answers, her voice low.

"This is Elliot Reed. I hate to bother you, but I'd like to come get Belle."

She hesitates. "Yeah, she just passed out. I don't mind if she spends the night here."

I narrow my eyes. Although I can't quite put my finger on it, there's something in her tone. "That won't be necessary. We'd hate to impose."

"Oh, it's no imposition."

"It would be for me. I hate owing people one."

"Elliot! I would never presume to call on this...like it was some kind of *favor*. I'm doing this for my friend."

"I appreciate the sentiment, but I'm going to bring my wife home where she belongs," I say, even as an internal alarm goes off. Who wants to look after a girl who's blacked out when she can pass her off to someone else without an ounce of guilt? I put steel in my voice. "Your address?"

Traci gives it to me. She isn't stupid, and she probably knows if she doesn't give it to me, I have other ways of getting it.

I hang up. "I'm going out."

"Okay," Nonny says, oblivious, which is exactly how I want her. "But I may not be home by the time you're back. I'm going out with Jennifer tonight."

I scowl. I don't remember that. "To do what?"

"Hang out…maybe watch a movie."

"Okay. But text me when you get there and again when you're on your way home."

She gives me a careless salute with two fingers. "Aye, aye, sir."

Now that guardian duty's been taken care of, I go to Traci's apartment. The drive feels interminable with the Friday evening traffic. I keep thinking about all the bad things that could happen to my wife, then tell myself none of them will, since she's with a friend. Traci may have been a shitty friend—and I still don't like her. However, she won't do anything stupid when she knows I'm aware of who my wife is with.

By the time I reach her place, a cold sweat has filmed my back. Traci opens the door. She's in a pink baby doll, her feet bare, and I raise both eyebrows.

"Come on in," she says.

A section of her hair wrapped around her finger, she twists this way and that as I walk inside. Every time she changes position, she tilts her head and arches her pelvis. If she's doing it on purpose, she's trying way too hard to be sexy.

The first thing I notice is my wife, prone on the couch. Her breathing is shallow, and she's so pale that I wonder for a moment if she's fainted. Her brows pinch as though she's in pain, and a hand is resting on her belly. There are smeared spoons and a couple of wine glasses on the table.

The one nearest my wife is empty. Lipstick marks on the rim match the shade on Belle's mouth.

The scene tells me everything I need to know about what occurred…except it can't be right. I turn to Traci. "What happened?"

"Annabelle and I shared a bottle of Chardonnay, and she passed out after only two glasses. Cheap date, right?" Traci tries a laugh, but it doesn't come off. "I should've been more careful and made sure she wasn't drinking more than she could handle. I'm her friend. It's my job to keep her safe."

I merely stare at her. Her eyes are overly wide, and she keeps running her teeth over her lower lip. I don't remember it being so fleshy, I note with clinical detachment.

When I continue to peer at her without a word, she clears her throat and shrugs, the gesture pulling the fabric over her braless tits. My eyes narrow at the display.

"Don't be too hard on her," she says. "I won't tell anyone."

I dismiss her with a nod and pick Belle up. She feels so slight and delicate in my arms. I open my hand. "Her purse."

"Here." Traci gives it to me, plus a plastic bag with Belle's shoes.

I leave without a word, carrying my wife down to the car. As I arrange her in the passenger seat, I get a good whiff of alcohol on her and stop. What the fuck? I bring my nose closer to her and sniff. She definitely smells like some kind of dairy and wine.

Just what the hell happened? My mind refuses to believe she actually consumed even a drop of alcohol. To her drinking means losing control, and that has heavy consequences. She'd no more give up her full faculties than jump out of a plane without a parachute.

Something very fucked up took place in the apartment. I'm this close to barging back up and demanding the truth, but my wife needs me more.

Tomorrow. I'm going to hear what happened from Belle herself tomorrow.

Annabelle

I GROAN SOFTLY. MY SKULL FEELS LIKE IT'S BEING pressed from all directions by a great, crushing force. The room's too bright; I place a palm over my eyes, trying to prevent my eyeballs from exploding.

I'm on a bed. The mattress dips, and my stomach roils at the motion. A warm hand checks my forehead temperature, and I turn into it, moaning a bit.

"Where am I?" I say, but given how thick my tongue feels in my mouth, I'm pretty certain the question is garbled beyond recognition.

"Home." Elliot's voice. *Thank god.* "Here. This should make you feel better." He helps me sit up and drink some kind of flavored water. I make a face at the odd, artificial taste, but he's relentless. "All of it. It's electrolytes. You need 'em."

"Why?" I croak.

He gives me a couple of aspirins and waits until I down both with the disgusting water. "Traci says you drank until you passed out. Two glasses of wine."

I frown, but it makes my face hurt. Shaking my head is absolutely out of the question. "But I didn't. I had an iced tea and some ice cream."

He helps me lie down again and scoots over, pulling me into his arms. I sigh at how nice it feels to be held, and burrow my face into his neck, inhaling the soap and clean, freshly showered skin.

"Can we turn off the light?"

"There's no light to turn off. I also left the blinds down."

"Then why does it feel so bright in here?" I whisper.

He doesn't answer. Instead he strokes my scalp and back, gently massaging the tender tissues. It isn't often I'm the one being taken care of, and it makes me feel important…and loved.

"What happened after work? I thought you supposed to go to a bar, but you were at Traci's apartment."

"We were going to do happy hour, but something happened with the market, so most of the guys couldn't come. I didn't feel like staying and thought we should just reschedule, but Traci said we should go hang out at her place. Her roommate was out of town, so it made sense." I place a hand over his chest, feeling the slow, even movements of his ribcage expanding and contracting with every breath. It comforts me for some reason, and I keep talking. "I had this super-rich ice cream and iced tea. She had wine with hers. But then I started to feel bad and wasn't sure if I could drive home because I was dizzy."

"So that's why you texted me."

"I didn't." I know that for sure, although I have no clue how Elliot knew I was at Traci's. "Maybe Traci did." My memories are sort of unclear, like a scene playing out behind a thick layer of fog.

He goes still for a moment under my palm. "Remember anything else?"

"No. I just felt really bad, that's all. But I swear I didn't drink." I bite my lower lip. "You know why I don't…"

Elliot knows the whole sordid story. He is the only person—other than me and the boy who raped me—who knows what happened. Unlike my rapist, Elliot also knows what happened afterward—the unwanted pregnancy and the mess I made of my life.

"Shhh…" He kisses the crown of my head. "I know, beautiful. Don't think about it. It's way, way in the past."

I close my eyes. "Sometimes it feels like it was just moments ago."

His arms around me tighten. "Bad memories often seem that way, but don't give them so much power over you. You overcame a lot, and you're stronger for it." He caresses my cheeks, the touch like a butterfly fluttering over a flower. "You are so much stronger than I am. I didn't know what strength was until I met you."

"I let people push me around. Mr. Grayson… Then you…" I flush then quickly add, "Not that I think badly of you."

"It's okay. I know I've been an asshole. But you didn't just give in because you were weak. You made your deal with Grayson because you had Nonny to protect. And you pushed back against me as much as you could. I just happened to be better armed, and winning for me was like taking candy from a baby—unfair bullying."

"Well I'm glad you did, because otherwise I would've never given us a chance. Despite what you think, you're not a bad sort, Elliot. Otherwise I would've never felt anything for you."

He sighs softly and kisses me on the forehead again. "Get some rest, Belle."

Some moments later I go slack, secure in his arms. Elliot does not relax.

TWENTY-THREE

Elliot

I LEAVE MY WIFE SLEEPING AGAIN AND GO INTO my home office. The idiots my client is employing have screwed up the model again. I have no idea how my client found them, but they have the logic of a two-year-old with a frog's ass for a brain.

My phone is silent at the moment, but it won't be for long. I turn my focus to the overall structure of the model. The analysts put in way too many damn exceptions, and of course if you do that, it doesn't work. They were supposed to look for a pattern that fits the greatest number of people, not predict how everyone on the platform behaves. People with their idiosyncrasies are, on the individual level, unpredictable. And just like you can't apply a general aggregate level behavior to an individual and have it match perfectly, you can't apply an individual behavior pattern to a group with millions.

I suddenly sit back. Something hasn't been right—other than my wife being passed out after drinking—and it finally dawns on me. How the hell can Traci afford a place like that? There is no way Gavin pays her enough, and from what I understand, her parents lost almost everything in Belle's father's Ponzi scheme.

Maybe she has a sugar daddy… But then why did she act so coquettishly around me?

Follow the money.

The anonymous tip comes back to me. Maybe it wasn't about my wife but about the people around her. I had Paddington check Traci and Dennis out, but not do a detailed workup on their finances.

Quickly, I text Paddington, rectifying that. He confirms my request, as usual. I tap my fingers on my desk. How am I going to get my wife to stop seeing Traci until Paddington comes back with information I've requested? They work together, and I know Traci's been ingratiating herself with Belle, who's been too lonely and isolated over the last two years to reject her childhood friend.

My phone goes off, jarring me out of my con-templation. It's Ryder.

"Did you see that what-the-fuck article?" His words ring loud and clear through the Bluetooth piece hooked to my ear. "I say *article*. It's more like…tabloid diarrhea or something."

"I thought you didn't read tabloid trash."

"I don't, but my publicist forwarded it to me since it involves you and Wife Number Three." Ryder curses under his breath. "I haven't shown it to Paige—no reason to upset her—but god. 'According to an unnamed source,' my ass."

I press my lips together. I appreciate the outrage, and I don't want to fess up to being the unnamed source. If any of this shit blows up, I don't want Ryder dragged into it. "Well. What can you do?"

"I have an excellent attorney for this kind of stuff."

"There's the Streisand effect," I point out.

"Argh. Well…I don't know. But you gotta make them pay."

Hmm. Maybe Ryder has a point. Besides, I do want as many people as possible to read the damned article. "Maybe a lawsuit is just the thing. Make it as big as possible."

"No," Ryder says. "You're supposed to make it go away quietly." He pauses. "That's what you want, right?"

"Hold on a minute."

I open a browser. The "article" is more like a titillating gossip piece with the photos I supplied. The "reporter" did a good job of spinning everything into an over-the-top exposé with a salacious undertone suggesting a fucked-up and forbidden obsession on Annabelle Underhill's part. I skim the writing. The piece starts from our initial dating, then to her marriage to my father, her divorce, her second marriage to Stanton and now her quest to break Belle and me up so she can take her place by my side as Mrs. Elliot Reed. The photos add authenticity.

I check some social media sites. There's no point in putting something like this out there if nobody hears about it. Thankfully, it's one of the top trending topics. Given the unexpected market movement yesterday, I've been bracing myself for disappointment.

Smiling with relief, I pour some scotch and silently toast myself.

"Are you there?" comes Ryder's concerned voice. "It's not that bad."

"You're right. It's not."

"Who did you piss off to get that shit smeared everywhere? My team had no clue somebody was going to do this. They never noticed anybody digging." The terse note in his words does not bode well for his people.

I feel bad, since they couldn't have known. They most likely never suspected I would betray myself. "I'm actually relieved it all came out."

Ryder doesn't speak for a moment. "Uh... what?"

"Everything in the article is true."

"Jesus." He huffs out audibly. "Even the closet incident?"

"Yup."

"What the fuck. Does your wife know?"

At the mention of my wife, tension creeps into my neck and shoulders. I roll my neck around. "Does it matter?"

"That depends. Do you care?" Ryder knows why I married Belle in the first place. He married his assistant Paige for the same reason, although that's a moot point now that he's in love with her and they're having a baby together.

"Of course I care," I say. "Look, this may work out for the best."

"How come?"

"Didn't you hear?"

"About what?"

Huh. Maybe Paige hasn't told him. "Number Three threatened Belle."

"With what?" Ryder sounds incredulous.

"She said she'd release more dirt on her."

Ryder snorts. "Like you would care."

"I don't, but my sister-in-law does."

"Aw, shit. I totally forgot about her. Nonny, right? Nice kid, but a little sensitive."

"Typical teenager. Everything's life or death."

"I was never like that."

"Because you have the sensitivity of a mule on morphine. And she's not used to the kind of lifestyle we lead." I lean back in my seat. "I don't want her hurt. Aside from Nonny being a nice kid, it upsets my wife."

"So…I guess you actually have feelings for her?"

"I'm starting over with her."

Ryder is quiet for a moment. "As in?"

"We don't have a contract anymore."

"*What?* You voided the prenup?"

"Yup. Gonna see where things lead."

"Damn. You're serious." Ryder sounds incredulous…almost aghast.

I scowl. "Got a problem with that?"

"No, I think it's wonderful…assuming that's what she wants too. Just don't do anything stupid."

"Hey, pretty boy, you're talking to a genius here."

"Don't damage yourself for her," Ryder says seriously.

I have to smile. "So you do know."

"I suspected when you didn't seem too upset about the article. Now you just confirmed it."

I shift in my seat. I forget Ryder is extra perceptive when it comes to me. We've been tight for a long time, and he knows me better than most.

"Women don't care if you have a wild side or if you do stupid shit, like fucking your new stepmom in a closet, when they're doing a temporary thing for fun. But for something more permanent, they want a guy who's more stable. The article damages Number Three, but it doesn't exactly help you either. Dad's gonna be pissed."

"Fuck Dad. He's already pissed. Why do you think we all have to marry like this?"

"Number Three's going to retaliate."

"Not a problem, so long as she moves against *me*."

I hear someone walk by on the other side of my office door. Nonny went out with her friends after breakfast, saying she wouldn't be back until dinner time. What's Belle doing up? She should be resting.

I go outside. My wife is in a robe, cinched tightly around her waist. She sinks onto a couch, her phone clutched in her hand. She looks up at me.

"Gotta go," I tell Ryder, and hang up.

Her dark green eyes are unfathomable as she raises her phone. "Is this all true?"

Damn it. I shove my hands into my pant pockets. "Yes."

"Everything?"

I nod.

"My god." She licks her lips. "How… Why would she release this? It makes her look *awful*." She stares at the screen. "She was so smug when she told me about the closet incident… She claimed it was a sign you still wanted her."

Embarrassment heats my cheeks, and I look away. "No. Actually, that was one of the lowest moments in my life."

After the ceremony was finished, I finally confronted her in private. When she told me how much she regretted marrying Julian—because, of course, her heart really belonged to me—I told her to prove it. She kissed me, her mouth open and skilled, and I let her. That seemed to encourage her, and she pushed me into the closet where her wedding items were stored and where I then fucked her brutally. She was on birth control, so I didn't worry about getting her pregnant. All I cared about was payback.

"Elliot, believe me. You're the only one for me," she whispered into my ear, her panting breath nauseating against my skin.

I pulled away with open distaste. "Keep telling yourself that while you dance with Julian with my cum in your cunt."

Her face twisted into an ugly mask as I tucked my cock back into my pants and walked out. The shallow satisfaction lasted only a few moments until I started worrying about a possible STD. *Stupid, stupid, stupid.* For all I knew, she'd ridden every schlong in the state.

Thankfully, my health check came back clean. But I would always associate the closet incident with an idiotic loss of control on my part. *Never again.*

"One of her lowest, too, I'm sure," Belle says softly, pulling me back to the present. I feel her gaze like silk over my face. "She didn't have to make the incident public... You did this, didn't you?"

"Yes."

"Why?"

"To make it clear she has zero chance at success. She needs to know that we're not getting back together...and that I won't let her threaten you. She'll be too busy dealing with her husband to bother us for a while."

Belle nods. "The part about her husband physically abusing her, and her wanting your help to divorce him... Is Stanton going to believe it?"

"He will once he checks the authenticity of the photo with her showing me her bruised arm. Every picture in the article is real. Also, he's going to discover very soon—thanks to an anonymous tip—that his wife has been using the PIs on his retainer to surveil you."

"*What?*"

"That's how I knew about your meeting with Dennis. She's been sending me photos. Anonymously." I snort. "Like that would stop me from finding out who was behind them."

"So…all the issues we've had, they weren't all because of Mr. Grayson?"

I shake my head. "No. I don't know how—or if—he fits in with her plan. Maybe they worked together and maybe they didn't. But I'm making sure none of our enemies can damage what we have. I'm cutting them down one by one."

"I wish you'd told me." She extends a hand, her palm open and facing up. "I would've helped you find some other way."

I take her hand, marveling at its delicate softness. "I don't regret it."

"But this is your private life. It should never have been made public."

"Belle, believe me. I'd endure far worse to protect you."

She brings my hand to her mouth and kisses the knuckles, her eyes closed. "You're more than I deserve, Elliot. Sometimes I feel like you're going to get tired of fighting my battles and just…walk out of my life."

I sit next to her and pull her onto my lap. "Shhh. I'm not fighting anyone's battle but my own. I'm not the kind of man who does things out of noble intentions. I only do things because I want to."

She sighs against my shoulder, and my hold on her tightens. If she were thinking straight, she'd immediately recognize that if she weren't with me, she would've never been Annabelle Underhill's target to begin with. A lot of what she's suffered is because of me—because we met...and I wanted her...and married her...and now because I want to keep her.

As she stays pliant in my arms, I thank every deity I know that she's too nice and probably too tired at the moment to realize just how bad I am for her. She thinks she has some ugly baggage, but none of that's about who she *is*, just the crappy circumstances she's been in.

But my baggage? I shudder. All my shit is stuff I did because I was too dumb to know any better. Fucking Annabelle Underhill right after she exchanged wedding vows with my dad...releasing a sex tape...and all the other stupid crap... Every time, it was just because I got a wild hair up my ass and said *fuck it*.

If Belle could think straight even for a second, she'd bail. Vanish faster than a hummingbird.

TWENTY-FOUR

Annabelle

NONNY'S EYES WIDEN WHEN ONE OF THE associates at the spa brings out a tray of chocolate-covered strawberries and places it in front of us. "Are they for us?" she whispers, as masseuses knead our feet.

I nod.

Before I can say more, she snatches one off the silver tray and gobbles it up. "Oh my god," she moans, the words muffled by chocolate, "this is so good!"

"Swallow before you talk." My smile ruins the rebuke. It's difficult to be upset when she's so happy.

I realize we've never had any girl time together. She was too young, then our parents died…and I never had any extra money to spoil her with. Perhaps the need to scrimp became too ingrained, because I never even thought about doing something like this with her until Elliot surprised me this morning.

"All prepaid. Just go have fun," he told me as he kissed me sweetly after a session of very thorough lovemaking.

"Oh my god, you've *got* to try one, Anna." Nonny hands me a piece.

We enjoy the blissful chocolate. After a moment, Nonny says, "You okay?"

I give her a frown. "Of course I'm okay."

"It's just… I saw that thing about Elliot and his ex."

I sigh. She'd have to be living in a cave not to have seen it. Even if Elliot were just an average Joe, Annabelle Underhill's husband is a big deal in the business world.

"Everyone has an ex they'd rather forget about," I say neutrally.

"Who's yours? Dennis, right?"

I force a smile. "Something like that. Now hush and enjoy your foot massage."

Nonny nods, pulls out her phone and starts typing.

My mobile buzzes a moment later. I give her a sideways look, but she's got her eyes closed.

Sure enough, there's a new text on my phone. *Do you think Elliot cared about the other Annabelle?*

I guess there's no avoiding it. *Probably. No reason to date her otherwise. We all think we care about our significant others until they turn out to be all wrong for us.* I hit send.

How do you know they're wrong for you?

I turn to her. "Are you dating someone?"

"Well...sort of." She shrugs, her cheeks flushed. "That guy from algebra."

"Who's also in your history class, right?"

She nods. "He's cute and super nice. But don't tell Elliot, because he'll get all overprotective. I want to wait until, like, our third month before saying anything to him."

"Okay. I can do that."

"So...?"

Right. Her question. "When the initial attraction cools a bit and you can actually hear yourself think again, you'll know."

"What if it never cools?"

I purse my lips. "Then maybe it's true love."

She starts texting again.

My phone buzzes. I look down, then still at my sister's question. *Did it happen for you and Elliot?* I raise my head and look at her, suddenly unsure why she's asking. "Nonny..."

She raises a finger, then types again. *I mean the cooling thing. I know you guys fought at least once.*

I sigh. *People occasionally fight. You and I fight sometimes too.*

But you said our bond is greater—blood and all. I'm your family forever.

A tight lump forms in my throat. I swallow, then answer, *Yes, you are. But that doesn't mean what I have with Elliot is any less. I love him, Nonny.*

What about him? Does he love you, too?

I think—I pause, wondering what he feels about me. He hasn't said the L-word, but surely he feels it. Why else would he have ripped up our contract? I delete what I wrote and just type, *Yes.*

I watch her expression as she reads my text. Her mouth curls into a brilliant smile. She turns to me. "I'm so happy for you, Anna. You deserve happiness more than *any*body."

"Everyone deserves to be happy."

"Not the way you do. I know what you gave up for me."

"I didn't give up a thing for you," I say as the skin around my eyes grows hot. "I did what any older sister would've done, and I wanted to do it. It was no trouble."

"You could've let someone foster me."

"Over my dead body." I exhale slowly so I don't start crying. "If you love someone, nothing you do for them is really a sacrifice."

She reaches over and holds my hand. "I love you too."

I squeeze hers back. Moments like this I can believe my life will always be perfect...with a fairytale ending.

Elliot

BELLE IS OUT WITH NONNY GETTING A MASSAGE and having her nails done. I encouraged them to indulge—I could sense they needed some sisterly bonding time, plus I wanted them to treat themselves. I love the way my wife glows after a good pampering.

Meanwhile, I shop. I don't generally shop for gifts myself, but I can't have my assistant do it when it's for my wife's birthday next week.

The problem is I'm not sure exactly what I want to get her. It has to be something very special. Not jewelry—too obvious. Beyond that, price isn't a consideration. My wife knows I have money, and getting something expensive will appear thoughtless. Unlike most women, she isn't overly impressed with my bank account.

Perhaps something sentimental and sweet.

Photos? Music, maybe? She might enjoy a concert...or sports. I realize I know very little about her likes, and I feel guilty. I should've spent some time getting to know her along with all the seduction, as enjoyable as that is for both of us.

I get a text from Paddington. *AU in L.A. and coming your way. Will arrive in twenty minutes.*

I almost ask how he knows where I am, but it's his job to know. I call him.

"Yes?" he says.

"How quickly can you set up surveillance?"

"What do you want?"

"I want you to record our conversation."

He doesn't miss a beat. "It's illegal in California to record without her consent," he says matter-of-factly.

"So make sure to have plausible deniability."

"I can do that, so long as you don't think about using it in court."

"It won't be for something that silly." Court won't stop someone like Annabelle Underhill.

I fool with my phone, checking the market news while making my way slowly to a café. Annabelle's got to be having me tailed, since she couldn't know where I am otherwise. I want our scene to take place in a very public venue with no expectation of privacy.

The café I have in mind is faux-Italian. The coffee is horrible—especially if you've been to Italy—but it has a small outdoor seating area, and is generally busy enough. It'll do for what I have in mind.

I tell the server I want an outdoor table. He tells me one's just opened up. Serendipity.

Without looking at the menu, I order cappuccino and a blueberry scone. The waiter leaves, and I keep fooling with my phone. It doesn't take long before a shadow darkens my table. I look up.

"Hello, Annabelle," I purr.

"You fucking bastard," she spits.

I put down my phone and look at her. Her dark hair is swept up; perfect makeup covers her furious face. Sapphires glitter from her ears and throat, and the sleeveless violet dress she wears looks spray-painted on. The color reminds me of the fading bruises on my wife's body, and my mood darkens instantly.

I note with derision that Annabelle's arms are unmarked. Stanton has probably never laid a hand on her.

What a way to squander the one bit of leverage she had over me. Not that it would've meant a lot once I knew what she was after. I owed Marlin, but not that much.

"If you must insult me, at least have the decency to sit down first so I don't get a crick in my neck." I turn my attention back to my phone.

She takes the seat across the table and slams her palm down. "You think you can get away with that article? I'm going to sue you for libel."

"It's libel only if it's untrue."

"Oh no. There will be consequences for publishing shit like this."

"What? You think I did it?"

Her eyes flash with a moment of uncertainty. "Didn't you?"

The display of anger is just too damn delicious. I shrug with an arrogant smirk. "Yeah."

"*Why?*"

"I don't like people threatening my wife. It was a reminder you have lots of dirt too. I just scratched the surface."

"No. You used up everything."

"Oh, I doubt that. A woman like you always has more dirt. I just have to keep digging."

The server brings my order, and looks at Annabelle questioningly. She shakes her head, the gesture jerky. I hand the waiter a fifty to leave us alone, and sip my drink. It's actually not too bad. "Are you upset because Stanton finally decided to divorce you?"

"You'd like that, wouldn't you? But no, he hasn't. And he won't. That disgusting old man thinks he's in love with me."

"Pity. I'd love to see him throw you away like yesterday's garbage. My wife and I could read about it together in bed and laugh."

Her face is so red, she looks like a boiled

lobster. "When I get rid of him, it will be on my terms, not his. And your stupid cunt of a wife will be gone by then."

There is such viciousness in her tone that my hand almost jerks as I reach for the scone. "And how will that happen?" I ask casually. "I'm not divorcing her. Unlike you, my wife is quite happy as a married woman."

"Divorce isn't the only way to get rid of unwanted spouses. People sometimes have accidents, especially when they're clumsy."

Annabelle's eyes are entirely too gleeful. My gut goes cold.

"So it *was* you who pushed my wife down those stairs," I say, hoping to draw her into confirming it.

"And what if I did? Who you gonna tell?" She sneers. "I'll just deny everything, and it'll be he said, she said. Too bad your little mouse didn't break her neck. That would've been so satisfying."

Fucking psycho. Anger twists my lips, and it's all I can do not to crush the scone. I'd much prefer to close my hand around her throat, but I can't. I'm playing for something bigger and more important.

She thinks she's so clever. It'd be funny if she weren't morally bankrupt. It won't be my word against hers. There are only four people who know about my wife's accident: me and Belle, Elizabeth and the staff member who found my wife at the bottom of the stairs. I don't consider the hospital staff, since Belle was admitted under an assumed name, thanks to Elizabeth's quick thinking. She didn't want me and Belle to be gossip fodder.

"People call me a genius, but clearly they're mistaken. It's amazing that I ever thought you were worthy of my affection," I say. "Don't bother scheming. If you were the only woman left in the world, I'd become a monk."

"You say that now, but you'll change your tune by the time I'm through."

"No, Annabelle. It's you who'll be ruined by the time I'm done."

"Is that a threat?"

"Consider it a promise." I slip a few bills under the coffee cup, enough to cover my food plus a tip. "Don't ever come near me or mine again."

TWENTY-FIVE

Annabelle

MOST PEOPLE HATE MONDAYS, BUT NOT me. I can't believe how exciting it is to have a job I actually look forward to. I hope I never lose this feeling.

Since I'm having lunch with Jana, I pick out a conservative ruched knee-length dress in the shade of green that brings out my eyes. If I remember correctly, green is also a good color to convey confidence, trustworthiness and all sorts of great qualities that I want Jana to associate me with.

I bump into Traci in the elevator. She's again in a not-quite-appropriate-for-work outfit. Guess she hasn't gotten over her crush on Gavin yet. I feel bad for her; it's got to be twice as tough when they're working so closely together.

Traci moves closer until we're standing only inches apart. "Hey, how you feeling?" She peers at me.

"I'm fine."

Her shoulders sag with relief. "Oh, good. I was so worried when you passed out. I swear I thought Elliot was going to bite my head off when he saw you like that."

I cringe. "Sorry. He's very protective. I'm sure he was upset with me, not you."

She nudges me with an elbow. "Don't ever pass out after a glass of iced tea again."

My face heats. "I won't."

"Good. And your secret is safe with me. I won't tell anyone how much of a lightweight you are."

I give her a small, sheepish smile.

"Other than that, how are you holding up?" Traci asks.

"What do you mean?"

"That article? About Elliot and his ex-slash-stepmom?"

My smile falters. "Oh. Well…it is what it is." I didn't think about my coworkers reading the article. I should have.

"Don't worry," Traci says. "Most people here don't take that stuff too seriously."

"Really?"

"Oh, sure. Look at the kind of rich and famous clients we have. Dirty gossip is par for the course."

That relieves me somewhat. Elliot isn't famous the way his actor brother is, but he is in the public eye. The elevator reaches our floor and we part, me heading for Jana's office, and her for Gavin's.

Jana's standing at her desk, looking down at a readout. She's in a black jumpsuit, paired with a patent leather belt with a golden buckle. Her fingernails are a glossy red, and stilettos add over three inches to her height. She studies me for a moment, and I shift my weight.

"Is…there something wrong?" I ask.

"No. There are your tasks." She gestures at one of the smaller tables near her desk. A sticky note is on top of a pile of papers. "Get them done before lunch."

"Sure. Do you need to me to make an appointment?"

"Hmm?"

"For lunch?"

She shakes her head. "Not necessary. The restaurant I go to always has a table for me."

"Got it."

I grab everything from the table and take it to my cubicle outside her office. Most of the stuff is related to the surprise treasury dump from Friday. Guess she didn't get to her "prior engagement."

I finish filing all the papers and proofread a prospectus for grammatical errors and typos. Suddenly I'm aware of someone watching me.

"You look super sexy when you're working." Elliot grins.

My mouth parts. He's the last person I expected to see. And he looks pretty sexy himself in a casual chocolate-colored shirt and expertly tailored slacks. As I drink him in a hot flame ignites within me, as though we didn't spend way too much time in the shower together earlier this morning.

"What are you doing here?" I start to get up, but he waves at me to stay seated. "You have an appointment with Pete?"

"Nope. Just happened to be in the area and thought…why not drop by?" He hands me a basket of sunny yellow daisies. "To brighten your Monday."

"It's already bright with you here."

"Well, yes. But for when I'm gone."

The unexpectedly boyish grin leaves me breathless. Without thinking, I stand and give him a kiss on the mouth.

"When's your lunch break?" he asks, his gaze on my lips.

"Can't. Jana's taking me out."

"So cancel."

"Elliot! You know I can't do that. You'll just have to be patient until tonight."

"You are a cruel, cruel woman, Mrs. Reed."

I tap the center of his chest with a gentle

finger. "If you come by tomorrow, maybe I can arrange something."

He gives me an exaggeratedly lusty look that makes me giggle. I start to say something, but then realize that murmurs are welling up around us.

My coworkers are swiveling their heads and looking toward the hall leading to the elevator bank. I let my gaze wander in the same direction, wondering if someone super famous is leaving.

I gasp. It's Dennis, with a security guard on each side of him. Holding a box, my ex drags himself forward. His face is bloodless, his lips pressed so tight they have no color. Strong emotion shines in his unblinking eyes.

"Oh my god," I whisper.

Elliot moves closer and puts a hand around my waist. I lean into him, but I can't stop staring at Dennis. What happened? He's too careful to screw things up badly enough to be fired.

He stops, then suddenly turns around and gazes at the cubicles and offices. Some people look away, but not everyone. His eyes meet mine, and hatred blazes in them. A corner of his mouth twitches, then he actually snarls.

His inarticulate fury lances me all the way to the core. Shaking, I take a step back. Elliot's arm tightens around me.

The guards pull Dennis into a waiting elevator. He doesn't exactly resist, but he keeps his burning eyes on me the entire time. Finally, the doors close.

The whole event took no more than a minute, but it felt like forever. My legs trembling, I plop down rather ungracefully into my seat.

Elliot crouches in front of me. "You all right? You look a little pale."

I blink and drag in a breath. "Yeah. I'm fine. Just…surprised."

"Why?"

"He's just an intern. What did he do so wrong that he's being humiliated like that?"

Elliot snorts. "My take? He's overly ambitious and too impatient. It takes years of hard work to make something of yourself, but he wasn't willing to wait."

"How do you know?"

"He lied." My husband's voice is flat.

I flinch at the lack of mercy and understanding in his tone. "He just wanted a fresh start," I murmur, recalling what Dennis told me.

"Lying isn't a fresh start. It's a shortcut." He takes my hands in his. "You're cold." Concern darkens his eyes. "Want me to get you some coffee? Tea?"

"No. You should get going." I put a hand on one strong shoulder. "Thanks for coming to see me."

He kisses me on the forehead, then searches my face. "Call if you don't feel well, okay?"

A smile curls my lips. I can't stay upset when Elliot is looking at me so tenderly. "Yes, Daddy," I whisper, more for my benefit than his. I feel like I'm falling so deep that I may never come out.

His gaze narrows. "Stop provoking me… unless, of course, you want me to toss you over my shoulder and cart you out in front of everyone."

I laugh, and he kisses me and walks away. The second he disappears into the elevator, the electric charge in the air vanishes. I turn to my work, resolving to focus. I need to give it a hundred and ten percent if I want to get done by lunch.

At noon sharp, Jana comes over. Her expression is neutral, but I can sense something's bothering her.

"Jana, is there something I can help you with?"

"Our lunch. I hope you didn't forget."

"Of course not." I close my laptop and grab my purse.

She sticks her lower lip out appreciatively. "Nice flowers."

I flush. "Thanks."

The restaurant she takes me to is a block away from the office. It's a delightful Japanese place that specializes in sushi and tempura. The interior is bright with natural wood and paper lanterns, and the air holds faint whiffs of sweet vinegar, hot oil and ginger. The place is bustling with the lunch crowd, but a hostess in a bright red and yellow yukata smiles widely at Jana and takes us to a private room in the back.

The hostess takes off her wooden Japanese sandals and gestures us in. Jana removes her stilettos, and I toe off my pumps and follow her into the room. It's big enough for a party of four. The flooring is Asian straw matting that feels cool against my soles. The seats have high backs, but no legs. The table is very low, but there's a square hole dug into the floor where we can lower our legs.

We're immediately served cold, unsweetened barley tea. Jana orders a sashimi lunch set, and I get seafood and veggie tempura since I'm not brave enough to do raw fish.

"It's unfortunate things have changed. No more lunch drinks," Jana says casually. "You might've benefited from a couple."

"I don't understand." What did I do to make her think I'd need a drink?

"I saw the little byplay between you and Dennis."

"Oh."

"You know him?"

"Well…yeah." I clear my throat. "We grew up in the same town. I actually dated him in high school."

Jana nods. Our food arrives soon after, and she picks up a slice of red tuna and dips it into wasabi-green soy sauce. She uses her chopsticks as expertly as she navigates the market. I'm slightly awed.

"Is that going to be a problem?" she asks suddenly.

I startle, then realize she means me and Dennis. "No. We aren't that close anymore."

"Good. It's best you don't talk to him or have any other contact."

"Why not?"

"He's a dishonest son of a bitch, and he did something he shouldn't have. He's lucky the only thing Gavin did was fire him. He could've been criminally charged if Gavin wanted, and trust me, the boss and the DA's office are tight."

The shrimp tempura turns to dust in my mouth. I can't believe Gavin would be so vindictive about the small lie about who Dennis's father was. He seemed so nice during dinner at home…but then that was with his pregnant wife. He might not show his ruthless side to family and friends.

"We can tolerate mistakes, but we don't tolerate betrayal."

"Betrayal?" I repeat, dumbfounded.

"He tried to finagle a job at another firm… using our client list and market positions."

I gape at her. "But how…? He's—was—just an intern."

"I don't know, but it doesn't matter. He got access somehow, and I'm pretty sure this means we're going to implement more enhanced security protocols. I'm certain he had help." She eats another piece of red tuna, her eyes on mine.

The way she's studying me is a little alarming. "Jana…do you think I had something to do with it?"

"No. If I did, you would've been escorted out with Dennis. But keep your head down and don't do anything that draws unnecessary attention to yourself. And do eat your tempura before it gets cold. It won't be nearly as good."

I reach for another piece, my mind churning. Dennis has his share of faults, but betraying his employer seems crazy. He said he really wanted to work at owm. Why throw it all away on a stunt like this?

Jana offers a few pieces of advice on how to handle some of the divas at the firm. I try to pay attention; it's important, plus I feel like she may actually quiz me later.

"Most significantly," she says, "if you can't handle something, you come to me. Actually, come to me about everything. I hate surprises."

"Even good surprises?"

"Even then. Just imagine: someone says,

'Great job,' and I have no clue what they're talking about."

I see her point.

"Your job is to do what I tell you and be loyal. To *me*, if that's not clear. And my job is to bring you along and protect you."

"But I'm just a junior assistant. I don't rank that high."

She munches on a piece of pickled ginger root. "So?" She peers at me. "You aren't going to be a junior assistant forever, right?"

"No."

"So how are you planning to advance if you don't have somebody mentoring you?" She glances down at her clean plate. "Ready? I have a meeting in ten."

"Sure."

She pays, and we leave. As we walk back, my phone rings. Jana glances at my purse. "Take it. I'll see you upstairs. Get three copies of the light crude analysis memo ready for my two o'clock. The research team should have it."

"Sure. See you soon," I say to her back as she walks briskly away. She always moves like she's five minutes late to a meeting that will alter the course of history.

I plunge my hand into my bag and pull out my phone, already hitting the green button. "Annabelle Ree—"

"You *fucking bitch!*" Dennis's rage explodes in my ear.

I flinch and almost drop the phone.

"It's all your fault! I told you! I told you!"

"You stole from the company," I say.

"I didn't steal shit. You fucking cunt! If you just did like I told you, I would've been fine."

"I'm going to hang up now. Don't ever contact me again," I say coolly, remembering Jana's warning. Elliot has never liked Dennis either. And right now I have zero reason to be compassionate.

"I'm going to make you pay!" my ex bellows. *"Dad should've shot you too!"*

My hand flies to my mouth. My stomach knots, and the lunch I had with Jana roils threateningly. I clamp my jaw, my breath hissing through my nose. There's no way I'm throwing up on the sidewalk less than a block away from the office.

Heartrending pain and wrath battle inside of me. Wrath starts winning. If Dennis were in front of me, I might actually launch myself at him to rip his face off.

"Listen to me, you son of a bitch," I hiss. "It is not my fault your father was a murderer. It's not my fault you lied on your job application, and it sure as hell isn't my fault you tried to betray Gavin and got caught. Want to blame somebody for the mess you call a life? Why don't you look in the mirror? And the next time you contact me, I'm going to sue you for harassment, mental anguish and anything else I can make stick." I hang up, then power down my phone. My hands and legs are shaking, and it's an effort to remain upright.

I blink away sudden tears. The memory of how I lost my parents floods me, bringing a fresh wave of pain.

I take a seat on a bench and breathe deeply until I'm calm enough to go back to work. Then I throw myself at my mountain of tasks, trying to shove Dennis's hateful words out of my mind.

TWENTY-SIX

Annabelle

B Y THE TIME I'M HOME, I'VE ALMOST FOR-
gotten the ugly phone call. Dennis is hateful, maybe even a little deranged, and I
won't let him ruin my time with the two people I
care the most about in the world.

With a smile pasted on my face, I open the
door and walk in. "I'm home!" I call out, dumping
my purse on the counter.

"Hey." Elliot gives me a quick kiss on the
mouth.

I grab hold of one muscled arm and kiss him
back. The greeting makes the odd and disturbing
day at work worth it. It's impossible to stay trou-
bled when I have a hot husband waiting for me at
home. Especially when he's in a one of those tight
workout shirts that shows off his thick chest and

ridged abs, and jeans that mold to his butt, and when I can smell the warm, clean skin that I want to nuzzle for hours…

But instead of being affectionate or salacious, he looks agitated when he pulls back.

An alarm bell clangs in my head. *Dennis again?* "What's wrong?"

Elliot takes a step back. "The details of the deal behind our marriage became public half an hour ago. And it's trending."

"What are you talking about?"

He hands me his phone. I read the article.

GREEDY BILLIONAIRES CLAMOR FOR MORE, the headline proclaims in capital letters.

The rest is just as lurid, but the basis for the ridiculous spin is accurate. It details the deal Julian has with his children, and how Ryder and Elliot married already to get paintings that are worth millions.

Why marry for a reason as crude as money when they already have so much? the article asks toward the end.

"Oh my god, how did they find out?"

"My guess is Annabelle Underhill. Paige said she seemed to know."

"Is this some kind of payback for the exposé?"

"Probably." Elliot puts his hands on my shoulders and pulls me gently toward him. "I'm sorry."

"I'm sorry too. What are we going to do?" I hug him, drawing strength from his warmth. "Oh my god, *Elizabeth*. She'll be hounded by men. And your brothers…"

"Lucas and Blake can handle themselves. But Elizabeth…" Elliot runs a hand over his face. "Yeah."

"How's Nonny?" Given that she hasn't come out to greet me, she can't be reacting well.

"She's at a friend's. Maria, I think. But first things first."

He leads me to the dining room. Chinese takeout with my favorite sweet and sour chicken and shrimp fried rice is waiting for me. He has duck and some stir-fried greens.

"You actually want to eat?" I ask incredulously.

"Can't fight on an empty stomach. Sit down." He pulls out a chair. "Please."

I sit. He's right; not eating will only hurt me. He opens the sweet and sour chicken and pushes it my way, along with some utensils.

"How are we going to fight?" I ask. "The deal is true."

He points to my food. "Eat, woman."

Making a face, I pop a piece into my mouth.

Only then does he say, "We have to make people believe it's not true."

"You're going to lie?"

"We don't have to lie. The premise that our father is forcing all of us to marry in the next six months to inherit the paintings is already pretty far-fetched."

"But true."

"That's not the point."

I think it kind of *is* the point, but ask, "Okay, so what are you going to do?"

"We're going to talk with my siblings and figure out how best to approach it. As a matter of fact, we've been waiting for you to come home so we can make sure you'll be on board as well."

"I'm fine with whatever you decide." And I mean that. I trust Elliot will do what's best.

Cradling my face, he kisses my forehead. "Thank you for your faith in me."

"Let's eat fast, if they're waiting."

But even as I smile for his benefit, I feel queasy. This is Annabelle Underhill's second attempt to drag me through the mud. She promised she would. And I hate that her hatred of me is going to hurt Elliot and his family.

Elliot

IT DOESN'T TAKE LONG TO WRAP UP DINNER. Neither of us has much appetite. We pack up the leftovers and put them in the fridge for later, then go to the couch in the living room. We have three minutes to the call, and I dial in.

Others hop on within seconds. Ryder, Paige and Elizabeth are the first to join, then Blake. His voice is cold and low, and that tells me he's too furious to yell.

"Fucking Julian," he says. "It's gotta be him."

"Annabelle Underhill knew we had to marry," Paige points out. "She said as much at the charity dinner Elizabeth organized with Nate Sterling."

"If it's Annabelle Underhill, I'll take care of it," I say. Paddington sent me the recording. I'm forwarding it anonymously to Stanton Underhill, illegally made or not. After that, it'll be up to the old man to decide what to do about his psychotic wife, but I doubt he'll shrug it off. A man like him doesn't get to be where he is by being overly understanding and forgiving.

"How about Mira? Didn't she know?" Elizabeth says.

"She did," Ryder says, "but she wouldn't spill the beans. Her agent contract came with an iron-clad NDA. She might be a backstabbing bitch, but she wouldn't do something to make me an enemy for life."

Suddenly the line beeps, alerting us to another person joining the call.

"How the fuck did you get this to leak?"

My wife's eyes widen. I rub the back of my neck. "Hello, Lucas. I didn't realize you were going to join us."

"I wouldn't normally, but did you have to fuck this shit up? What the hell is wrong with you guys?"

"Inbox bursting with marriage proposals?" Blake says sarcastically.

"No. I was on the verge of… *Fuck!*"

"Just tell her the truth and get her to sign an NDA and prenup," Ryder suggests. "Women aren't stupid. They're gonna know if you're faking affection."

"Can't. It's *Ava*," Lucas says.

My jaw slackens, and I feel my mouth part. Belle looks at me blankly, but doesn't ask…for which I'm grateful, since I'm not sure how to explain Ava.

Ava Huss is Lucas's ex. Or that's the story from what I understand, but…

When Lucas had his accident—the one that left him scarred—Blake and I were the first people to show up at the hospital. She appeared, claiming to be Lucas's girlfriend of sorts. That was news to us. None of us knew Lucas was dating anyone. To be honest, he isn't the type to date anyone seriously. He fucks women. Not indiscriminately, of course, but he doesn't get involved. Ava vanished soon after exchanging a few unpleasant words with Blake at the hospital, and I assumed she was one of those pathetic, parasitical exes looking for an opportunity to worm her way back into his life...and his sizable bank account.

"I'm so sorry about that," Elizabeth says finally. "But we didn't do anything."

"Oh, I know *you* didn't, Elizabeth," Lucas says. "But Ryder and Elliot?"

"That's not fair," Ryder interjects. "You think I want this shit out there?"

"Don't you? It gets you media attention."

Ryder laughs. "'Media attention.' I'm already world famous, in case you've forgotten."

"Stop fighting," I say. "We have to do damage control, and it's got to come from me and Ryder."

"I'm supposed to trust you guys now?" Lucas snarls.

"We're the ones who are married," I say. "It'll sound better coming from us."

"So categorically deny everything?" Belle asks.

"No, that would be a lie," Blake says thoughtfully. "It's always best to fight truth with truth."

Lucas says, "Not a terrible idea, except the truth doesn't help us here."

"Everyone knows Elliot isn't the type to marry just to get a painting. And Ryder wouldn't marry his assistant over something as ridiculous as this...*and* start a family," Blake says.

"Think that'll be enough?" Elizabeth asks.

"It has to be. It's the only thing we can say."

"It's all about the delivery," Ryder says. "Definitely no written statement, at least not on my part. I'm scheduled to be on a bunch of talk shows this week to start laying the groundwork for promoting my next movie. So I can mention something there. Very casually, but with enough scorn to make people feel like idiots for believing the rumor."

"That's all fine and good, but when we get our paintings a year after all of us are married, it's going to confirm the rumor was right," Lucas says.

"Is anyone going to be keeping score by then?" I ask.

"Let's worry about that later," Elizabeth says. "What matters is taking care of this mess for now."

Although she speaks calmly, there is an edge to her tone that makes me worried. "You okay?"

"I'm fine. I just don't like having this out there. I've got enough problems."

I sigh. She has her share of stalkers and obsessive admirers whose single unifying characteristic is being oblivious to her distaste for them. This might encourage a few to take it a step further.

"Okay, then problem solved for now," Ryder says. "Elliot and I will deal with it; the rest of you sit tight."

"If you screw things up, I'm going to break your pretty face," Lucas growls.

"Fine. But when I fix the problem, you owe Paige an apology. She's rather fond of my face."

Lucas curses. But he's no longer yelling, so I know he's good…for now. "When are you marrying Ava?" I ask.

He laughs, but there's a manic edge to it. "After this shit? I'll be lucky if she doesn't spit in my face."

"Where are you?" If he's in town, I want to stop by and check up on him. My instincts warn me that Lucas is a step away from becoming unhinged, even though outwardly he seems to be keeping things together.

There's a pause. "With Ava."

I scowl at the non-answer. "You know you can trust us."

"I do trust you. That doesn't mean I want to share everything or want to see your ugly mug."

I sigh, but let it go. Forcing myself on him would only make things worse.

We end the call since it's late for Blake, and I want to spend some time with my wife. But first…

I hit two of my most active social media accounts and post: *Wow. Do I look like the type who gets married just to get a painting?*

Belle looks at my statement over my shoulder. "Will that be enough?"

"Should be." I toss my phone on the table.

"People know my reputation for not giving a damn about anything."

"Because they don't know you." She links her fingers with mine. "You care so much, you have to fake it."

I chuckle to disguise how unsettled her observation makes me.

She gives me a look. "Laugh all you want while I count the ways you care." She shifts, bringing a knee onto the couch. "You're kind to Nonny, which you wouldn't be if you didn't care. You're sweet to Elizabeth and worry about her." I open my mouth, and she immediately wags a finger. "Uh-huh. No. You don't get to deny it when you told me before dinner about how worried you were about her."

I snap my mouth shut.

"And you voided the contract between us, making what we have real. A man who doesn't care wouldn't have."

I raise my free hand and rest the palm against her face. She leans into my touch, her eyes on me.

"You have a big, generous heart." Her warm breath fans against my skin. "Otherwise I would've never fallen in love with you."

Her faith in me humbles me. Her love for me slays me.

And I know I love her.

No other woman will ever touch me the way she does. The things I felt when I first laid eyes on her—I called them lust. But now I recognize they were fate.

I press my cheek against hers. "I love you, Annabelle Reed."

She trembles slightly. Then lays a hand over mine and slowly pulls back so she can look at me. Her green eyes shimmer, and she's so beautiful it hurts.

"Elliot," she breathes out, and a stunning smile curves her lips.

I can't help it. I cover her mouth with mine. Her fingers dig into my hair, and I taste her sweetness, breathe in her loveliness.

And I feel so damn free.

After placing her arms around my neck, I grab her ass and stand up. Her shapely legs wrap around my hips with surprising strength. Without breaking the kiss, I carry her to our bedroom. Still without breaking the kiss, I manage to get her dress and bra off. She helps by toeing off her shoes. Her mouth is as desperate as mine. We finally break away to get my shirt. I fling it over my shoulder at the same time I kick off my flip-flops and pull my pants off with rough hands. My fingers unsteady, I divest her of her panties.

She stands before me, flushed and fully nude.

I take in the beauty of her body—the gentle slopes, the gorgeous breasts and tiny waist that flares out below. My heart beats erratically, and at that moment I finally understand why all those songs about doing anything for the one you love are so popular.

I would kill for my wife. But at the moment, I simply gather her up and lay her on the bed.

Her flame-red hair spreads around her, and I try to control both my breathing and the lust raging through me. I've never wanted a woman the way I want my wife right now.

"Elliot, I need you," she murmurs.

"I need you too." I kiss her again. *Go slow, idiot. Don't ruin it by rutting like an animal.*

Very deliberately, I run my fingers down her neck and shoulders, then caress the plump underside of her breast. Moaning softly, she arches into my touch—oil to my fire. I nuzzle against the tender skin at the crook of her neck and very gently stroke her tight nipple.

"My god, Elliot…" Her smooth legs move restlessly against mine.

"Let me make it good for you, beautiful."

I pull the nipple into my mouth, sucking strongly. She cries out, her fingers digging into my hair, her spine arching. Her legs widen in silent invitation, but, with supreme control, I ignore that. I want her mindless with pleasure and crying out my name. I want her to know nothing matters but us—what we have, what we can have.

I let go and watch the wet tip of her tit bead tighter at contact with the cool air. My mouth wraps around the other nipple, while my hand travels along her taut stomach. The muscles jerk, and I stroke her firmly, quietly communicating I will take care of her.

"Elliot, you're killing me," she moans.

I laugh darkly against her. "Good."

Gripping my hand, she drags it down between her legs and presses it against her slick folds.

Damn. She isn't just ready. She's soaking wet. My dick is so hard I feel like it's going to shatter at any second. Gritting my teeth, I pull my hand away from her, then lick the sweet juices from my fingers. She watches me, her eyes dark, pupils so dilated there is hardly any green left. Her tongue flickers. My body hardens more in response, and I can feel pre-cum dripping from my cock.

Belle takes a drop with the tip of her index finger and puts it in her mouth. So damn erotic that I feel like the top of my head is about to blow off.

I move down her body wound tight with anticipation. I spread her thighs wide, then nuzzle the soft skin near the apex. Her feminine scent is stronger and headier, and I love it.

I love her.

A whimper pulls from her throat, and I grin wickedly before closing my mouth over her clit. She presses a palm over her mouth, and I pull back. "No hiding, Belle. We're done with that."

Biting her lower lip, she fists the sheet underneath her. Her clit is slick and swollen and so damn sensitive. One, two…three broad strokes using the flat of my tongue and she's climaxing, her body flushed, her face twisted in bliss. Feeling her come against my lips is more satisfying and sublime than any drug. I keep pushing her, this time thrusting into her with two fingers. Her entire body tenses, winding tight, then she comes again with a sharp cry.

"Elliot… Elliot…" She chants my name almost mindlessly, her voice drugged with ecstasy.

I know what she wants, but I do not relent. I crave her pleasure more than I crave my own, and I flutter my tongue against the sensitive tissue, the highly responsive bundle of nerves, gripping her pelvis to keep her where I want her. The sound tearing from the back of her throat is more animal than human, and I growl with satisfaction and need.

Finally I sheathe my dick in a condom and drive into her. Her cunt is swollen, but so completely wet that I glide in with ease. She wraps her legs around my waist, heels digging in, urging me to move.

Supporting my weight on my elbows, I link

hands with her and kiss her deeply as I slam into her again and again. Her fingers squeeze and she whimpers against my lips. She's so damn primed, I know she's close to another orgasm.

And I want to give it to her, watch her shatter beneath me.

I pull away and change the angle to give her the extra stimulation she needs. Her face is glowing, and her eyes start to glaze over with another impending climax.

"I love you," I say between panting breaths. "I love you."

She unravels with my name on her lips. Only then do I relinquish control and let an awesome orgasm barrel through me. I've never felt one this powerfully. The force of it is almost frightening, and it destroys me from the inside out. But I'm okay. I'm with Belle.

I roll to my side, pulling her with me so she's lying on top. "I love you," I say again. I feel like I need to make up all the times she told me she loved me and I didn't say the words back.

"I love you too," she whispers, then kisses me on my chin. "I couldn't ask for more in my life."

"I could."

She blinks. "Well, aren't you the greedy one…"

"What's greedy about wanting to live happily ever after with the love of my life? Telling you I love you is just the first chapter."

"Who would've thought a man who ordered me to suck him off for three grand could be so romantic?"

I cringe. "Can we not talk about that? I didn't know I'd fall in love with you back then."

"I know." She hugs me. "I don't care about how we met. I'm just glad we did."

My arms tighten around her. "So am I. So am I."

TWENTY-SEVEN

Annabelle

THE NEXT THREE DAYS ARE LIKE SOMETHING out of the happy moments in Disney movies right before everything goes to hell in a handbasket. Since my life isn't a movie, I'm sure it won't implode, but…part of me can't stop thinking about Dennis's horrible words, especially at work.

Dad should've shot you too.

He was probably furious at having been fired. He thought Elliot, as Gavin's close friend, would be able to do something to help him keep his internship, but not even Gavin's mother would've been able to help after the theft.

As I leave work on Thursday, hair on the back of my neck bristles. I scan the lobby. Expensively dressed people mill about, and four security guards in navy-blue uniforms stand by two exits. One of them is older, but the other three are young and look like they hunt wolves with their bare hands.

I shake my head at myself. Dennis said those things, but that doesn't mean he's actually going to do something. He's always been on the impetuous side, with a generous dollop of roughness, but I just don't see him as someone who might use deadly force.

Everyone thought Mr. Smith was an affable guy, too...until he opened fire on your parents.

I shove the thought aside and get into my car in the underground garage across the street. The one in the OWM building was unavailable when I arrived. Something about a minor incident in the garage, although I don't know exactly what happened. There hadn't been any time for gossip before Jana dropped an Everest-sized pile of papers on my desk and told me to go over every single one of them for information about potentially lucrative leveraged buyouts.

When I arrive home, I dump my purse and crumple onto the couch.

"That bad?" Elliot teases.

"Ugh," I moan. "My god. I didn't know a firm like OWM could generate so much paperwork. I thought only lawyers did that."

He laughs and arranges us so I'm lying with my head in his lap. He undoes my ponytail, fanning my hair over the soft fabric of his camouflage shorts. The bright green shirt he wears is loose, but can't hide the impressive breadth of his powerful shoulders.

And just like that, all my fears disappear.

He is perfect, inside and out. And he's mine through the love we have for each other.

I look up at him with a slightly bemused smile. Reaching up, I brush the tip of my index finger over his chin.

He catches my finger and kisses it. "What are you thinking?"

"That I'm lucky to have you. We don't travel in the same social circles. We should have never run into each other."

"It's not luck, it's fate. I was meant to run into you, and you were meant to be mine."

"For a logical man, that's awfully whimsical."

His eyes darken, and he lowers his head. "A better word would be 'grateful.'"

My breath catches, and I tilt my face, my body warming with anticipation. But before our lips can touch, Nonny bursts out of her bedroom. "Anna, can I have a twenty?"

Elliot straightens with a sigh. "Your sister has shitty timing," he mutters. "I'm getting her a credit card."

"Don't even think about it." I give him a stern look, then turn to Nonny. "What happened to all your money?"

She shifts her weight from side to side, not quite meeting my eyes. "I…bought some candy bars."

Elliot gapes at her. "Were they wrapped in gold?"

I have to agree. Her allowance is exceptionally generous, especially given that Elliot pays for her clothes, food, all school-related activities and so on.

"Some junior high school kids came up to sell stuff… You know, for a fundraiser? So I bought, um, three boxes."

"Good god." Elliot shakes his head. "You're going to get diabetes."

I lay a hand on his thigh. I know why she did it. She used to have to sell stuff too, and she was always the worst salesperson in the class. "All right. Bring me my purse."

She does. I fish out my wallet and pull out a twenty. A card slips out of one of the pockets and falls on the floor.

Nonny takes the money. "Thanks."

"Don't mention it, but next time buy one *bar*, not three boxes."

"Okay. Sorry."

Before I can grab the card, Elliot reaches down and picks it up. His face pales when he reads what's on it. He glances at me sharply, then turns to Nonny. "Do you mind giving us a few minutes?"

Her quizzical gaze darts between us. "Um… sure." She walks off to her room, watching us over her shoulder the entire way.

As soon as the door closes, Elliot sits me up and gets to his feet. "How the hell do you have this card?"

His voice is seething with fury, and I flinch. Cold fear flows through my veins. This is the exact tone he used when he found out about Mr. Grayson.

Elliot

MY WIFE'S FACE TURNS PALE SO FAST, I WORRY that she may faint without giving me the answers I want.

"What is it?" she whispers, her lips barely moving.

"*Keith Shellington.*"

Her eyes don't register any recognition. But how can that be? *She has his card.*

"I don't understand," she says finally. "Who is Keith Shellington?"

"He's the fucker who stole from me and Lucas. The embezzler I told you about." I wave the card in her face. "This didn't jump into your wallet on its own." *Grayson and now this…* I want her to explain what the hell is going on. Tell me what I need to hear to make the nasty pit in my gut go away.

"Let me see it." She takes the card from my hand and reads the name and phone number on the heavy stock. She shrugs helplessly. "It's a guy I ran into outside a sandwich shop two or three weeks ago."

"What were you doing there?"

"Having lunch with Traci. We were just saying goodbye when he bumped into me and spilled coffee on my clothes. I told him it was fine, but he was all apologetic and gave me this card to call him in case I couldn't get the stain out. He said he would replace the dress. He seemed to feel really terrible about it, and I didn't… Elliot, I had no idea he was the man who stole from you."

I can feel my eyes narrowing. The story is too ridiculous and contrived to be believed. Keith couldn't have known she would be at that particular place at that particular time. He doesn't even live in L.A. And for him to just conveniently run into my wife out of millions of people in the city?

No way.

Then I finally register the bloodless, glassy-eyed expression on my wife's face. Her slim arms are wrapped around her legs, and she's watching me like a prisoner awaiting execution.

She's horrified at having been found out.

The thought rams into me with the force of a wrecking ball, and my knees almost give. I curl my hands into fists, my body vibrating with a cocktail of emotions—bitter disappointment, anger and grief.

I mentally count to ten. I have to calm myself or I'm going to fuck everything up. I tunnel my fingers into my hair.

Is my love so shallow that I don't trust her?

Even when my discovery has turned her face into a rictus of panic, she's lovely. I want to protect her, tell her I can fix everything, that nothing will be different because—in spite of everything—I still love her.

Love.

Belle's story is very, *very* hard to swallow. Even Nonny could come up with a better lie. At the same time, life is complicated, and has its share of ridiculous coincidences. If it were anybody but Keith Shellington's name on the card, I wouldn't think twice about what she told me.

As the moment stretches, her teeth dig into her shaking lower lip. I crouch before her and gently free her lip with shaky fingers.

"Do you want me to pack my things?" she whispers without meeting my gaze.

"What?" I couldn't have heard that right.

She finally looks up. "I can't do what we did after you found out about Mr. Grayson. I just can't!" Unshed tears shimmer in her eyes. She blinks rapidly to make them go away, but they spill over her cheeks anyway.

The sight cuts like jagged glass. The realization that I crushed her like that eviscerates me. She hasn't been dreading the discovery, but my reaction. And my accusatory tone must've gutted her.

I'm such a fucking douchebag. I don't deserve her even though I have no intention of letting her go. Ever.

I reach out and hold her fragile shoulders. "You won't have to." I kiss the corner of her mouth and taste the salt of her tears. "I trust you."

"But… I thought…"

"It's a choice, Belle. And I choose to believe you."

"You aren't going to wonder later?" The words come out garbled and fast, almost unrecognizable. "That I made a fool out of you?"

"No. We said we loved each other. I can't love you without trust. And faith."

She exhales sharply and collapses in my arms, hot tears streaming down silently. I hold her, running my hands over her delicate back. "You have to stop crying or you're going to make yourself ill," I whisper into her hair.

She merely clutches me harder.

"If not for me, do it for Jana. She'll be despondent without her assistant tomorrow." That earns me a watery laugh. "I'm sorry I hurt you so badly."

"I don't want to think about the past."

I understand that. But I need to face *my* past. "Belle, even though I trust you, Keith's running into you was no coincidence. I don't want that son of a bitch sniffing around me and my new family. I need to confront him."

She pulls back. "Is there anything I can do to help?"

"There is…if you're sure."

Her eyes flash. "He stole from you and is apparently trying to get between us. So yes, I want him to at least say 'sorry' to your face, now that he's been found out."

I smile. I don't have the heart to tell her how unlikely that is. He's a fucking rat—an ungrateful, traitorous rat. "Contact him and tell him you couldn't get that stain out. He'll ask to meet. Let him set the time, date and location. That's it."

"What if he just offers to send money instead?"

I shake my head. "He won't. He went to a lot of trouble to meet you in person."

"All right, if you're sure. I can call him right now, actually." She takes her phone out and starts to enter his number, then stops. "I don't think I can talk to him while hiding how I really feel about him."

"Then don't. Text him."

She nods and types a few things. I don't try to look at what she's writing over her shoulder.

Toying with her hair with my fingers, I study her fierce face. Despite the upcoming confrontation with Keith, I feel as light and worry-free as a cloud in a sunny sky, because nothing can destroy what we have so long as we love and trust each other.

TWENTY-EIGHT

Annabelle

I STRETCH MY NECK AS THE LAST CONFERENCE call of the day ends. It was a long one with some overseas clients whose English was so thickly accented that I had a hard time deciphering what they were saying. Still, I managed to take a copious amount of notes as Jana instructed.

"I'll type them up right away," I say, gathering my legal pad and pen from the table in my boss's office.

"Unless your handwriting's so bad that you won't be able to make your notes out on Monday, you can go home," Jana says.

I glance at my watch. "But it's only four." And as far as I know, Jana doesn't believe in cutting the workday short unless there's a good reason, and today being Friday isn't one.

She settles behind her neatly organized desk. "Tomorrow's your birthday, so I'm letting you off early."

"Oh. I didn't…" I forgot about that. I stopped celebrating the last two years, mostly due to the lack of funds and just…not having any reason to when things were progressively becoming bleaker. "How did you know?"

"As your boss, it's my job to know. And next year, I'll get you a present other than letting you go home early." She gives me a small smile. "Happy birthday."

I beam at her, absurdly pleased at her bringing up next year. I haven't really thought that far ahead. Even though by then I'll be in school again, I would love to work part-time at OWM.

"Thanks, Jana. Have a great weekend."

Her smile widens, and she turns her attention to whatever's on her laptop.

I grab my purse and pull out my phone, about to call Elliot, then remember he's meeting Keith at four thirty. Hmm. How long will that take?

Pursing my lips, I tap the side of my phone. I don't want to sit around until he's done. Seems like a gross waste of my special extra hour off.

Dropping the phone back in my purse, I make an executive decision. I'm going home to freshen up. If we can, we'll go out. If not, then we'll stay in and order some Thai and watch whatever looks good on Netflix while snuggling. The perfect plan for a Friday evening before my birthday.

As I head toward our penthouse, I make a quick detour—only a few blocks—so I'm driving past the building that houses Keith Shellington's office. It's an impressive skyscraper with reflective glass sides glittering in the sunlight. I can't see anybody inside, but my mouth dries anyway. Apprehension slithers down my spine as I sit at the red light. Keith's using me to target Elliot seems so far-fetched. At the same time, it does feel…odd that he bumped into me right outside Galore and spilled all that coffee. It was almost as though he was waiting for me…

Now I wish Elliot wasn't confronting the man, or at least that I was going with him for backup, but that's being silly. Elliot made it clear he needed to do this to put all the past baggage behind us. I don't want to ruin what we have with groundless fears.

Besides, they're meeting in Keith's office. What's the worst that can happen? Raised voices and some nasty, heated words? Elliot can be hot-headed, but I doubt things will get physical.

By the time I'm home, I'm feeling better, almost convinced that things will end well between the two men. Nonny's still not back from school—I remember her saying something about sleeping over at her friend's today, and that's totally fine with me. I want her to have a great high school experience. She deserves that.

I drop my purse on the kitchen counter and get a big glass of cold water. Maybe I should call a few restaurants and see if we can get a reservation rather than waiting until Elliot comes home to see what we should do. If we decide not to go out, we can always cancel.

I take my phone out and unlock it just as someone knocks at the door. I wonder who it could be. The front desk doesn't allow people to come up unless they're on the approved list or they can show that they have legitimate business—like express delivery.

A quick look at the intercom screen shows a guy in a T-shirt with a local florist's logo on the chest and a cap with the same logo on his head. His face is tilted down, and he's fooling with a small tablet for delivery confirmation signatures. He's also holding a large bouquet of flowers— roses, lilies and some others I don't recognize.

Elliot. He must have ordered them for tonight, I think, ridiculously pleased at his thoughtfulness.

After grabbing a few small bills for a tip, I open the door. Holding the bouquet in front of his face, the deliveryman pushes forward with enough force to make me stumble back. Once inside, he kicks the door closed and drops everything on the floor.

My body goes numb, and the money slips from my fingers.

"Hello, Annabelle."

Elliot

IN DEFERENCE TO MY WIFE'S WORK SCHEDULE, Keith is meeting her in his downtown office near OWM at four thirty on Friday. That means I need to select my attire with care. Office drones don't suspect anything so long as you look like you belong there.

So I chose clothes that say *entrepreneur with an edge*. A black silk V-neck shirt. Impeccable black trousers. Black loafers. No jewelry except the wedding band.

I step out of the elevator and take in the vestibule. Sand-blasted letters on the thick glass doors read SHELLINGTON FUNDS. The receptionist's desk is gleaming, a computer and a phone sitting on the spotless surface. The golden color scheme is a bit much, but I suppose if you want to make it look like you have the Midas touch, you gotta do what you gotta do. And Keith, it seems, has done well for himself since I last laid eyes on him.

The secretary outside his door is a slim brunette who looks remarkably like Annabelle

Underhill. If I didn't know better, I would've thought she was Wife Number Three's long-lost sister.

She gets up at the sight of me. The blue dress she has on is tight but covers everything adequately. "Hello. You are…?"

"I have an appointment. Annabelle Reed."

She does a double take. "Annabelle…? Uh…"

"I know. Mom really wanted a girl." I wink at her and walk into Keith's office before she can stop me.

The room is spacious, with a decent view of the city. The focal point is a giant desk, which is cluttered with paper and three laptops. Two couches face each other, with a coffee table between. A decanter half full of amber liquid and three empty glasses are on the tabletop. Some things don't change. Keith was never one to keep his workspace tidy.

He swivels in his chair. Shock registers in his gray eyes, a wide smile slipping from his lips. The change pleases me immensely.

He's thirty-nine, although he can pass for forty-five. He sports a thousand-dollar haircut, his jaw shaved clean. His charcoal-gray suit fits well, but it can't hide the fact that he's a skinny bastard with a soft body.

I take an empty seat. "You're moving up in the world. Offices in L.A. now."

"Just opened three weeks ago." He pulls out his phone, texts something and places it back on his desk. "Sorry about that. But you know how it is. The market waits for no one."

"Get tired of Chicago?"

"Nah." His clasped hands rest on his belly. "Expanding the business."

"You mean broadening your base to steal from."

"Tomayto, tomahto." His lips twist. "Where's your wife?"

"She had to work late."

"A beautiful girl...although I think your interest is more due to the fact that her name is Annabelle."

Did he know about Annabelle Underhill even before the exposé? The way that secretary out front looks may not be an accident.

As though he's reading my thoughts, he says, "Oh yeah. I know all about Annabelle Graham. Oh, sorry, Reed. Oh damn, I mean Underhill." He throws his hands up theatrically. "Who the hell can keep track of a woman who marries so often?"

His tone is just a tad too bitter, and a sneer twists his mouth.

"You had a crush on her." I throw it out to test my theory.

"Wasn't a crush back then. It was love, and I borrowed that money to give her what she deserved."

My jaw drops. "You stole from me and Lucas for *her*? That conniving bitch?"

"Well, I was young. Didn't realize she was such a cunt back then. And it isn't stealing if you plan to pay it back."

"Tell that to your clients and see what they think." *Jesus*. It's difficult to process the information. I never suspected he had feelings for Annabelle Underhill.

Then I realize something. She wasn't just cheating on me with my dad, but also with Keith. That little bitch. A woman like her doesn't change. Perhaps I should surveil her and send proof of her current infidelities to Stanton as well.

"My clients worship the ground I walk on. And you can't prove I did anything wrong," he says.

"Only because you pinned it all on your assistant."

"Pssh. That cunt was reporting every move I made to Annabelle. She got what she deserved."

He's a complete asshole. But he's also free with information. Probably dying to tell me all about how clever he really is, and I'm willing to oblige. I want to know everything he's done. Even if I can't pin anything on him, I can try to use what he's telling me to foil him. "So why did you pay for my wife's living expenses? What did she do to deserve that? Or do you have a crush on her, too?"

Keith shrugs. "She didn't do anything. It was her father."

"What?"

"Aaron Key was my mentor when I came out of college. Nice guy, although not the sharpest tack in the carpet, if you know what I mean. But he taught me a lot about covering my tracks, especially when money is about to go missing. He was always so damn sneaky. When I heard about his death and that he was survived by two daughters, I had to look them up. Without the benefit of his instruction, I wouldn't have made it this far. So—out of the goodness of my heart—I decided to help them out some until they could get back on their feet."

"Through Grayson."

"I wasn't going to associate with them myself. I might've had some uses for them later."

"Like sending the oldest my way to marry me?"

He smiles. "Something like that."

I lean back, steepling my fingers. "How did you know I needed a wife in the first place?"

"Well, it's a funny thing. Your newest stepmother was more than a little peeved about the deal your father made with you." He shakes his head. "You really should've gone to her wedding. Pissed her off to get snubbed like that."

"Tiffany?" This is getting Kafkaesque. "How the hell do you know her?"

A shit-eating grin splits his face. "Her mother invests with me. When Tiffany was in town, we all decided to have dinner to discuss her money situation. She's smarter than people give her credit for. She knows the Julian gravy train won't last forever, and was eager to tell me all sorts of things about her marriage. Wasn't happy at all to think about those paintings going to you kids. I guess they're worth quite a bit of money."

"They are," I say to keep him talking.

"Yeah. So anyway, it wasn't long before I came up with the idea of telling your former love interest and mine, Annabelle Underhill, about your sudden need to marry. You know, just to see what she would do to kill the good thing she has going with Stanton."

"How would knowing about me do that?"

He laughs and shakes his head. "Elliot, Elliot. Such a genius with computers and such a moron about people. Annabelle has always been obsessed with you. I mean, don't ask me why. No accounting for taste, eh?"

"She can't be that obsessed. She tossed me over for Julian."

"What can I tell you? Greed is a marvelous thing. But it just about ripped her apart to have to choose between you and Julian's fortune."

Damn. That explains so much. I can feel the pieces of the puzzle falling into place.

"But now you have money!" Keith goes on. "And you got it after she was already married to your father. Oh, the irony!" He laughs again. "And I knew that that fact, along with your dad's forcing you to get hitched, would be more than the poor girl could resist. All I had to do was point her in your direction." He makes a pistol with his fingers and pretends to shoot me with it. "Pow. It'll be amusing to watch her flail around, even though she won't go down easily," he continues. "She knows all there is to know about your wife, and she's going to do everything she can to get rid of her competition. She is positively obsessed with the need to have what she believes she deserves: you."

His unnaturally bright eyes send a nasty feeling coiling around my gut. He doesn't give a shit about Annabelle Underhill. Or Belle, for that matter. He wants to see *me* fall.

"But it won't matter if that doesn't work," he says. "I have other pawns in play. It's really too bad your wife is such a poor judge of character."

He's so damn smug. Then another detail clicks into place. Belle said she ran into Keith after lunch with her friend. "Traci."

He nods, pleased that I've figured it out. "She's a great lay. The poor ones tend to be, because they really love your money. I'm sure your wife is good in the sack, too."

My teeth clench. "Don't drag my wife into this."

"But she's already in it, just like her little friends."

Friends?

"I help Traci get a job at owm; she helps her high school crush get an internship. Of course that boy's an idiot, trying to get me to hire him as an analyst by stealing the firm's data. Like I would hire a known traitor. Besides, what would I do with owm's positions? The timing's all wrong, and I know Gavin likes to play the market danger-ously." He tsks. "I had to let Gavin know. It was only right…even though it would mean that Idiot Boy blamed your wife for his misfortune. So sad."

I feel cold, as though I'm covered with a layer of frost. I recall the pure venom in Dennis's expression as he looked at Belle on his way to the elevator with the security personnel.

"Amazing what young people will believe when they feel grateful and trust that you'll always have their best interests at heart." Keith is entirely too gleeful as he lays a dramatic hand over his chest.

The pit inside me grows bigger and uglier.

"Dennis's obsession *is* troubling, though. After all, he once crossed a line with your wife that most decent men wouldn't. He blames her for that, too, since she was unreceptive to his advances when sober. What's a man to do in a situation like that except take advantage when she's inebriated?"

A low growl rises from my chest as a killing rage pumps through me. *Dennis* is the rapist from all those years ago? "*Fucking bastard.*"

Keith sticks his lower lip out. "Pretty much. And he'll cross the line again. Just the kind of person he is. I'm going to enjoy it when he does because you love her. You thought you were being smart and freeing her from my clutches when you paid Grayson off, but all it did was let me know how much you love your little wife."

"Dennis isn't getting anywhere near Belle," I grate out, standing up. "And this conversation is over. If anything happens to my wife...if she so much as breaks a *nail*, I will fucking destroy you."

"Is that a fact?" Keith gets up slowly. "What are you going to do? Have me arrested? I haven't done anything illegal, just like I didn't do anything illegal before...except you still decided to fuck me over, keeping *my* millions for yourself." He laughs in a way that makes the hair on my neck stand. "Tell me something, Elliot." Humor vanishes from his face, leaving a hard mask. His voice is low and soft as he whispers, "Where's your wife now?"

Terror like I've never experienced before slams into me. My heart accelerates, blood roaring in my head. It's the same tone he used when he told me I'd never find any hard evidence tying him to the embezzlement because somebody else was responsible, except this time his eyes are glittering with sinister intent. Pulling out my phone, I run out of the office.

I have to find my wife before it's too late.

TWENTY-NINE

Annabelle

DENNIS TAKES A MENACING STEP FORWARD, and I retreat, keeping my eyes on him. "What are you doing here?"

"Giving you my regards in person." His face twists. "You fucking bitch. *You ruined my life!*"

Fear spikes, my heart hammering as I tell him, "You got fired because you stole the client list and the firm's positions to take them with you to a competitor."

Anger vibrates through him as he glares at me, moving closer. "And it's because of *you* I had to do that!"

I back away slowly, air rasping in and out. I'm alone, and I'm weaker and defenseless. Panic flutters in my belly. For all I know, Dennis has a gun.

My eyes flicker to his waistband, but I don't notice anything that could be a gun under his shirt.

"I told you to get your husband to back off," he says roughly. "But no. He had to get Gavin involved. I told you *all I wanted* was a fresh start!"

"But you lied. You didn't think that would stay a secret forever, did you?"

He isn't listening. "You wouldn't let me live my life because you're bitter about the way your parents died. Guess what? Your parents might as well have murdered mine. They were the dirty ones."

"My parents didn't deserve to be gunned down like animals!"

"They got exactly what they deserved! If your dad hadn't tricked mine into the Ponzi scheme, my family wouldn't have been destroyed. *It's all your fault!*" Tendons stick out from his neck as spittle flies from his mouth. "I should've fucking killed you when I had the chance, but no, I was too damn stupid to do it."

For a brief moment, I wonder if he was the one who pushed me down the stairs at Elizabeth's function, but that doesn't make any sense. He couldn't have gotten in, and it wasn't the kind of party you can just crash.

"Your cunt is too small a price to make up for what you've done to me."

I gasp. "You…! *You're* the one."

"Oh yes. And you're so much less destructive when you are lying prone, unconscious. That should've been your permanent state, and I'm going to fix that now."

He lunges. I scuttle toward the front of the couch, putting it between us. He feints this way and that, but I manage to keep out of his reach. My pumps are cumbersome; I kick them off and manage to throw one at his face. He ducks, but the second one hits him on the top of his head.

"Bitch!" he bellows, his complexion crimson. He tries to hurdle the couch but catches a foot on the back. As he falls, I run toward the second level to the master bedroom.

Dennis comes after me. I barely make it. I wish I were far enough ahead to lock him out of the bedroom, but he's too quick. I throw a bottle of lotion I left on the nightstand at him, and that buys me seconds. I dash to the other end of the suite for the doorway leading directly to the pool.

I run across the terrace until I'm on the other side of the pool. The area surrounding the water is covered with textured tiles warm from the sun.

Dennis sneers. "So this is how you've been living. Fucking cunt. You don't deserve this." He flings his arm in the general direction of the penthouse. "This kind of life… It should've been mine! You stole it from me!"

NADIA LEE

I shake my head. "You have no idea what I've been through."

"I don't give a shit. You'll pay for what you've done." He picks up a half-empty bottle of scotch and a glass Elliot must've left on the poolside table and hurls them onto the hard tiles where I'm standing. I cover my head and cry out as they shatter on the ground around me. Bits of glass glint in the afternoon sun.

"Now where you gonna go?" he taunts as he makes his way toward me.

Sweat trickles down my skin. I know what it means if he gets a hold of me. Screw it. Cut feet are better than death—or worse.

Gritting my teeth, I leap to my left, trying to avoid the jagged pieces as much as possible. A few still dig into my bare soles, and I gasp, faltering for a moment. The pain is worse than I expected.

I start moving anyway. My blood smears the ground, and I know I won't be able to run for long. But it doesn't matter; Dennis jumps and catches my wrist roughly, yanking hard. I slip, and my head hits the edge of the pool. The world starts spinning.

God, I can't go like this. I am not letting a shithead like Dennis end me.

Dennis's foot connects with my ribs, and I gasp in pain and immediately curl up. He does it

338

again, and this time I go with the brutal force and fall backward into the water.

I hold my breath and kick upward, but something heavy lands on me. Hands close around my neck; a knee presses against my back. I flail, my lungs desperate for air. My head and feet throb, and I see red unfurling around me as my vision starts to go dimmer and dimmer...

...until I'm submerged in utter darkness.

Elliot

"Where the fuck is my wife?" I yell into the phone as my Maserati peels out of the garage.

"Home," Paddington answers in his usual blasé tone, apparently unperturbed by my profanity.

"You sure? She's not answering." And Jana said she left work an hour ago.

"Quite certain. I tracked her phone, and I know she took it with her today."

His records would show where she's been all day. Paddington's very thorough.

I hang up and dial 911.

"Nine-one-one. What's your emergency?" comes a professional male voice.

"I need you to send a couple of patrol cars." I give them my address.

"What is the problem, sir?"

"My wife. I think she's in danger."

"Think? What—"

Damn it. I don't have time for this bullshit. "Just send somebody over. Please!"

I drive as fast as I can. I'm almost to my building. It's a small relief when I see the main entrance. I'm out of the car instantly, tossing my keys to the dumbfounded security guard outside. "Move it if you need to!"

A couple is about to enter into an elevator. I push them out of the car. "Sorry. Take the next one!" I yell as I press the close button repeatedly.

My hands start to shake, and I squeeze my eyes shut.

The elevator pings, and I open my eyes. Panic surges; the door is ajar. Flowers are scattered on the floor along with some paper money, the couch is skewed and my wife's pumps are lying haphazardly in the living room.

I rush inside. "Belle!" I cry out, searching. She's nowhere on the first level.

I take the stairs three at a time to the second, where I hear water splashing on the pool deck. I run out. Broken glass litters the side of the pool. The ground is smeared with blood, and I make out two bodies in the water.

Without any hesitation, I dive in. A stroke later, I'm over Dennis. Inhaling deeply, I wrap my arm around his neck and pull hard. Belle's face comes out of the water, but she's not gasping for air.

No, no, no. I can't be too late.

Dennis struggles, but he's no match for me. I'm fresher, and adrenaline-fueled panic gives me extra strength. My fingers dig into his sopping hair, and I yank his head back, give him a vicious right hook to the jaw and push him under. A killing rage sears through me, and I see the son of a bitch through a red haze. This is the animal who raped my wife when she was fifteen and pinned all the crap that went wrong with his life on her. Scum like this deserves to die a horrible dea—

Something brushes against my arm. I flinch and see Belle's red hair spread out around me.

It snaps me back to reality. What the hell am I doing? Killing Dennis will only make me a murderer, and won't do a thing to help my wife.

I leave him floating and drag Belle out of the water. My heart is in my throat, panic and denial rising. She's not moving, and her skin feels so, so cold. When she's on the ground, I finally notice blood seeping from a gash on her head. "My god, my god." She's not breathing, she's deathly pale, and *she's not breathing*.

I get on my knees and start CPR. I dimly notice uniformed police officers coming to the pool.

"Hands in the air!" one of them yells. He's holding a gun trained on me.

I look up. "Help me. My wife. Please. She's not breathing."

He puts the gun away. "Oh, shit."

His partner requests medical assistance on the radio, and I do the only thing I can—I resume CPR.

Please breathe, Belle. You have to breathe!

Every second that passes is like a knife slicing me open, but I continue compressing her chest and giving her the breaths she desperately needs.

Suddenly Belle coughs up water and curls up to her side, wheezing roughly. *Oh thank god.*

"Hey, beautiful, I got you. You're safe." I pull her into my arms, my hands shaking. *She's going to be okay.* She's coughing and breathing, and doctors can fix everything else. I'll make sure of it.

One of the cops gestures at Dennis, who's dragged himself over to the edge of the pool. "Who's that?" he says at the same time his partner asks, "What should we do with him?"

I open my mouth to answer, but it's my wife who rasps out, "You can take him straight to hell."

THIRTY

Annabelle

IT TAKES TWO DAYS BEFORE I FEEL WELL enough to get out of bed. It doesn't help that my period started right as the hospital was running tests to make sure no permanent damage had been done, although the bit of embarrassment and cramping were the least of my problems. The head injury worried my doctor and Elliot, but it didn't turn out to be anything serious. It just looked bad because of the blood.

Nonny was inconsolable when she learned about the attack. "I should've been home on Friday," she sobbed at the hospital. "Then maybe he wouldn't have done it."

I squeezed her hand. "If you'd been here, you would've been hurt too. I'm just glad you were away and safe."

It took some convincing before she calmed down, and I specifically instructed her to go on like nothing had happened. "Otherwise you're letting Dennis win. You don't want that, do you?"

Her face set stubbornly. "Hell no!"

I grinned. That's my sister.

Our bedroom at home—I refused to spend a second more than I had to at the hospital—is full of flowers from my in-laws, except Julian and his wife, and my coworkers from OWM. Gavin, his wife Amandine and Jana all come by on Monday to see me, and I assure them I'm fine and will be back at work soon.

"Make her listen to reason," Elliot complains. There are dark circles around his eyes, and he hasn't shaved since Friday. "I'm trying to get her to take a month off, but I might as well be talking to a piece of cookware. Teflon cookware."

Jana raises an eyebrow.

"A month is ridiculous!" I say. "I'm going to go stir crazy."

Jana turns to me. "Point taken. But if you don't take at least two weeks off, you're fired. I heard you cut your feet. It's going to hurt to walk."

"Yes, ma'am," I answer meekly, and Elliot relaxes…a little, and shoots a look of gratitude her way.

She glances at her watch. "I have to get going.

Take care of yourself and don't come back until you feel not just fine, but *great*."

"Yes, ma'am," I say again to her retreating back. Jana has that effect.

"Traci's fired," Gavin says after Jana's gone. "She's also under investigation for her role in Dennis's attack."

I gape at him. "Traci? No way." I didn't catch every detail about what prompted Dennis to attack and who helped him. At first I was too happy to be alive, then the doctors were busy poking and stitching me up…and then I was just too exhausted. But *Traci*…?

Gavin nods. "Unfortunately, it's true."

"She's the one who helped Dennis get hired, and she's been keeping tabs on you," Elliot adds. "Apparently she's always liked him."

"But I thought… She had such a huge crush on Gavin."

Gavin stares at me, dumbfounded. "She did?"

"Yes. Why do you think she dressed like that?"

"Gavin *is* a better catch than Keith Shellington," Elliot says with a sympathetic glance at Amandine, who merely sighs. I must look puzzled, because he turns to me and says, "Traci was sleeping with Keith."

"Oh my god."

"He's under investigation too. For inciting everything," Elliot says.

"Can they get him?" Elliot gave me the broad strokes of Keith's role while I was at the hospital, but I'm not too optimistic about him paying for it. He didn't actually *do* anything.

"Maybe, maybe not." Elliot purses his mouth. "Hard to say at this point."

Amandine adds, "It doesn't matter what the police find. He's finished."

"How?"

"He's already made enemies out of Elliot and his brothers and sister. Gavin, too, which means he's just antagonized lots of wealthy and powerful families. He won't be able to sneeze without somebody watching over him to make sure he doesn't break any laws."

Part of me wants him tossed into a dungeon, the key thrown away, but a bigger part of me is just glad this is over. Sighing, I lean back against my pillows.

"We should get going," Gavin says, helping Amandine up. "And *you* should get some rest. When you're well, we'll have dinner together again."

I smile. "I'd love that."

Elliot walks downstairs with them. I close my eyes in the now quiet room. The doctors prescribed a bunch of painkillers, but I refuse to take them. I want my mind clear.

My feet ache, my ribs are bruised and hurt like the dickens when I move the wrong way, and the gash on my head is ugly and throbbing. But I'm alive, and Elliot and Nonny are safe, and that's all that matters. A few drowsy moments pass, and then a thought fleets through my mind, and I frown.

"Why are you scowling?" Elliot says, reclaiming his spot next to me.

I snuggle next to him, grateful for his solid presence. "Because you were right about Traci and Dennis. If I'd listened to you, maybe things wouldn't have gotten this bad."

"It's not your fault they betrayed your trust and friendship, Belle." He kisses me tenderly on the temple. "They're the bad guys here. Don't blame yourself."

I place my hand over his chest, comforted by his warmth and his scent. His heart beats steadily under my palm.

"Saturday was your birthday."

"I know."

"I ordered this really special cake."

"With a gigolo inside?"

Elliot laughs. "No, you dirty-minded little minx." He flicks the tip of my nose. "It was a genuine cake with strawberries and flowers on top, made with real German chocolate. Had to toss it, though."

I sigh. That cake sounds wonderful. "It's okay."

"I'm going to order another when you feel better and we can have a small party. But since it would be cruel and unusual to deprive you of cake until then, I got you this." He produces a beautifully wrapped pink box and hands it to me.

Eyebrows raised, I tug at the satiny ribbon and carefully open the box. Inside is a chocolate cupcake with intricate frosting that looks like hearts and stars. "Wow," I say.

"It's no ordinary cupcake," he explains. "Inside is a gooey center full of pure dark chocolate."

"Ooh, yummy." I smile.

"Here." He pulls the cupcake out, sticks a golden candle in the center and lights it. The small flame bathes both of us in a warm glow.

I grin. I don't care about the injuries…or the near-death experience. This is the best birthday ever.

He sings "Happy Birthday." I can't help but smile at the mellow baritone of his voice. Is there anything this man can't do?

Nope, I think. He's perfect. And he's all mine.

When the song ends, he looks me in the yes. "Make a wish, Belle."

I tilt my head, gazing up at his face. "I don't need to make a wish." I kiss him on the mouth. "I have everything I could hope for already."

His throat works, and emotions flit through his dark gaze. Laying his forehead against mine, he shares the air I breathe. "God, I love you, Annabelle Reed."

"I love you too, Elliot."

Elizabeth

I sit in the darkened study in Ryder's mansion and wait. My brother is out with his wife, so I'm the only one here, along with a few of the household staff. They don't bother me, though. They're busy running the fortress Ryder calls "home."

I count carefully as the clock on the wall ticks each passing second. Finally, at eighty-four, my phone rings.

"Lizichka," a gravelly and slightly accented male voice says. "You called?"

"Yes, Tolik. You read the article about Julian's deal with us, I presume?"

His grunt conveys a wealth of disapproval and concern. "Nasty business."

"It's certainly not ideal." Which is why I am forced to make this call. "I want everything there is to know about my father and Wives Numbers Two through Six."

"What are you looking for, Lizichka?"

"Leverage. Something to fix the situation. Like you said, this is nasty business."

"What about that man at the dinner?"

I inhale sharply. If he hears, he doesn't let on. "Ignore him. He has nothing to do with this," I manage.

"As you wish."

"Thank you, Tolik."

AN UNLIKELY DEAL

Coming March 2017...

Turn the page for an early sneak preview...

THE BOY

THE BOY IN THE GARDEN IS NO MORE THAN four. He is a handsome child, with bright brown eyes and the silkiest of dark chestnut hair. His black shirt is neatly pressed—thanks to the housekeeper—and his blue denim pants are tidy as well, except for a streak of dirt from the yard where he wrestled with his twin.

He takes hold of his mother's soft, manicured hand with his own, sticky with sweat and candy from earlier. She flinches and tries to pull away. When he doesn't let go, she yanks her hand from his grip and stares at her palm with distaste. She takes out a handkerchief and wipes it.

His gaze rises to her face.

"'Ommy?" he says when she ignores him.

She sighs. "It's *M*ommy, not 'ommy." Her voice is impatient.

"I love you!" he declares as though he isn't

bothered by the correction, looking up at his beautiful golden mother with a cherubic smile.

She shakes her head. "What did I say about manipulation?"

"What's 'ano'olation?"

"*Manipu*lation," she corrects him again. "When you say things like 'I love you' to get the other person to say it back. Manipulation. Putting pressure on someone."

The smile on his face slips. He just wanted her to know how much he loves her.

"You're being needy," she continues. "Needy children are the worst. Why are your hands so grubby?" She opens and closes the palm he held, then wipes it again.

He looks down. "I'm sorry," he whispers.

She doesn't acknowledge him. Instead, she wrinkles her nose and disappears into the mansion.

The boy remains standing in the garden, unsure and alone.

ONE

Lucas

I DO NOT MAKE A HABIT OF REMINISCING about my exes. Nor do I make a habit of stalking our former haunts.

So it is with the greatest annoyance and puzzlement that I find myself back in Charlottesville, Virginia. I have nothing there—no friends, no business interests. Well...there's that house. I should put that on the market and move back to Seattle permanently, but somehow I can't bring myself to do so.

For fuck's sake, just sell the place and get the hell out of here. Cut all ties.

Rain water drips down my jet's windows as the plane slows on the tarmac. The cabin crew hands me a spare umbrella.

My assistant had my Mercedes dropped off at the airport yesterday before starting her vacation. I claim the car—no luggage this time—and run a rough hand over my face. My left leg aches. I should probably move to someplace where the sun shines all year long.

Instead of going to my own home to soak the throbbing limb in hot water, I drive to the duplex, park across the street like a fucking stalker, and watch the sad little building through the rain-blurred windshield.

She doesn't even live here anymore, but somehow I keep coming back. Like a damned boomerang.

The bitch kicked you to the curb when you were at your lowest. Fuck her.

Yes. Fuck her. Forget she exists. Get myself a hot chick to fuck so I can move on. Scarred or not, I am young and rich. It's no problem to get a willing girl.

The duplex's exterior could use a fresh coat of paint and a bit of landscaping, but the management company won't do anything until the place looks like a dump. They know just as well as I do that college kids don't care all that much about curb appeal.

The scuffed blue door stays stubbornly shut. It was raining when we had our first real date and she let me pick her up from her place.

In my mind's eyes, I see the door opening, Ava stepping out with an umbrella. She's in a long-sleeve shirt and old jeans with frayed hems and stitches, and her feet are encased in a pair of black boots she bought on clearance at a department store the year before. I quickly put an open umbrella over her to shield her from the icy raindrops and lead her to my car. I don't want even a drop to touch her soft, warm skin.

Idiot.

No matter how much I will it, Ava isn't coming out. She left me two years ago. She couldn't have made it clearer that she didn't want anything to do with me.

A pretty blonde walks by on the other side of the street, a bright orange, white and navy blue umbrella showing her school spirit. Her white UVA med school shirt stretches across young, perky tits. The skirt she's wearing is short and shows off long, shapely legs. Her canvas shoes are wet, but she doesn't seem to mind.

Med school. Must be smart. And she's easy on the eyes.

But my body remains coolly uninterested. It's as though after the accident, somebody flipped my libido switch off…leaving me deadened to one of the best pleasures in life.

If I were the superstitious type, I'd suspect that Ava cast a dark spell on me before she left.

The muscles in my left leg twinge, and I rub the thigh with an impatient hand. It acts up every time it rains, even when I'm seated. Maybe the pain's making it difficult for me to get interested. I'm not a masochist.

The blonde knocks on Ava's old blue door, and a boy comes out. They hug and kiss. The view twists something inside me.

What the hell am I trying to accomplish by coming back?

I pull out and drive away. It's over.

It was over two years ago.

For a so-called genius, it's taking me an awful long time to accept that fact. I can deal with numbers and patterns. But figuring Ava out… That has always eluded me.

No time for that bullshit. Let her go. You have three months left to find a wife.

The muscles in my neck tighten until they feel like steel. The idea of marrying anyone spikes my heartbeat, and the roast-beef sandwich I had for lunch churns in my gut. If it were just me, I'd say to hell with everything. But if I don't marry…if all of us don't get married, none of us are getting our grandfather's damned paintings.

I don't fucking *want* a wife. I'm not like my brothers. Pretty Boy Ryder found one—well, he felt compelled to marry his assistant after knocking her up. My twin Elliot found a stripper to marry for a year. But I can't let my brothers and sister down. My sister Elizabeth in particular would be devastated.

The paintings are rightfully ours. If Grandpa had had a better lawyer—or a better brain for business—they would've come to us rather than our asshole father, who is now using them for his twisted amusement. Julian is a borderline socio-path who likes to watch people weaker than him squirm at his command. It enrages him that he can't fuck with us—his children from his first wife are too wealthy and well-connected, and Elliot and I made our own fortunes when we were twenty-one.

I drive past the guard manning the gated community in Charlottesville. He merely nods. The lush verdant lawn stretches endlessly, trees big with branches that stretch far. The leaves are still a vibrant jade, but a tinge of orange, yellow and red has started to creep in, a discordant signal to the end of summer. Homes are stately in stone and brick, with elegant white-framed windows. Beyond them is a golf course, which I never used.

I only bought an "estate" here because it had an acceptable house for sale. Ava was studying at the University of Virginia, and flying back and forth between the east and west coasts didn't appeal. That's ten hours per round trip I could've spent with her. Seattle didn't have anything for me. Still doesn't, which is why I haven't moved back after finishing my treatment at the UVA hospital.

My home sprawls on one level and comes with seven bedrooms. Perhaps it was divine providence that the only place available was a one-level house. Going up and down the stairs with my injuries would've been difficult, especially on days when I was wheelchair-bound.

I park my car in the three-car garage. On the other side is a silver Lexus that's barely three years old. I don't drive it, but I make sure it's well maintained.

You should get rid of it. She's not coming back.

Shaking off the gloomy thoughts, I step out. The black waxed surface of the Mercedes is like a mirror, reflecting my white, strained face. I take the time to smooth it into a calm mask and slip quietly into the house.

"Welcome home, Lucas," Gail says in greeting, her voice as gentle as a spring breeze. She eyes my face. "Something warm to drink?"

I shake my head.

Her thin-lipped mouth thins further because I'm not letting her mother me, but I ignore her displeasure. In her early sixties, Gail is my full-time housekeeper. Despite my parents' disapproval, I don't insist that she put on a maid's uniform or any such bullshit. She's old enough to dress herself; right now she's in a light blue sweater, jeans and white sneakers.

She goes to the kitchen counter, her cloud-like gray hair glinting under the recessed lights, then almost immediately returns with a white envelope.

"This came for you."

Moments like this, I miss Rachel. My assistant would've thrown it out without bugging me with it, but she's on a well-deserved week-long vacation in the Bahamas.

"You can toss it. It's junk," I say without taking a closer look.

All legal documents that require my attention go to my attorney. Things that matter come to my inbox. My bills are paid automatically through direct debit, and invoices are forwarded to my assistant. Only garish advertisements and pitiful offers of credit end up in my mailbox.

"I thought that at first, but it doesn't look like junk." She hands it to me. "Here. See for yourself."

Left without a choice, I take it. It's as big as letter-sized paper folded in half, and the material is stiff and waterproof. The outside doesn't have any stamps or indication of where it's come from. It merely has a name—LUCAS REED—in all caps.

Maybe it isn't junk after all. "Thank you," I say and take it to my office, trying not to limp.

My left leg is shorter now, even though the surgeons did their best to minimize the discrepancy. I can usually manage to disguise it, but on days when my leg muscles throb, it's hard to hide my uneven gait.

I close the door to my home office and slump in the armchair that faces the cold and black fireplace. The mantel has a framed photo of me and my brothers and sister, taken while we were exiled to fancy European boarding schools. People call it "education," but that's just a euphemism. There aren't any pictures of Ava and me together. We never took any, and I don't remember why. I wish we had.

For what? To burn them? Delete from your phone's memory? Would that have made it clear that she's gone?

I tug at the little red-tipped section on the corner, and the envelope comes apart easily. Glossy photographs spill out, landing in my lap. I pick one up.

A young female pedestrian on a stone bridge crossing a river. Wind tosses her long and wavy platinum blond hair. The color of her eyes is ice blue, which never seems to fit because they're too warm. Her facial bones are delicate, her lips soft. She's always been frail looking; just a tad too thin, as though she grew up without enough to eat. That hasn't changed from the way the pale pink dress fits her, a slim white belt cinching her small waist.

My fingers go numb. Ava.

Heart hammering against my ribs, I flip the picture over. Nothing on the other side. I pick up the rest of the photos, but none of them have a message for me on the back.

Suddenly a thought bleeds into my mind. All of the photos are candid shots. Someone's been watching her.

Stalker?

My gut goes cold. My sister Elizabeth has had her share of problems with assholes who didn't understand the meaning of no. But this feels different. Why would a stalker send me Ava's photos?

I dig inside the envelope for clues. My hand grasps a piece of paper.

Le Meridien Chiang Mai, Thailand, it reads. Underneath the name of the hotel are dates— today, tomorrow and the day after—and an itinerary for a flight from Chiang Mai to Osaka via Seoul on Korean Air. The flight doesn't leave until almost midnight two days from now.

If I leave now, I can be in Chiang Mai before the departure.

I pick up the photos again. I didn't see them before, my focus on Ava's face, but the signs around her are in Japanese. I still remember a few hiragana and katakana characters from way back when I spent a semester in Tokyo.

So why Chiang Mai?

I toss the photos on the floor and throw my head against the back of my chair. I never, ever go after exes. *Never.* Not like some lovesick fool with my heart on my sleeve. I might as well cut off my dick and carve LOSER into my face with a nail.

But I'm entitled to closure. It won't be begging if that's all I want…and maybe a pound of flesh for all I've suffered in the last twenty-four months.

On its own volition, my hand reaches into my pocket and pulls out my phone. My fingers move across the smooth surface and dial my pilot, who's ready to go 24/7.

"Sir?"

"Chiang Mai," I say. "ASAP."

I head straight to the garage. No time to pack.

JOIN MY NEWSLETTER AT HTTP://WWW.NADIALEE. net/newsletter to be notified when *An Unlikely Deal* is out!

ABOUT NADIA LEE

New York Times and *USA Today* bestselling author Nadia Lee writes sexy, emotional contemporary romance. Born with a love for excellent food, travel and adventure, she has lived in four different countries, kissed stingrays, been bitten by a shark, ridden an elephant and petted tigers.

Currently, she shares a condo overlooking a small river and sakura trees in Japan with her husband and son. When she's not writing, she can be found reading books by her favorite authors or planning another trip.

To learn more about Nadia and her projects, please visit www.nadialee.net. To receive updates about upcoming works from Nadia, please visit www.nadialee.net to subscribe to her new release alert.

CPSIA information can be obtained
at www.ICGtesting.com
Printed in the USA
BVOW09s0901080418
512775BV00001B/50/P